# BLAME IT ON THE VODKA

Blame it on the Alcohol: Book Three

---

## FIONA COLE

Copyright © 2022 by Fiona Cole

All rights reserved.

Cover Designer: Najla Qamber, Qamber Designs

Photographer: Regina Wamba

Interior Design: Indie Girl Promotions

Editing: Kelly Allenby, Readers Together

No part of this book may be reproduced or transmitted in any form or by any means, electronic or mechanical, including photocopying, recording, or by any information storage and retrieval system without written permission of the author, except for the use of brief quotations in a book review.

This is a work of fiction. Names, characters, businesses, places, events and incidents are either the products of the author's imagination or used in a fictitious manner. Any resemblance to actual persons, living or dead, actual events, or locales is entirely coincidental.

*To Kelly.*

*I don't have words.*
*Other than, thank you.*

## Playlist

Drinks - Cyn
Like I Can - Sam Smith
Moment of Weakness - Tenille Arts
Bad Bitches - Lil Jon, Kronic & Onderkoffer
when the party's over - Billie Eilish
Real Talk - Angie K
Telephone - Lady Gaga (feat. Beyonce)
Bill Murray - Matt Nathanson
Hiding - Florence + the Machine
Lover to Lover - Florence + the Machine
If There Was No You - Brandi Carlile
The War Is Over - Kelly Clarkson
You Are the Reason - Calum Scott
There's No Way - Lauv (feat. Julia Michaels)
Guilty - Paloma Faith
River Lea - Adele
Like That - JP Saxe
Sky Full of Song - Florence + the Machine
Forgive Me Friend - Smith & Thell (feat. Swedish Jam Factory)
Kill - Jimmy Eat World
that way - Tate McRae

unbreak - Camylio
Can I Sleep in Your Brain - Ezra Furman
One More I Love You - Alex Warren
Please Notice - Christian Leave
I Lost a Friend - FINNEAS
Shrike - Hozier

## Prologue

RAELYNN

"Wanna fuck?"

My lips tipped in my best fuck me smile, growing a little sinister the longer he took to respond. Maybe he hadn't heard me. Except I knew he had by the way that sexy muscle in his cheek twitched at my bold words.

I probably should have flirted and batted my lashes before propositioning him, but that wasn't me, and I didn't like beating around the bush.

Just as my patience almost snapped, he finally turned my way, adjusting his gaze down to my height. I wasn't short, but he had to be well over six feet—packed in with muscles I'd been fantasizing about licking since I saw him standing in the corner of the frat party. I'd studied him subtly until curiosity got the best of me, and I had to know if he was just as big everywhere else.

I could almost taste the salt on his skin. I slid my tongue along my lips in anticipation and was rewarded when his eyes landed there first. Then, finally—*fucking finally*—they lifted to mine. Across the room, they looked muddy, but less than a foot away, they cleared to green, barely rimmed with a deep brown that matched my eyes.

It was fate.

I'd felt his eyes on me all night, and I was ready to feel his hands, too.

Would he be soft? Hard? Or would he—

"No, thanks."

Like a record screeching to a halt, my fantasies stumbled over the unforeseen roadblock and started to crash.

"Excuse me?" Surely, I heard wrong.

"No. Thanks."

His deep, rumbly response curled around my senses, sending shivers up my spine, only serving to piss me off more than how much his shocking answer already did. Trying to hide my reaction, I stiffened, pulling my shoulders back and looking as regal as every etiquette class taught me to. "What do you mean, no thanks?"

His lips—those perfectly shaped lips—tipped into the most delicious smirk I'd ever seen a man pull off. "You don't hear that very often, do you?"

"Never."

I was Raelynn Vos. No one turned me down. If I wanted you, I had you. I didn't say it with arrogance but with confidence. I was hot, and I knew it. I'd been in college for two years, and I'd worked my way through the campus population, searching for who I deemed worthy.

And this specimen before me screamed more than worthy. His attention over the past hour stroked along my spine, almost begging me to come get him. Yet, there he was, turning me down.

"Sorry to be your first," he apologized.

"Don't be," I said, rolling my eyes away to scan the room. "I'll find someone better."

"Doubt it. I'm the best."

I snapped my attention back to him, hating that he got a reaction from me. Hating that his confidence only made him sexier. "Arrogant much?"

"Just honest."

With a scoff, I forced my gaze away again. Across the room, I saw my out when my best friends, Vera and Nova, came into view. "Whatever. I have better things to do. Bye."

Walking away, I waved my hand as if I was shooing him off, and I hated that—even though I didn't turn back—I knew he was watching me with that same damn smirk.

"Asshole," I muttered.

"Who's an asshole?" Vera asked, fingering the pearl necklace she never took off.

"That guy back there."

"Why's he an asshole?" Nova asked. For a second, my calm friend's eyes flashed as fiery as her hair.

"Ugh. He turned me down."

Both sets of eyes shot to me—wide, mirroring the same shock still reverberating through me. I'd met Nova and Vera at the start of college, and we hit it off, complementing each other perfectly. In all the time I'd known them, I'd never not gotten someone I wanted.

"Like, did he know you wanted him?" Vera asked.

"Uh, yeah. I very clearly asked him if he wanted to fuck."

"Jesus, Rae," Nova chided, her cheeks now matching her hair.

I shrugged it off, trying to be aloof when I was anything but. "Whatever. There's a whole ocean of fish. I'll just find another one."

Locking my smile firmly in place, I ignored the warmth that had followed me since I walked in, knowing it was the brooding stranger's gaze. He no longer existed to me, and I headed to the dance floor to prove it.

One hour later, and I had option number two eating out of the palm of my hand. Was he as hot as Mr. Big and Arrogant? No, but he was better—if for no other reason than he was lucky enough to have his mind blown by me. I dragged him up the stairs and headed to a random door, hoping to find it empty. His tongue worked against my neck, and I already had plans for it elsewhere. A shiver slid down my body as I swung the door open. We stumbled through, only to find it occupied by a couple against the wall.

Rather than freeze, another shot of adrenaline hit me harder. One long leg wrapped around the guy's waist as his hand worked between her legs. Looked like they were just getting started, and I could get down for some voyeurism.

At least, I thought I could until the door shut, pulling the guy's attention over his shoulder, and familiar green eyes slammed into me.

"What the fuck?" I shouted. *How dare he.*

The guy's brows shot up.

"Hey," the girl shouted back, getting her leg down to stand tall and indignant. Pretty impressive, considering her dress still hung at her waist.

"Sorry to interrupt. You're stunning and absolutely gorgeous. I mean, those tits. I could have a wild night with you any day," I said with a wink. Then I shifted my attention back to the guy, dropping my smile. "But what the fuck?"

I did my best to build my fellow women up, and if I wasn't so perplexed, I would have felt bad about cockblocking her.

"Uh, can we find another room?" Option Two muttered behind me.

"No. I'm busy," I answered, not bothering to turn and face him.

"Whatever," he muttered, leaving. Not that I cared. I was too focused on figuring out why the hell this guy turned me down.

"Do you mind?" Mr. Big and Arrogant asked.

"Yeah. I fucking do."

"Jesus Christ," he muttered.

"Now, explain to me why you very obviously want to fuck, but still decided to turn me down." That muscle in his jaw ticked again, and I knew there had to be an explanation just waiting to come out. Probably one he didn't want to admit, but dammit, I needed to know. I just had to push a little harder to get it. "You would have been lucky to have me. I'm fucking awesome."

A groan rumbled from deep in his chest and grew until it spilled from his gritted teeth. "Did you ever think I realized that, and that's why you're not some random girl up in a room with me for a quick fuck?"

"What?" the girl and I said in unison. Although, her screech drowned out my shocked gasp.

"Fuck this." The girl shoved Mr. Big and Arrogant back and covered her chest.

Before she could storm out, I doled out another compliment because I was all about women supporting women despite the fact that I was chasing her off. "You're amazing, by the way. Don't let him get you down because you can do so much better."

She narrowed her eyes but also gave a nod of camaraderie and understanding.

As soon as she left, I turned to find him buckling his pants. "Seriously, what the fuck?"

His words played on repeat like an echo, only serving to increase my confusion the more I thought about them. He *didn't* want to fuck me because I was too awesome? I was so confused.

"Listen," he started, running his hand through his short, dark blond hair.

God, he was hot. The way his arm flexed, testing the restraints of the black T-shirt—totally drool-worthy.

"I saw you across the room almost as soon as you entered."

"I noticed."

"Arrogant much?"

He smirked, throwing my words back at me from earlier, so I returned the favor. "Just honest."

"Well, when I saw you..." He took a deep breath and looked me up and down, setting me on fire all over again. "Maybe I realized you're more than just a fuck."

Now it was my turn to wear the shocked look. Sure, I had lots of guys wanting more from me, but usually, it was more sex. I never gave them a chance to ask for more outside of that. Maybe if I cleared that up, we could move on. "Well, I don't do more than fuck."

His face pulled to a frown as if I was an intense math problem he wanted to solve. After an uncomfortably long time, he finally asked, "Do you do waffles?"

"What?" I shook my head, struggling to process the random question.

"Waffles. If I can't fuck you, then I'm going to eat," he explained with a shrug.

"You can fuck me all you want."

"No. If I can't have more, then I won't fuck you."

"Ugh," I groaned. The way he calmly drew the line in the sand pissed me off, but waffles did sound good, and I was so done with this party. "Fine. Feed me waffles."

"Awesome." If I thought his smirk was a force to be reckoned with, it was nothing compared to the full smile that almost knocked me off my feet. *Damn.*

"Let's go then."

"Wait. What's your name?" I asked.

"Wondered if you'd get to that."

"Playing hard to get?"

"Nah. I'm pretty easy."

"Could've fooled me," I deadpanned.

"I'm Austin."

"Raelynn."

"Well, Rae, let's go eat."

My nickname rolled off his tongue without me even telling him that's what my friends called me. I liked it. And with less hesitation than I should've had, I followed him out, sending a quick message to the girls.

We were silent beyond the basics of eating out. *What are you getting? What's your favorite thing to get here? How do you like your coffee? Do you like lemon in your water?* I wanted to be disappointed by the turn of events, but when the salty, buttery, sweet waffle hit my mouth, I regretted nothing.

"What are we doing?" I asked around a mouthful of waffle.

He huffed a laugh at my mumbled question, taking the time to finish his bite before answering. "We're becoming friends."

"Friends?"

"Yeah. I now know you like cinnamon waffles, coffee as black as your soul, and no lemon in your water. We're getting to know each other."

"Yeah, I've learned you're stubborn as hell."

"I can be. What else?"

"You like nasty-ass blueberry waffles, a mildly okay preference of coffee with more than enough cream but no sugar, and you like an obscene amount of syrup on your pastries," I said, cringing at the soup-like mess on his plate.

"See. Friends," he exclaimed proudly. "People who like each other, but don't fuck."

"Ugh." I balked at the explanation because I wasn't sure there would ever be a time I didn't want to fuck this man. He was every fantasy come to life.

"You obviously don't have friends."

"Excuse me, I have plenty of friends. Asshole."

He held up his hands, laughing. "Okay, okay. You don't have *guy* friends," he specified.

"True," I conceded.

"Cool. Then I'll be the one to show you the ropes—now pass me the bacon."

"Fuck, no. I love bacon," I said, grabbing the piece and shoving it in my mouth before he could reach it.

"You're the worst friend ever," he said, laughing.

"Oh, you just wait. I'll show you."

## Chapter One

### AUSTIN

"Fuck me."

That stupid red sports car shined like a beacon of light, screaming conceited asshole everywhere it went. And there it sat, warning me that the dinner Rae invited me to wasn't just her family and me. No, it was me, her family, and her *boyfriend*.

I couldn't even think the word without cringing.

Stalling, I pulled out my phone to check my messages.

**King:** Want to grab some dinner?
**Me:** Can't. I'm about to walk into Rae's house to have dinner with her family.
**King:** What's it called when you're pussy whipped without having any pussy?
**Me:** Fuck you.

I played football with King in college. Other than Rae, he was my closest friend, and he liked nothing more than giving me shit about my relationship with Rae. Ignoring his response, I opened the next message.

**Gma:** Maybe you can come visit after your weekend in Vegas.
**Gma:** Grandpa told me to tell you to not do anything he wouldn't do—which isn't much—so have fun.
**Me:** I'll definitely be there.
**Gma:** Bring a girlfriend with you.
**Me:** Only when I'm serious.
**Gma:** Okay. We love you.
**Me:** Love you too.

I could feel her sigh of disappointment all the way through the text message from miles away upstate. However, she knew better than anyone how I felt about relationships.

Before I could change my mind and reverse out of Rae's winding driveway, I killed the engine and knocked on the door.

Rae flung it open and slammed into my chest point two seconds later. On reflex, my arms wrapped around her petite frame, finding the familiar grooves of her ribs, losing myself in the points where her fingers pressed into my back. We'd hugged a million times over the years, but each one stole my breath.

Just as quick, she backed up, dragging me inside before gently closing the door.

The golden chandelier hanging high in the foyer shined down like a spotlight, illuminating her sharp cheekbones and thick lashes.

"Thank god you're here."

She brushed back her hair, the highlights like flashes of gold—just like her shoes. She wore all black, except for those sparkly-ass shoes. That was Rae. She appeared regal and untouchable, but when you looked close enough, when you gave her the time of day, her bold personality exploded like a fireworks finale.

"Nova is finishing up the tour, and Vera bailed on me for her adorable, chubby, little baby. Blech."

I cocked my brow, knowing damn well that she loved that baby, and *blech* was the furthest thing from the truth.

"You have Bodie," I reminded her.

This time when she said blech, there was an added eye roll, leaving no doubt she meant it. She didn't leave me room to call her on it, though, because in the next instant, she turned and motioned for me to follow her.

"Austin," Rae's dad, Kenneth, greeted. He stood from the table with a wide smile, coming around to greet me. I offered my hand, but he quickly brushed it away and pulled me in for a back-slapping hug. "I'm glad you could make dinner. Now it's a true family dinner."

"Wouldn't miss Ida's cooking for the world." I winked at Rae's mom as she rounded the table and pulled me in for a hug almost as tight as Rae's.

When Rae and I started our friendship all those years ago, we went all out. She took me home whenever she got the chance, and I melded with the Vos family as if they were my own.

Bodie half-raised from his seat to reach across the table and deliver a weak handshake. He didn't like me. Not even his forced lawyer smile could hide the disdain in his cold blue eyes.

"I hear you're headed to Vegas next week," Kenneth said from his seat at the head of the table.

"Yes, sir."

"Make sure you take care of our girl here. Especially since Bodie can't make it."

It filled me with petty joy every time his eye twitched over my close relationship with Rae and her family. He'd probably fully unmask his hatred and hit me in the face if he knew how much I truly loved her and would happily snatch her from him if she'd ever want me for more than a night.

"I'll make sure Rae at least stays out of jail."

"All parents can ask for," Ida added, laughing. She shook her head, meeting Kenneth's eyes with a shrug.

I'd never met two parents who supported their child to own who they were as much as Rae's did. Not that I had great examples to go by. I never knew my mom and my dad kicked off when I was a teen. Thankfully, my grandparents took my brother and me in, and that was when I learned what true support looked like.

"I'm sure it can't be easy sticking to a *friend's* side when you're single in Vegas," Bodie said. "Especially for someone with such a rural background. The bright lights must be a little distracting."

For a moment, I imagined cutting through his snide remark with a biting comment of my own. Instead, I managed to bite my tongue—a skill I'd had to learn well. My temper and acerbic tongue got me into more fights than I'd like to admit. As much as I wanted to take Bodie down a peg, it didn't serve any purpose than to provide a rush of victory, quickly followed by the fallout.

"I think I'll manage," I grit out.

"Besides," he continued, turning his attention to Rae. "My girlfriend is a good girl. She won't get in trouble."

I held my breath, waiting for Rae to scoff at Bodie complimenting her like a dog. Except she didn't. The air slowly seeped out as I watched the wild woman I knew give a pinched smile before emptying her half-full wine glass. When he rubbed his hand along her neck, she stiffened, her shoulders tensing up to her ears. It wasn't until he finally pulled away that she relaxed again, only to snatch the bottle of wine to refill her glass.

I waited for her to look up so I could gauge her reaction—try to read what went on in her head, but she never looked up from the table. By the time she finally did, a blank wall stared back. Over the years, we got so good at reading each other that we didn't always need words. I used that now and cocked my head, asking her what was wrong. It was only then that she softened and smiled, giving a careless shrug like nothing had happened.

Except it did, and I couldn't brush it off as easily as her. I couldn't ignore the way it happened more and more frequently. I noticed it first when she was around Bodie, but lately, it extended to when she hung around me and the girls.

The Rae that greeted me so exuberantly in the hallway disappeared a little more each time I saw her, and I didn't like it. I just didn't know what to do because any time I brought it up, she shut me down.

Maybe her increasingly tepid personality had to do with her dad's campaign. Kenneth had always been in the public eye because of his company, Vos Industries, but now that he'd shifted his attention to running for Senate, eyes were on the whole family—especially Rae. Although Kenneth made his stance on his daughter being a free woman who could have fun without being held to a double standard quite clear. So, blaming the change in her on the campaign didn't really add up.

"Kenneth," Bodie called. "Have you given any more thought to possibly using Morgan Law Firm as your political lawyers?" Kenneth tried to respond but didn't get beyond opening his mouth before Bodie held up his hand. "I know, I know. You have the law firm you've worked with for years, but they focus on corporate law, and Morgan Law can provide a fine focus into what you need. Rae knows how great our firm is."

He looked to her to back him up, but she picked that time to bring the glass back to her lips, only offering a small smile and nod in support—if you could call it that.

Bodie's jaw ticked, and his nostrils flared. He looked ready to snap at her lack of words, and it brought me to the edge of my seat.

"I appreciate your offer, Bodie. I'll be sure to talk it over with my staff and keep it in mind."

"Of course."

"Rae, I saw your photo pop up online when I was scrolling through the society pages," Ida said, turning the conversation.

Rae relaxed just enough to put down her glass. "Yeah, I figured appearing at the restaurant opening would garner enough attention to talk about our plans to raise money for the shelter."

"I'm pretty sure the jacket without a shirt underneath was what got you all the attention," Bodie muttered.

Rae's lips tightened, but she merely swallowed and stuck to talking to her mom about their plans. A lot of people assumed Rae was nothing more than an airhead who liked to party and be fashionable, but she knew mainstream marketing like the back of her hand, which made her such a huge asset for anyone wanting to get their name out there.

Thankfully, that was the last bitchy comment from Bodie, which allowed conversation to flow from there through the rest of dinner. Kenneth asked me about work and the new marketing design I was in charge of. I always gave him my full attention, but any time there was a gap in conversation or when Bodie took over, I used the opportunity to watch Rae.

We were friends—best friends—because I refused to be anything other than important to her, and if I gave in to having sex, she'd use me up and never give me a chance for more again. I watched her hop from one man to the next, and I didn't want to be another had-been on her list.

"Well, we should get going. I have an important meeting, and Rae needs her beauty sleep," Bodie announced.

Everyone managed a laugh, except me. God, I hated him.

A hate that only grew when I walked out to the foyer to find them arguing after Kenneth held me back to ask me about a marketing project, and Ida went to the kitchen. Steel shot up my spine when I caught the way Rae's shoulders curled in under her dropped chin. Bodie towered over her with a clenched jaw and flushed face.

"Everything okay?" I asked, my voice cold as ice, fists clenched and ready to kill him.

Bodie stepped back, giving Rae enough space to stand up tall again. She watched Bodie before turning to me with that same wall dropped down over her eyes. I wanted to kick it down. "Everything's fine," she answered blandly.

"Well, sunshine…" Kenneth walked in, interrupting before I could push for more. "I'm off to bed." He wrapped Rae in a hug with a kiss on her head. "Bodie, it was good to see you."

He shook Bodie's hand but gave me another back-slapping hug. Another win.

When Bodie went to shake my hand, I squeezed harder than before—a warning of sorts. He tried to squeeze back, but I outweighed him by fifty pounds of muscle, and he didn't stand a chance. I didn't bother hiding my smirk when he pulled back with a grimace.

"You coming?" Bodie asked Rae.

"In a minute. Can you get the car heated up?"

His jaw clenched when he looked at me and back to her. "Yeah."

"Thanks for coming tonight," she said as soon as Bodie left.

"You mean, thanks for saving you from a night with just your parents and Bodie?"

She rolled her eyes. "Well, if you're going to be a whiner about it, then I guess I won't give you the other thing I invited you here for."

"What thing?" I asked, narrowing my eyes, looking her up and down for any signs of a gift pocketed away.

"Are you going to stop being a baby?" she taunted.

"No."

"Ugh, fine," she ceded like I knew she would. "I'm too impatient to not give it to you anyway."

"I know," I laughed.

With a glare and a smile, she slapped my shoulder before digging through her purse. "Aha!" she proclaimed.

I took the white envelope and opened it while still watching Rae bounce from foot to foot like a little kid. I was so distracted by each sway of her body that it took me a moment to process what the tickets were for. "Holy shit, Rae."

"I know."

"How did you get these?" I asked.

"You mean, how did I get exclusive opening night tickets to Hamburg Stacks art gallery showing that don't go on sale for another month?"

"Opening night?" I parroted.

"Yup, the only night he'll be there."

"Holy shit."

"Do you love it?" she asked, looking more excited than me.

"Hell, yes, but there are two tickets here. I guess I'll have to find someone to go with," I teased.

"I don't freaking think so."

"But you hate art shows."

"I don't *hate* them. I find them a little boring, but you love going, and I love going with you. And I love watching you love art, so of course, I'm going to go."

My heart pumped a little harder. I was damned lucky to have Rae in my life in any way. "Thank you."

She smiled like it was nothing, and I pulled her in for a hug, pressing a kiss to the top of her head. Her arms held me close, and I basked in the moment, not allowing myself to linger too long.

*Friend.*

"So, the flight leaves at twelve-fifteen?" she asked, stepping back.

"Yup. Do you want me to Uber to the airport with you?"

"Nah, I'll meet you there. Besides, I'll still be packing by the time you get to the airport seven hours early."

"Please," I scoffed. "I'll only be there six and a half hours early. The airport doesn't open until six."

"You're ridiculous," she laughed.

Taking a chance with the moment alone and light mood, I shifted the subject. "Is everything okay?"

"What do you mean?" she asked.

"With you and Bodie."

Her eyes dropped. "I mean, he's annoying, but I'm fine."

"You sure?"

"Austin," she started, finally meeting my eyes. The Rae I knew and loved stared me down, but something was missing. "It's me. If anything wasn't fine, I'd crush him."

"Yeah," I answered, but not with the same exuberance I should have.

"By the way, I was thinking of booking the full spa package for when we get to the hotel."

"That sounds fun for you."

"Oh, no. You're coming with. I'm thinking facials and pedicures."

"Rae…" I warned, but it was drowned out by a much sharper voice.

"Raelynn. Let's go," Bodie snapped from the door.

She jumped but quickly covered it with a wink and a gun. "It's already mentally booked, therefore it has to happen. I can't wait for our spa day."

"You're lucky I like you," I groaned, following her out.

She blew me a kiss before ducking into the car. I caught it like I always did and slapped it on my cheek, loving her smile—wishing it was a real kiss goodbye and not the air kisses we used as a joke.

I wished for a lot. I wished Rae was more than my friend, but she didn't do relationships. Not really. What she had with

Bodie was a farce, and the only thing I had on my mind was marrying her.

Nothing less would do.

Unfortunately, anything more than sex was never on the table, and as much as I desired her, fantasized about every inch of her—about what it would feel like to be inside her—I'd rather have a lifetime of friendship than just a moment of bliss.

I hated the way he'd been such a shock to the solar plexus when Rae actually called him her boyfriend. She'd explained it as an experiment. It made sense since he'd been so absent in the beginning. But as the months went on, he was always there, and now it all felt like a ruse for a campaign photo op. Anyone who knew her, knew she didn't really want to be with him, and as much as I tried to convince myself it was just for looks, something pricked at my conscious that more lingered beyond the surface.

Although, maybe that was just my complete and utter disdain for the prick.

## Chapter Two

### RAELYNN

"I still don't think you should go," Bodie said, making his way to my liquor cabinet.

I almost said something about drinking *my* alcohol before noon but thought better of it. Instead, using my time to shove my last few things into my carry-on. The quicker I packed, the quicker I could leave and be away from him.

I'd avoided him over the last week since dinner at my parents. He'd been more on edge lately, and our drive home had been filled with a heavy silence between snappy words.

I hated it.

I was Raelynn Vos. I didn't hide from anyone.

At least I didn't use to.

But over the last year, a lot changed—like Bodie. The boyfriend that hadn't seemed too bad to have for parties and photo ops—who hadn't cared what I did most of the time, slowly changed to caring a lot. He'd shifted from aloof to a stage five clinger who got increasingly angry when I wasn't available to him.

His moods were another change—one I didn't want to think about.

"It's my best friend's wedding. I have to go," I explained, rolling my eyes behind his back where he couldn't see.

"It's a Vegas wedding. It's...tacky," he scoffed.

"Well, I'm happy for them to be able to squeeze it in with his hectic schedule."

Bodie ran his hand through his shaggy hair. The dirty blond waves slicked back, and I remembered how much that same move had drawn me to him in the first place. I liked that his hair brushed the collar of his shirt. I'd wanted to feel it against my fingertips when I ran them along his neck. I wanted to know if it was as soft as it appeared when I fisted my hands in it while he ate me out. I'd wanted to know if he was as muscled all over his body as his arm looked when it flexed across the club. The exact same move as now.

Except now, I looked at that same move with dread—realizing it hinted at his agitation more than anything else.

"I know, I know." He took a deep breath before facing me, showing some effort to calm down. "It's just hard thinking of you in Vegas without me. It's so risqué. Especially with *Austin* there."

He sneered Austin's name, unable to hide how much he hated him.

"You know there's nothing going on." How could he not when I'd explained that Austin and I were just friends about a million times?

"I just don't like the way he looks at you."

Obviously, he didn't take the time to notice the way I looked at Austin. I couldn't help but ogle all his muscles and brooding sexiness that poured off him. Not that I'd ever do more than look. Austin was my best friend—sometimes closer than the girls. He was my Instagram boyfriend who took all my photos. Austin was my Netflix and literally chill. No amount of sheer sex on a stick could ruin that.

When Bodie went back to pacing and took another swallow from the glass, I took the opportunity to go in the kitchen and snag a water bottle. I lived in a decent-sized apartment in New York, but his attitude took up too much space, making it feel as cramped as a tiny loft. "You have nothing to worry about," I explained, struggling to keep the exasperation out of my voice.

I was tired of the conversation.

I was tired of Bodie.

I just wanted him gone—preferably forever, but I said I'd stick it out a little longer. At least until the end of my dad's campaign. I knew my dad didn't care if I was single, but everyone knew family played a huge role in voters' thoughts. I could be wild, but with a steady boyfriend by my side, it was more acceptable.

I turned back to put my bags by the door when I collided with Bodie's lean chest. My heart jumped into my throat, choking back the yelp of surprise—only to start beating a mile a minute. He wasn't as tall as Austin, but the way his brows slashed down his angled face created a sinister look—one I'd come to avoid at all cost.

One I couldn't get away from now as he cornered me. With every step forward, I took one back.

*Shove past him and tell him to fuck off,* a lingering voice from before Bodie encouraged, but I'd learned to ignore that voice, and slowly it faded to almost nothing.

"It would make me feel better about our relationship if you supported me more. It was embarrassing how you didn't speak up at dinner."

I wanted to say that I didn't think his volatile attitude was a good choice for my dad. Instead, I dug deep for calm and said, "My opinion isn't going to change his mind about your offer."

"A little effort wouldn't hurt either way."

His gritted words were my only warning before he gripped my arms too tightly. I tried to jerk back, but my back hit the counter, and I was trapped as he closed the space between us to nothing. I hated that I winced, having no doubt his fingers were leaving bruises.

Despite the show of weakness, I held his stare. I might have fallen from the fuck-you-woman I'd been and avoided him when I could, but I didn't cower. I made sure he knew I saw him and what he did.

The crease between his brows softened, and he sighed. His grip loosened, but he didn't let go, instead rubbing over the sore spots. "I just...I don't want you to go, and I'm being touchy about it."

"I get that, Bodie, but I *am* going." I infused steel into my words, making sure he knew I wouldn't back down.

Like the flip of a switch, his grip tightened even more than before. "Maybe you could care a little that I'll miss you. That would be nice."

*Nice?* He wanted *nice?*

The sharp pain radiated up my arms and into my chest, sparking to life a dangerous flame. A flame I'd once grown to a beautiful fire until he came along and squashed it. Until he came along and slowly sprinkled it with water until it could be cowed into submission before I even knew what was happening.

*Nice?*

The word reverberated like an earthquake in my limbs, mixing with the fear his ominous glare flooded through my veins. It spread like goop, taking me over. I hated the feeling. I hated this. I hated him. I hated that I was in this position to begin with.

I *knew* better. I *knew*.

Old Rae snapped back before common sense could stop me. "I don't care if you'll miss me, Bodie. I'm not here to soothe your precious ego."

As soon as the words left my mouth, I knew I'd made a mistake. His cold eyes flashed with rage before shuttering to an ice I'd never seen before. If I thought I was scared before, it was nothing compared to what swallowed me whole when he shoved his hand into my hair, fisting the strands tight.

"Then maybe you can soothe me in other ways," he grit out, pulling my head back.

The lips I hadn't minded when we first kissed landed on mine roughly. Bodie had lost his temper before, but never like this.

Adrenaline shot through my limbs, giving me the strength to shove him back. "No."

But I wasn't strong enough. I barely created any distance before both hands were back, shoving me hard, slamming my back against the counter. The sharp pain hit so hard, my legs gave out. I would have gladly fallen, but his grip held me upright.

"Why do you do this?" he growled. "Why do you push me to this point? Would it kill you to be a little fucking nicer to me?"

"Stop." I tried to infuse strength in my command, but my body trembled, leaving me almost pleading.

"I'm so sick of this shit. I'm sick of not being able to reach you. All I want is a little bit of commitment from you. I want more, and I can't reach you."

Emotions swirled through me like a roulette wheel of fear and determination, leaving me to wonder which one would win out.

But I knew exactly which would win this time.

I was Raelynn Vos. Knowing the chain leashed around his anger held on by a rusted link, I decided I didn't care. I decided that if that chain broke, I'd go down as no one other than me. "Because I don't want you to reach me. I never did," I confessed with a cruel coldness coating my words.

*Chink.*

I met his eyes as the last bit of metal gave way, unleashing a whole new fury. I made sure he knew I saw him even as I watched his hand pull back, ready to strike.

But before he could land his blow, a knock at the door froze all motion inside the apartment.

"Miss Vos," my favorite concierge, Gus, called from the other side of the door. "Your car is here, and I wanted to see if you needed help with your bags."

God bless Gus and his over-achieving, sweet heart.

Bodie's fists unclenched, clenched, and unclenched one last time before both hands fell away. His cold stare melted, giving way to regret—just like always. Next came the silent pleading for forgiveness. There was also a plea to turn Gus away, but I didn't fucking think so.

"Yes, come in," I shouted.

Gus entered, all smiles, and I almost ran to place grateful kisses all over his wrinkled cheek. Pushing off the counter, I held back my wince from the twinge in my back and used the polite etiquette my mother taught me. "I have a bag in my room, if you don't mind."

"Yes, ma'am."

As soon as he rounded the corner, I leveled a glacial glare at Bodie. "Leave," I demanded.

"Rae," he pleaded with his hands out. "I'm sorry. You know—"

"No. No more."

"What do you mean, no more?"

Seeing my chance—my out, with Gus coming back any second, I latched on to the opportunity with both hands. "We are done."

"What do you me—" He winced and shook his head as if he was trying to make sense of it all, grasping at straws. "But the campaign?"

"I'm sure if I *explained*," I said slowly, full of meaning. "My father would understand."

For the first time, fear entered Bodie's eyes, and I liked it. "No…"

"I won't. I don't need to." The longer he looked scared,

the more powerful I became, realizing he was just human. A giant, mean, waste of a human, but just a man capable of fear like anyone else. "Because if you ever lay your hands on me again, I'll fucking cut them off and feed them to you."

He opened his mouth before slamming it shut. Again, his hand dug through his hair as he looked around for a solution to pop out from behind the curtains. When he didn't find what he was looking for, he reverted back to what he knew. He leaned in, curling his lip to deliver an ominous promise. "This isn't over, Raelynn."

He stood upright just in time for Gus to come back out. Lifting my chin high, I met his promise with uncaring disdain. "Please see Mr. Forrester out," I requested Gus. "I'll be down in a minute."

"Yes, ma'am."

Thankfully, Bodie didn't argue, and I'd never been so happy to close the door on him than ever before—for the last time.

The lock clicked loudly in the empty apartment—I was alone. Finally.

The chaotic storm fled my body, taking my fight with it.

I collapsed to the floor. My chin dropped, and my hair hid my face. It was only then that the tears came.

How had I gotten there? How had I reached a place I'd vowed to never ever be in? I'd watched my mother crawl her way out of a life she hated when I was young, and I swore I'd be stronger. I swore I would never let anyone break me. I swore I knew better.

It hadn't started this way. It started as one night. Usually, that was it before I went looking for someone else, but a couple weeks later, it happened again. Then someone snapped a picture of us before dinner. It was only after the reporter dug into his background that I realized what an asset he could be. *Socialite Raelynn Vos Dates the Good Guys, Turning the Numbers Up for Kenneth Vos.* It was through various outlets that I discovered he was a pastor's son, the perfect date for all the events my dad needed us to attend to boost his campaign.

Bodie had been distant at first, almost uncaring, while he focused on starting his career at a new law firm. It'd been the perfect arrangement. A commitment for the papers without an actual commitment that took too much from me. Then things changed.

Somehow Bodie slipped under the radar. He used slow tactics and small changes that were almost undetectable until it was too late.

*And I let it happen.*

But I wouldn't anymore.

Wiping away any evidence of my tears, I brushed my hair back and lifted my chin, raising myself back to my feet.

I was Raelynn Vos. No one fucked with me, and Vegas shined on the horizon—the perfect opportunity to prove it.

## Chapter Three

### AUSTIN

For the five-millionth time during our flight, my eyes strayed from the movie playing on the tiny screen to the woman beside me. By the time the credits rolled, I couldn't even recall the name of the movie I'd watched so little.

After all these years, you'd think I'd have had my fill of looking at her, but it was never enough. The last couple hours, I'd studied the way her lashes cast dark, alluring shadows along her sharp cheekbones. All of it softened by the pouty lips I could draw from memory. The lips I *had* drawn from memory more times than I could count. But it was never enough.

"Folks, we're about twenty minutes out. The weather is sunny and a cool eighty-two." The pilot's announcement crackled through the speakers, halting my perusal of Rae when her eyes fluttered open.

I feigned interest in the random ads scrolling across the screen while simultaneously watching her readjust from the corner of my eye.

"Hey," she said in the sexiest sleep voice.

An ache bloomed in my chest, both sharp and warm, when I took in her sleepy smile. She blinked, pulling me into her heavy-lidded, warm chocolate eyes. The ache grew, expanding to my cock when she stretched her arms high, pushing the full curves of her breasts against the simple white T-shirt. I almost laughed at the description. Nothing was simple on Rae.

"Sleep okay?"

She collapsed back, sinking into her seat. "Like a rock."

"That explains the snoring."

"Stop it," she gasped, jerking her shocked face to mine.

"Don't worry. I bought everyone drinks—on your tab—to make up for the horrid sound."

"I hate you." She laughed, knowing I was joking.

That's the way it was between us, just two friends bantering back and forth. As much as I wanted her as my everything, being the guy who got this side of her wasn't bad at all.

"Feel better after your nap?" I asked.

Rae showed up to the airport quieter than I'd ever seen her. When I asked if she was okay, she merely waved her hand, shooing the question away and adding a forced smile, assuring me she was fine. She'd barely looked at me while we waited for our flight, but I swore her eyes carried a tinge of red from crying. Everything inside urged me to push—to fight—but she kept shutting me down, and I had to respect it. I'd reminded myself that Rae was strong and didn't take any shit. I didn't have to worry about her.

Unless we were landing. Then the strong, fearless Rae openly showed signs of fear.

The hum of the wheels rumbled below, and as always, her slim fingers latched onto mine. Rubbing my thumb along the silky skin of her hand, I gave a reassuring squeeze, reminding her that with me, she was safe.

I fucking loved landing in planes with her.

By the time we got our bags, the Rae I knew and loved was back in full force. Even the quieter version that had made an appearance over the past year had vanished. This was the Rae from college—wild, crazy, and ready for anything.

"Here, take my pic."

I groaned and rolled my eyes but dutifully took the phone she shoved in my hands.

"You know you love it."

"Hardly."

I hid my smile behind the phone, watching her move and pose while I snapped picture after picture. Somehow, over the years, I'd become her Instagram boyfriend—the guy who climbs the tree and lays on the ground while holding all the bags just to get the perfect picture for Instagram. Not that I minded watching her move from pose to pose.

"Okay, now you come take one with me," she ordered.

Not bothering to fight, I stood by her side and held the phone out to capture us both. I followed her lead through a range of motions, starting with a sultry stare that had us both laughing. When she looked off, lips pursed, and her brow raised, I snagged a piece of her dark hair and laid it over my mouth like a mustache.

"That's the one. Pure perfection," Rae exclaimed.

"What can I say? I learned from the best."

She flipped her hair dramatically before heading out to our waiting car. On the drive to the hotel, she did her social media thing, and I pretended to answer emails but couldn't keep my eyes off her. Something about her seemed lighter—like a switch had been flipped, or a weight had been lifted. Whatever it was, it made me want to be light and happy with her.

But when a message came through from my brother, all thoughts of happy vanished.

"What's that frown for?" Rae asked, taking a break from her phone.

"Johnathan," I muttered, the only explanation necessary.

Her face scrunched up in commiseration. "How is he?"

"Fine. Just asked me to place a bet for him while I was in Vegas, which I will most definitely not be doing."

"Is he still married to that one girl…Krista?"

"Definitely not. Although, he married another woman, Corinne, soon after their divorce."

"How did I miss that?"

"It was a little after graduation when you were traveling and honestly, another marriage isn't much to talk about."

She shook her head. "It's amazing how different you two are. One who seems to marry every year without much ambition, and the other who says he's going to wait for *the one* and has more talent in his finger than most people have in their entire bodies."

"You know I only want to get married once," I reminded her.

"I know, I know. No need to explain," she said with a laugh.

I never went into the details of why I only wanted to get married once, but we'd talked about it before. She romanticized it like some kind of Disney movie and rather than correcting her about how it had more to do with standards than romance, I played along.

"Besides, we're here," she announced.

We hopped out of the car, and I passed a tip to the valet before we made our way to the front desk.

"Are you sure you don't want to just share a room," Rae asked. She waggled her brows and even blew an air kiss.

"And be assaulted by you?"

"Oh, come on. I'd make it worth it."

I struggled not to react when Rae jokingly threw herself at me. It was a game to her, and in a way, it was a game to me too. A game of determination and willpower. Part of me wanted to take her up on her offer, just to watch her face when I pulled her to me and whispered in her ear all the filthy things I wanted to do.

But I didn't. Instead, I scoffed as if I'd never dreamed of how she'd make it worth it.

"Fine," she sighed. "How about a facial?"

"Hard pass."

"Oh, come on. I brought your favorite—mango coconut."

"I'd hardly call you forcing it on me that one time my favorite."

"Ugh, fine. But you're missing out."

"I think I'll survive."

The concierge handed us our keys, his eyes bouncing between us to keep up with our banter.

"What time are we meeting?" I asked once we got on the elevator.

"Concert is at seven, and Parker goes on at nine-thirty-ish. The wedding is after that."

"Okay. I'll meet you down here before the concert. Just text me when you're ready."

"Okay, just stop by if you change your mind about that facial," she called through the closing doors.

Shaking my head, I laughed all the way to my room. Just as I walked through, my phone vibrated, and I braced myself for a message from Rae, instead finding a message from my grandma. Skipping a text message response, I hit the phone icon and gave her a call.

"Hey, stranger."

"Hey, Grandma. I just wanted to call and let you know I landed safely."

"Good. Was it a good flight?"

"Perfect."

"Oh, good. I'll let Grandpa know."

I smiled, imagining her walking through the house looking for him just to let him know I made it okay. They were the type of people that waited up until I let them know I made it home okay from their house. They stood on the porch, waving while I backed out, and didn't go back in until I was out of sight.

They were the type of people who stood by their son as he kept fucking up his life.

They were the type of people to take in two boys after their father died.

They were the type of people I strived to be like—to make proud.

"When is the wedding?" she asked excitedly.

"Not until late tonight. They have a concert to play first."

"How romantic," she gushed.

"Not many people would call a Vegas wedding romantic," I laughed.

"Oh, it's not the location," she said like it was obvious. "It's the promise to each other—the commitment they're making to love one another through thick and thin. Marriage is so important, so no matter where it happens or how, the meaning is always the same. Just because it's not big and fancy doesn't change the importance of the vow you take."

I'd heard the speech a thousand times, but it always made me smile. Grandma and Grandpa had been married for almost fifty-five years. An impressive goal to emulate—especially coming from watching Dad marry again and again and again. I had perfect examples of what I did want in life and what I didn't.

How their son could be so different always surprised me. Dad had married eight women before he finally kicked the bucket. None of them stayed long or cared much for my brother and me, but having the rotating door in our house left enough of an impression to know what I didn't want. When our grandparents took us in, I got to see what a real marriage was, and I idolized it.

"Yeah. Parker and Nova don't need much. I know they're chomping at the bit to be married."

"The life of a rock star," she sighed dramatically. "Well,

I'll let you go. Make sure to send pictures. Especially of you and your date."

I laughed at her hint. "It's just Rae."

"Ah, yes. Why don't you two date?"

"Because Rae doesn't date," I answered in rote. We'd had this conversation too many times to count. They'd only heard me talk about Rae and seen a handful of pictures. Somehow we never managed to make our schedules match up the few times they came to visit, but loved her regardless.

"Such a shame. You two make a cute pair."

"Thanks, Grandma."

"Either way, take lots of pictures and tell the happy couple congratulations from us."

"Will do."

I hung up and looked at the time. Three more hours to kill.

I considered taking Rae up on her offer—if for no other reason than to see her, and *maybe* because that one time I really did love the smell of whatever gunk she put on my face. In the end, I decided to give myself time to build up my defenses. Rae and Vegas screamed temptation. She'd flirt, and I'd look away to hide the fact that I was really imagining pinning her to the wall.

But she had a boyfriend, and we were just friends.

I'd need time alone to remember that before I did something we'd both regret.

Like say fuck it and give in.

---

WATCHING Parker and Nova say their vows—even in front of Elvis—filled me with happiness. The love they had for each other bubbled over, filling the room, making everyone smile and tear up. This was a couple that would stand the test of time.

"Such a wimp," Rae muttered at my side once we all stood outside congratulating the couple.

"Says the girl with watery eyes," I muttered back.

"She's my best friend. These are happy tears."

"Yeah. I'm just happy for her, too."

She paused, and something about it made me look down just in time for her to look up. "Sad it's not you?" she asked, a tinge of edge to her tone matching a curious flare behind her thick lashes.

I'd formed a friendship with all three girls, but I was closer to Nova than Vera. We both liked art, giving us something to talk about, comparing the difference in our interests. She was more of a classical artist, while I took the route of graphic design. Rae made jokes about us nerding out and how we should just sleep together and get it over with. I'd roll my eyes and brush off the comment, but this time was different. This time had a sharper bite to her words—maybe a bit more honesty.

Was she…*jealous?*

But for Rae to be jealous, she'd have to see me as more than a friend—she'd have to want more. She'd have to want me for herself, and that wasn't something Raelynn Vos did.

Cutting that useless line of thought, I shot back with my own banter, giving her the most intense stare while biting back my smile. "Hardly. We know there is only one friend I'd marry." I almost choked at the way her eyes widened. "King, of course."

Her sigh of relief was audible, allowing her shoulders to drop from where they'd pulled tight a second ago. "You two would make a cute couple," she joked.

Her reaction was all the proof I needed that thinking Rae could be jealous was the most absurd idea ever.

"Hey, Emerald," Brogan called to Rae, cutting off our banter.

Rae turned to one of Parker's band members with a

bored, who-the-fuck-are-you stare, but I noticed her lips twitch—a clear sign she wasn't nearly as irritated as her haughty glare led to believe.

When Rae didn't melt at Brogan's feet like any other woman in the world, he smiled, holding up his hands in surrender. "Raelynn," he corrected.

"Thank you," she answered with a demure smile. Rae wasn't a woman who answered to nicknames. Especially from someone she knew damn well knew her name. Especially not a nickname as lame as the color of her dress.

I stood back, watching Brogan try to lure Rae in, doing my best to mask the jealousy pulling my jaw tight. I should've been used to her flirting with others, but it still screwed my muscles too tight. Thankfully, I at least knew she wouldn't be going home with him. I'd watched her strut away with men since we met, but it never got easy. Not even when I found a woman to lose myself in. But tonight, I didn't have to worry because she had Bodie. I hated the douchebag, but he was a solid cock-blocker.

Everyone started talking about their plans next, and I considered tossing Rae over my shoulder so I could have her all to myself. However, that plan was dashed when Brogan spoke up. "Evan just texted me about a party at the Bellagio."

"I'm down with that," Rae jumped in.

The look Brogan gave Rae was textbook—the one any guy got when he thought he was going to get lucky with the bombshell in front of him. I didn't fucking think so. "Don't you have a boyfriend you should call?" I interjected, hoping to dash Brogan's hopes and get Rae and me back on track for a night alone.

"You're not her boyfriend?" Brogan asked.

I narrowed my eyes, trying to figure out if he was that arrogant or that dumb to flirt with a woman so openly when he thought their boyfriend was standing beside them.

Before I could ask, Rae answered, "Nope. He's just my forever wedding date."

My lip curled at the description. *Just.* I wasn't *just* anything.

"Well, then, by all means, come along," Brogan crooned, scanning her from head to toe. "I know I'd love to have you there."

I hoped that Rae would roll her eyes at his cheesy come-ons, but she stood there, eating it up.

*Fuck.*

Bringing up Bodie didn't work, and with each passing second, I saw my plans of just the two of us fading away. "I am not going to some random hotel party," I tried to reason with her.

Fail.

She shrugged. "Vera will go with me."

Vera stepped back with her hands up. "Girl, I love you, but Nico and I have plans. It's our first trip after the baby, and we're making the most of it."

Unphased, Rae stuck out her tongue. "Party poopers. Fine," she added with a dramatic sigh. "I'll just go alone."

"Austin," Nova said. I ruefully met her wide, pleading eyes, already knowing my fate. "Please. I don't want to have to skip out on my wedding night to make sure my best friend is safe."

"What?" Parker almost shrieked.

Nova gave him a not-so-subtle wink, assuring me I wasn't getting out of this.

"Fucking fine. I'll go," I grumbled, turning to point at Rae. "But we're not staying long."

She smiled in victory, and as much as I fought it, I couldn't help but smile back.

I'd go anywhere for her.

## Chapter Four

### RAELYNN

The party could have been one at college. A crowded room, drunk people grinding on each other, beer pong in the corner, and the occasional cheers and shouts mirrored everything I'd loved about frat parties. Except this one had top-of-the-line liquor and beer dispensed by a bartender. Add in the Vegas skyline twinkling in the distance, and I for sure knew I wasn't in Kansas anymore.

I giggled at my own silly reference.

"What's so funny?" Austin asked, standing tall like a centurion by my side.

"Me."

"You are pretty hilarious."

"What I think is funny is that we're at a celebrity party, and you've had all of one beer."

"Someone has to stay sober to keep an eye on you."

"Pssshhh. I'm a big girl, Austin. Haven't you noticed?" I put my arms up and shimmied, blowing him an extra pouty kiss. Euphoric victory shot through my veins when his eyes flicked from my lips to my breasts before looking away, a tinge of color heating up his cheeks.

"C'mon, Austin. Have a shot with me."

"I'm not doing shots. Shots with you lead to epic hangovers."

"But also, epic nights." He confirmed I was right with a smile but still shook his head. "At least have one drink with me," I coaxed with my best pout.

His eyes flicked to my lips again before holding up his beer. "I am."

I snagged the bottle and drained it. "Well, now you need another. C'mon. Vodka gimlets are calling our names. I know how much you like them."

"Might as well do shots," he muttered behind me.

But I didn't care because his big rough hand was in mine, and he didn't resist when I pulled him to the bar set up in the corner. I caught sight of Brogan off to the side with some woman's hands glued to his broad chest and mouth latched onto his. Good for him.

We'd been at the party for less than an hour before he gave up on seducing me. Those big hands had spanned my back as we danced. The scruff of his beard abraded my neck when he told me how much he wanted me. I almost let him have me, but when I'd glanced over his shoulder, my eyes collided with a brooding green, and Brogan ceased to exist.

Something about Austin's gaze sucked the air out of the room, leaving just the two of us. Something about the eyes I'd grown to know better than my own sparked differently—sparked something inside *me* differently. I'd almost stumbled, but Brogan caught me. When I looked back, the raw energy pouring from him was gone, replaced by the same bored look he'd been wearing since we got here. So, I brushed the moment aside and stuck my tongue out like a kid, earning a minor twitch of his lips.

I'd focused my attention back on Brogan—or tried to—but when he realized he wasn't getting any from me, he left with another girl—not the same one he currently had pinned to a wall. Not that I cared. I was having too much fun.

"Oh, wait." I held up my hand to stop Austin from drinking and dug through my purse for my phone. "Can you take a video, please?" I asked the bartender.

"Sure."

I looked around and assessed Austin, trying to figure out the best pose. "Sit on the stool," I ordered. With his usual dramatic sigh, he complied, bringing his feet to the bottom rung. I snagged the bottle of vodka and sat it discreetly off to the side. "Maybe they'll end up sponsoring me." I shrugged.

He smiled, watching for my next move. He always gave me shit with his eye rolls and groans, but he'd told me more than once that he enjoyed watching my mind work as I put together the perfect pictures. Everyone assumed I was a vapid, selfie-obsessed airhead, but Austin saw the art behind what I did.

"Whoa, whoa," he said when I pushed his knees apart to step between them.

"Calm down. Your virtue is safe," I joked. "I'm just trying to get close for the photo."

With a cocked brow, he relaxed and made room for me.

"I mean, your virtue is safe for now. Who knows about later?" I waggled my brows, loving the deep rumbling laugh. "Now, let's link arms and take our drinks."

He had to lean in so I could get my arm around his muscular one. The rough hair on his forearm tickled my skin, sending goosebumps all the way up my arm to my neck. It was either that soft caress or the way our foreheads almost touched. Or maybe it was how his eyes turned serious again, so similar to before, melting into an emerald green as they met mine. I always taunted him, loving the way he laughed and looked away as if embarrassed. But sometimes, he didn't look away, instead leaving me a pile of goo under the heat flaring in the depths.

There was no doubt that Austin and I were just friends, but the way he stared now made all the other times I turned to goo feel like standing beside a pile of embers compared to the raging bonfire burning me from the inside out now. Despite our friendship, being this close almost begged me to close the gap and finally taste him. Being this close had me desperately wondering what it would be like if he acted on the intense promise in his look.

*Just. Friends,* I reminded myself. As much as I wanted to eat Austin's delicious body up with my bare hands, I'd never do it at the risk of losing his friendship. Because I knew that if we ever slept together, he'd want more than I could give, and there'd be no going back.

So, friendship it was.

With a wink, I lifted my glass to my lips and sipped from the edge, watching him do the same.

"Perfecto," I announced to the bartender.

"I'm glad you approve." He smiled and handed my phone back.

"Better than your beer?" I asked Austin.

"Maybe a little," he answered, taking another drink.

"I'm always right. Now let's dance."

"I'm good."

"Ugh. Fine. Then you can watch."

Another flash of heat shot straight to my core but was gone in an instant. It was enough to fuel me out to the dance floor and put on a show. He watched every second, even turning down women that approached him. Every once in a while, I'd dance close and snag his hand to lead him back to the bar for another drink. After four or five, or maybe seven, everything lightened until I thought I'd float away.

The music, laughing, drinking, and dancing all reminded me of what I'd been missing. Bodie had called a couple million times, but I kept hitting ignore, feeling more and more free with each rejection. Euphoria mixed with the alcohol, and once I finally got Austin out on the dance floor, I used him like my own personal pole. Skimming my hands up my body and through my hair, I rolled my hips and turned, working my way closer.

I was about to curl my back into his front when a large shackle landed on my wrist. I jerked my head over my shoulder to figure out what Austin was doing to find him studying my arm with narrowed eyes.

"What is that?" he asked.

"What is what?"

His brows pinched more over stormy eyes. "Those bruises. On your arm."

My breath stuttered like I'd been punched to the chest. Wriggling my wrist free, I slowly lowered my arm, fighting for a calm I didn't feel. "I don't know. I get bruises all the time."

He didn't believe me. I saw it in the way his shoulders pulled back, and his nostrils flared. "Did Bodie do that?" he asked dangerously soft but loud enough for me to hear.

In the hard body preparing for battle in front of me, I saw a spark of concern—of pity.

*I didn't fucking think so.*

I could never admit to Austin what happened. I couldn't stand him looking at me like anything other than a powerful woman. I refused. So, I forced a laugh, tossing my head back. "Puh-lease. Bodie could fucking try."

He scanned my face for the lie, but I did my best to hide it. Slowly, his body relaxed, but the skepticism still lingered, waiting to be brought up again.

Wanting to shut it down for good, I set out to distract him —pushing harder than usual. Closing the gap, I rested my hands on his chest, sliding them up and around his neck and into his hair. I raised up on my tiptoes and brushed my nose against his chin, gasping when his hands gripped my waist, almost spanning all the way around.

When I glanced up, almost all the skepticism was gone. Only a little more to go.

"You know, Austin, what happens in Vegas, stays in Vegas.

We're both drunk and ridiculously hot. We could finally sleep together and pretend it never happened in the morning. We could blame it all on the vodka."

The last bit of doubt faded, being singed away by another flare of desire. For a second, I almost expected him to take me up on it, but then the usual deadpanned stare took its place. "I highly doubt your boyfriend would be okay with that."

"Lucky you, I don't have a boyfriend."

"What?"

"I broke up with him."

He shook his head like he was trying to jar something loose to make sense of it all. "When?"

"This morning. Or wait, yesterday morning, since it's after midnight."

"Why? What happened? Does your dad know?"

"Calm down, private eye," I said, laughing. "We broke up because I don't do serious, so it was only a matter of time. And the only other important thing you need to know is I don't have a boyfriend, so it's our lucky day." He still gripped my hips, but also looked more confused than anything. "So, how 'bout it, Austin. Wanna fuck?" I smirked, using the first line I ever said to him in college.

He studied my face as if actually considering it, and the plan to distract him turned into something more. My heart sped up, the possibility of Austin taking me up on a one-night stand sent almost too much adrenaline for my body to take.

With achingly slow movements, one hand released my hip to skim up my body like a feather, past my jaw to push a stray hair behind my ear.

He leaned in, and I held my breath.

"I would, but I will only sleep with my wife."

His eyes locked on mine, and time stood still.

Until his eyes twitched and humor sparked in the green depths, igniting a laugh I couldn't hold back. I snorted, and he quickly followed suit.

Before I knew it, we were both laughing with tears down our cheeks. "Is that the line you use on all the girls?"

Austin slept around as much as I did, just with the occasional relationship tossed in. He wanted a wife, but I figured he didn't want one yet.

"Nah, they came to me."

"God, you're such a slut."

"A slut that won't sleep with friends," he said with a pseudo-serious glare.

I gasped, putting my hand to my chest. "Poor, King. He must be heartbroken."

"He tries harder than you to get in my pants."

"Hmmm. Maybe we should team up to break you," I threatened.

"Psh. If we all got together, he wouldn't know how to handle *us.*"

"This is a valid point. We *are* crazy."

His mouth pursed, and brows pinched.

"Crazy awesome," I exclaimed, raising my hand.

Not one to disappoint and always knowing what I needed, he slapped my hand. I loved that he didn't question it. I love that he played along and enjoyed the games as much as me.

Still laughing, we made our way to the bar for another round, setting out to prove just how crazy we could be.

## Chapter Five

### AUSTIN

I DIDN'T MOVE A MUSCLE. I wasn't sure I could. Everything ached. Things I didn't even know could ache—ached. Drums—no. What was worse than drums? The whole damn Tran-Siberian Orchestra wreaked havoc in my head. The throbbing so intense, I couldn't even piece together the night or where the hell I was.

"Fuck." The soft whimper came from behind me.

Dread washed over my skin, leaving me to wonder who I brought home. Then the voice registered, and I realized I at least made it back with Rae. With superhuman effort and a groan that even hurt, I rolled to my back.

"What the fuck?" I wasn't even sure what I was questioning. How I could hurt so much? What the hell happened after we decided to move on to straight shots? How did we even get back here? "How much vodka did we have?"

As if a reminder of my mistakes, my head pulsed on the verge of exploding. I dug my fingers into my temples in a fruitless effort to ease the pain.

"Too much. Not enough. I don't even know," she answered, her groggy voice sounding as rough as I felt.

She rolled to her back, and we both stared at the ceiling,

side-by-side, wondering what the hell happened. I was hoping to maybe pass back out and wake up feeling more human, but nature called.

"I got to piss."

"So, sexy," Rae deadpanned.

"I turn on the extra charm just for you."

"Lucky me."

I rolled out of bed and watched her bat her lashes, her makeup still perfectly in place, framed by her arms stretched over her head, laying across the dark spread of her hair. Although, my attention shifted quickly when I got up, causing the sheet to shift, baring part of her full breast and the most perfect rosy nipple.

Like Pavlov's dog, my mouth watered at the sight. My muscles tightened, fighting the immediate urge to crawl back in bed and pull the hardened tip into my mouth. I stood frozen, waiting for Rae to figure out what had me so entranced, except her attention dropped down my bare chest, and it was only as my cock began to harden that I noticed the breeze against the sensitive skin. Looking down, I found my half-hard dick hanging between my legs.

"Holy shit," Rae breathed in awe.

"Holy shit," I shouted, snatching an extra blanket to wrap around myself. Thankfully, Rae did the same because fuck, it was hard to focus with her tits out. But then it left me with enough attention to start considering everything that could have happened.

Did we sleep together?

*Fuck.* The thought of sleeping with Rae filled me with a million conflicting emotions, but most of all, dread—for what it could do to our relationship or that I finally had her, and I couldn't even remember it. Feeling unsteady on my feet, I stood still and looked around the room for any signs of sex. No condom wrappers. No signs of things being knocked over.

No trail of clothes leading from the door in our urgency to get to each other.

No. I shook my head. We didn't sleep together. My mind wouldn't let me forget that—no matter how much alcohol I had.

"Austin, what the fuck is that?" Rae asked, more serious than I'd ever heard her before. She pointed her finger accusingly to where I gripped the sheet, and a flash of gold caught my eye. As if in slow motion, I raised my left hand. My head swam, the single line of gold around my ring finger blurring. A pinch started in my chest and bloomed to pressure building inside and out until I was sure I'd pass out.

It was her whimper that pulled me out of the haze to find her sitting on the bed, the sheet clutched to her chest with her right hand, as she stared at her left, taking in a gold band that matched mine. Time stood still, both of us clinging to modesty while reality set in.

"We did *not* just get married in Vegas," she whispered, almost like she was pleading with me to make it true.

But I couldn't.

"I think—I think we did," I answered.

My eyes bounced between the two matching bands. I took in the shiny metal that tied us together, and in all the chaos and shock, another emotion emerged—happiness. Before it could grow to anything other than a tiny spark, Rae started laughing. Slowly at first, almost a whisper of a giggle. Then it grew until she was folded over, wiping tears from her eyes.

"Why are you laughing?" I asked hesitantly.

She looked to be on the edge of a breakdown, and I could only imagine the havoc this was wreaking on her. Rae never wanted to be married. At least that's what she said. People always said the truth came out when you were drunk, so maybe she did want to get married on some level. While this probably wasn't in her plans, I'd show her how great it could be.

This wasn't in my plans either. It wasn't how I wanted it, but my grandma's voice reminded me that even a cheesy wedding in Vegas was still a marriage—still a commitment. It may not have been intentional, but according to those rings, we made vows, and I always promised myself I'd only do that once, and I'd mean it.

"It's a joke. Did you slip the ring on my finger while I was sleeping?"

"No, I wouldn't do that."

Her laugh took on a more panicked edge. "It has to be a joke, right? This isn't real."

The desperation coating her words hit me in my chest like a needle popping a balloon. As hope seeped from the hole, irritation and anger bled into the vacant space. She knew what marriage meant to me. She heard me swear countless times that I'd only marry once. As much as I tried to rationalize it, her laughter mocked me—mocked my beliefs. Trying to push past it, I took slow deep breaths and walked around the room, scanning every surface.

"What are you doing?"

"There has to be something—some kind of paperwork."

"There isn't because this is a joke."

The hole grew under her determination to believe it wasn't real. Shoving aside a lacy scrap of material, I unearthed a thick cream piece of paper.

"Certificate of Commitment," I read, holding it up for her to see.

She studied the words, taking in the gold embossed circle between our two signatures. My stomach sank right along with her hope of it being a prank.

On the back, a yellow post-it had barely legible words scrawled across it.

"Austin and Rae, the license will be filed before your heads hit the pillow. Maybe it was a tad too much alcohol, but I know love when I see it. Congrats on your happy marriage. Love, Elvis."

"Oh, my god." She groaned, sinking her head into her hands.

I set the novelty certificate on the table, running my fingers over the words.

*Commitment.*

*Marriage is so important, so no matter where it happens or how, the meaning is always the same. Just because it's not big and fancy doesn't change the importance of the vow you take.*

I hated watching Rae struggle to process what we'd done, but there wasn't anything we could do but face it. At least we wouldn't have to face it alone. At least we'd have our best friend by our side.

Hope flickered like a light at the end of the tunnel. Maybe it was fate that it all worked out this way, but no matter the reason, we'd make it work.

"We can—we can get it annulled."

Her words drowned out my thoughts like a record scratch. "What?"

"Yeah." Sitting upright like the idea was the perfect solution to bring her back to life. She crawled to her knees, still clutching the sheet. "We can get it annulled," she said again, more excited this time. "We're not stuck. People make these mistakes all the time. It's Vegas."

If her calling marrying me a joke was a pinprick to my chest, then her calling it a mistake was an atomic bomb. Memories of my father signing yet another divorce paper, laughing while telling my brother and me that that was the end of mistake number five, or six, or whatever number wife he was on, singed through the fraying ends of my calm. The frustrated tension exploded through my body, pulling my muscles tight, and I clenched my jaw to filter back the biting words I knew I could be capable of when cornered and hurt.

"It's a marriage Rae, not a mistake."

"We were drunk. It's not like we would have gotten married if we were sober," she scoffed. As if the thought of marrying *me* was the most absurd thing she'd ever heard.

The more she attempted to brush it off, the less I was able to hear my rational voice, the less I was able to fend off wild thoughts. Like the thought that she wasn't so upset about being married as much as she was upset about marrying me—the guy who didn't come from an elite background like she did, but who was always there for her. The one guy who never asked for more than what she was willing to give. The guy who never judged her. The guy who's loved her from the beginning.

"It doesn't matter if we were sober or not," I bit out.

"Uhh, yeah, it does. I'm pretty sure there's a law about it. Actually, I don't think they're supposed to let us get married if we're intoxicated at all. The Elvis guy could probably get sued."

She explained it away like it was his fault and not hers—like she didn't make the decision, so she shouldn't have to face the consequences. And when did marrying me become such a consequence?

My phone pinged from under the pile of my clothes. Needing a distraction, I grabbed it and immediately regretted it.

**Gma**: I didn't know you were serious with Raelynn. I'm not mad you didn't tell us, especially since you two look so happy. Call us when you get a chance so we can congratulate you both.

*Mother fuck.* How did she know?

I scrolled up to see if I sent anything, but the last message was about Nova's wedding. Swiping through my phone, I saw the massive amount of notifications on one of the apps, and it hit me.

Already dreading what I knew I would find, I opened Instagram.

"Shit," I muttered.

"What?" she asked distractedly, too caught up in her escape.

"You posted to Instagram."

"No," she breathed, falling back to her butt like the wind had been knocked out of her. "No, no, no."

She grabbed her phone, and I switched apps. "And TikTok."

As soon as I tapped the square, Rae's horrible singing voice filled the room. "Going to the chapel, and we're—" She broke to giggle when I picked her up to carry her inside. "Gonna get ma-a-a-rried."

The video cut off just as she looked to me, and I looked at her. I must have been drunk because, in that small glimpse, I saw all the love I'd been holding back pour out with one look.

She played the video, and I waited for her to see the end and know, but instead, all I got was another pained groan. "Fuck."

"My grandparents know."

I didn't need to explain more—she knew what my family meant to me, but I knew she planned to ignore it when she refused to look up.

"We can explain what happened. They'll understand."

"No." The word tumbled so easily from my lips without pause. I always said yes to Rae, but not this.

Her head shot up; her brows pinched in confusion. "No?"

"No. I can't. I—I can't get a divorce."

"It's not a divorce. It's just an annulment."

The tension squeezed tighter and tighter, pushing me to the limits. No amount of slow deep breaths could keep me from the edge. "No," I said harder. "I can't."

"Austin, we are not staying married."

Her voice hardened like mine, and it was the final straw. "Why?"

"Because I don't want to be married."

"At all? Or just to me?"

"What?"

"C'mon, Rae." My voice softened with the challenge, baiting her to react. "Which is it?"

Her mouth opened and closed, searching for words that never came. My lip curled into a sneer the longer she struggled. She met my eyes, and there was no hiding the piece of me I kept under lock and key. She took her time studying my face like she'd never seen me before, and I hated it.

Finally, she shook her head and laughed. "I'm not doing this. I'm getting dressed and calling my lawyer."

"No," I said again, standing my ground as she scrambled around for her clothes. "I'm not agreeing to this."

"Tough shit, Austin. It. Was. A. Mistake," she snapped, showing me a side of her I'd never seen directed at me.

It shouldn't have bothered me, but she threw that word in my face again. *Mistake.* A part of me screamed to stop. A part of me wondered if I was still drunk, but all I could see was her laughing and calling *me* a mistake—not just the wedding. That part of me won. "Then maybe you should act mature enough to accept the consequences for once in your life."

She froze before slowly turning away from her task and facing me with narrowed eyes. Her whole body pulled tight like an animal ready to pounce. "What?"

The snap of her t only served to add fuel to the flames, and I used a dangerous tone of my own to match hers. "For once, just deal with your decisions and stop expecting everyone else to cater to what you want to fix it."

She took a step forward, her anger much bigger than her small frame. "Excuse. Me?"

"Marriage may be a joke to you. Something you can erase away with enough money, but it means a hell of a lot more than that to me. Don't you dare assume I'll cater to your whim when marriage and having a wife means something to me."

"Oh, all of a sudden, you care about a wife. You fuck random women all the time."

"I didn't fuck you. Hell, you married me, and I still wouldn't fuck you like all the other guys do." Like a slow-burning firework, I ignited and whispered into the sky, making you wait for the explosion.

Rae's nostrils flared under her wide eyes, and I could've sworn she was seconds away from smoke coming from her ears. "Fuck you. Since when are you all about being with one woman. You go through as many as I go through guys."

"Just because I enjoy myself doesn't mean I don't know how to value and respect the tradition of marriage. But I know you struggle with the concept."

"What the hell does that mean?"

I laughed without humor, lost in the hurricane of fire all around us, spewing words that I didn't even mean. Her dismissal landed blow after blow, and I lashed out blindly to land my own. "You don't value anything but your freedom. You have no respect for anything unless it gets you what you want. You're a selfish, spoiled little girl."

"I am *not* selfish."

"Then how come you're acting like you don't know how much this means to me? I have no doubt it was your idea to get married in the first place. You're always pushing for us to fool around, showing no respect for our friendship. You probably used how much marriage meant to me to get what you wanted—just like you always do."

Her lips parted, sucking in the smallest gasp. I would have missed it if I didn't notice every detail about her. The furrow in her brow softened, and I almost softened with it. I knew I was hurting her, but I was too mad to stop—like a freight train off the rails.

"Fuck. You," she almost growled.

"You. Fucking. Wish." I leaned in and sneered each word.

Finally, she stumbled back. "Get out," she whispered. "Get the fuck out."

"Gladly."

Grabbing my clothes, I didn't even bother to change, taking the sheet with me.

With the slam of the door, it was like every ounce of anger that had pushed me moments ago stayed behind, leaving me empty.

Leaving me with nothing but regret.

## Chapter Six

### RAELYNN

"What are you doing here?" I asked.

More tears built when I got through TSA to find my two best friends waiting on the other side.

"Oh, please," Vera scoffed, yanking me into her arms. Nova wrapped around behind me, and as much as I fought it, more tears slid free. I was so tired of crying.

These two women weren't my best friends—they were my sisters, and I shouldn't have expected anything less than them bombarding me at the airport without even having to ask.

"Your flights don't leave for hours," I said, wiping away any evidence of weakness, sliding my sunglasses back in place. I didn't care if I looked like a diva, everyone could suck it today.

"The guys are meeting us later," Vera explained.

"But it's your first day as a married couple," I said to Nova.

"We have all the days ahead of us," Nova assured. "You need me because, apparently, I'm not the only one spending their first day married at an airport."

I winced. Nova usually stood back and observed until one

of the people she loved was in trouble, then she didn't pull any punches and went straight for the heart of it.

A golf ball-sized lump tried to work its way up my throat, but I forced it back down, somehow managing to choke out a simple, "Yeah."

"That's it? Yeah?" Vera asked, brows lifting high.

"What else can I say?"

"Um, how about everything? All the details. Where, when, why? How?"

Groaning, I pressed my fingers to my temple, willing away this fucking hangover.

"Do you want to get a drink?" Vera asked.

"God, no."

"Ohhhh," they said in unison, finally realizing my hangover.

It didn't take much to put two and two together.

"Come on. Let's grab a greasy lunch." Vera linked her arm with mine, and Nova took my suitcase.

They gave me enough time to order and devour every ounce of my burger before leaning back, arms crossed, waiting for answers. I gave them a rundown but started falling apart all over again when I got to the morning.

Two hands reached across the table, gripping mine, and I held on tight.

"I just...I don't think I can talk about it yet."

"Okay," Vera agreed without pushing.

Nova nodded along with her. I loved them both so much. They knew me better than anyone and knew exactly what I needed.

"Thank you."

"Of course," Vera cooed. "Besides, we know we'll get it out of you later, anyways."

The threatening words with the calm, soothing tone had me snorting. Which then made Nova snort, and then all three of us were laughing. I was the first to stop because it just hurt.

I had no other way of explaining it, but I was so sad that even laughing hurt.

*Fuck.*

"Just take some time," Nova said softly, seeing my turmoil. "Don't make any quick decisions when you're this upset."

I nodded but didn't confirm or deny because I knew as soon as I got home, the only solution was to call our lawyer and get this marriage annulled.

With one last hug, I said goodbye to the girls and boarded my plane, hating the empty seat beside me. Part of me had hoped we'd be forced to sit next to each other. I knew we wouldn't have talked, and our anger would've been palpable, but maybe it would have filled this void growing bigger and bigger each second away from him.

But he never showed, and I could assume he changed his flight to avoid me. After hearing all the words he spewed about me, maybe I shouldn't have been so surprised. Maybe the things he said in anger were the truth—the way he really saw me—as some spoiled, selfish girl.

*Was I?*

By the end of the flight, my headache had only grown, and I moved through the airport at lightning speed. When my car arrived, I exited the doors and scrolled through my contacts for our lawyer. I was so focused I didn't even register the first flash.

But when I heard my name, I jerked up to find a small crowd of photographers with their cameras pointed at me.

"Raelynn, where's your husband?"

"You and Austin have been friends for years? What changed?"

"Raelynn, how does Bodie feel about this?"

"Did you plan to get married while away?"

They peppered me with questions, and my usual confidence and quick wit were nowhere to be found. Thank god for sunglasses to hide my deer in headlights look.

"Rae," a familiar voice called behind me.

I looked over to find my father's secretary smiling next to a black Escalade. "Molly," I sighed in relief, darting over to escape the small mob behind me.

"Congratulations on your wedding," she exclaimed loud enough for the photographers to hear.

Her forced smile was so big it looked like her face would crack in half. Before I could ask her what the hell was going on, she pulled me into a big hug.

"Your father is so happy for everyone to hear the big news." She pulled back, holding my shoulders, and uttered through her stretched lips just for me, "Wave and smile."

Digging up my socialite skills among my confusion, I turned and gave a coy smile and finger wave before darting in the car. Molly followed, and as soon as the door closed, she settled back, dropping the fake smile for a look that screamed, you fucked up.

"Your dad is pissed."

*Shit.*

The whole drive, Molly pleaded the fifth while I tried to imagine and prepare for every scenario that could be waiting for me. I finally caved and opened my text messages, scrolling past anyone not listed as Mom or Dad. A chill ran down my spine when I spotted Bodie's name. Pausing with my thumb over his message, I considered opening it, thinking it would be better to be prepared—to see any danger coming, but then I reminded myself that I was free. I refused to change myself because someone wanted me to think of them as dangerous. Bodie was nothing. He couldn't hurt me anymore. I won.

Not even bothering to delete his name, I kept scrolling but didn't find anything from my parents besides a single phone call from early in the morning.

I imagined they wouldn't be happy, but they always supported me and my decisions—they always let me make my mistakes, and despite what Austin accused, I faced the consequences and did my best to clean them up myself. But this wasn't like my usual antics; this wasn't an individual consequence, and while most times, my decisions only blew up on social media and the occasional magazine, with Dad's campaign, I knew it'd show up elsewhere.

That was the variable that had me on edge as I opened the door to their house.

My mom shot up from her perch at the edge of the stairs with a look of disappointment and warning. The combination sent an ominous wave through my veins. I slowed my steps and tried to smile. She looked just as casually put together as always in designer jeans and a blouse, her makeup done to highlight the same brown eyes as mine, her matching dark hair styled to perfection.

"Hey, Mom."

She closed the gap and framed my face in her gentle hands. The familiar move comforted me, but the way she looked at me like she didn't know me washed the comfort away. In all my years, I'd never made her question me, except that one time in high school when I started that bonfire party, and the cops came. Even then, her look had been more *what the fuck* rather than *who are you*.

I almost broke down crying again when she pulled me into a tight hug and whispered that she loved me.

"Come on. Your dad is waiting."

"Do I have to? Maybe I can just escape to Mexico."

"I raised you better than that. We don't run."

"I know," I muttered but appreciated the reminder.

Dad turned when we walked into the office, clutching a glass of amber liquid. He scanned me from head to toe like he always did when I walked in. To make sure I was okay, he would tell me. *I'm just waiting for the day you come to me with a broken bone or missing limb.*

I waited for the usual nod of approval, but it never came. Instead, he studied me like my mom had. His pale blue eyes dulled with the dark shadows. His short blond hair stood up in odd places from roughly running his hands through it. If I hadn't known how bad it was before, I knew now. You could tell the level of stress Dad faced based on the amount of disarray his hair was in, and right now, it looked like a patchy spike design.

"If you want to day-drink, all you have to do is ask. You know I'm always up for it," I joked, desperate to lighten the mood.

The man who always had a smile for me since I was a little girl didn't laugh. His eyes slid closed before he jumped right in. "I've always been lenient with you, Raelynn. But this? Of all the times?"

*Ooookay.* Apparently, we were skipping the niceties. Well, as much as I screwed up, he had some explaining to do, too. "Well, you didn't make it any better when you had your secretary pick me up and pretend the marriage was real."

His head snapped back to me so hard I worried he'd have whiplash. "It's not real?" he shouted.

"No. I told you, I never wanted to get married."

His jaw hung open in disbelief. I stood there, trying to hold my chin high while he struggled to rearrange the situation in his mind.

"Holy shit," he muttered.

And there went his hand again, tugging at the already frayed ends of his hair.

"You would have known that if you had waited to talk to me instead of making your own plan."

"You didn't pick up your phone. What was I supposed to do?"

"Ignore it."

"Ha." He barked a laugh. "That's a little hard to do when you get married in Vegas. As if you aren't being watched closer than ever right now, you were in Vegas with Nova and Parker. There was no way you wouldn't get noticed. Add in social media, and ignoring it was the furthest thing from a possibility as I could get," he bit out, losing his patience.

He shook his head, looking away before downing the rest of his drink in one swallow.

For the first time in the twelve years since Dad adopted me after marrying Mom, his disappointment weighed on me. Like a spotlight burning down in front of a mirror I couldn't escape, reality sank in. I wanted to look away, but I couldn't.

I was disappointed in myself.

I messed up. The people who never got mad at me were pissed. There was no denying that I truly fucked up in a big way. Not with my drunken antics or bold personality that the media loved, but in a way that hurt the people around me.

"What about Bodie?" my mom asked.

I cringed, just his name like nails on a chalkboard. "We broke up."

"What? When?"

"The day I left. So, yesterday."

"Are things okay?" she asked so sincerely, it caught me off guard, causing the mask I always wore when talking about Bodie to slip. Her eyes narrowed at whatever mine revealed, and I quickly snapped the blank layer back in place. If I thought Dad was disappointed in me over the wedding, it wouldn't come close to how devastated my mom would be if she knew how long I'd stayed with Bodie after his first abuse.

"Yeah. It was time," I answered neutrally.

I realized my mistake when her eyes narrowed more. I wasn't neutral about anything. I was decisive and bold with my choices. I made them with passion, never with the shrug of a shoulder like I did then.

Deciding my dad felt like a safer option than my mom's scrutinizing stare, I addressed him. "Listen, Dad. I'll explain to the press, and we'll get it annulled. Your campaign pushes to remove the double standard, and men recover from things like this all the time—a woman can too."

He shook his head before I even finished pleading my case. "Rae, I'm already getting calls from investors and sponsors asking me if I'm the kind of man to support cheating. My campaign also focuses on loyalty and commitment. You had dinner with Bodie a few days ago, and now you're married to Austin," he explained. "This isn't as simple as explaining it away. Not right now."

Those last three words hung like a guillotine—ominous and my final downfall. "What do you mean, not right now?"

"You know I love every crazy antic you get up to. I support you to be independent and push the norms. I love that you are a bold woman, exemplifying to other women and younger girls that there is nothing wrong with forging your own path."

I did know that. When I was seventeen, I told him I never wanted to get married and to become the first female president to sleep around. He'd laughed and told me to do what made me happy as long as I was safe and respected myself.

We weren't laughing my antics off now.

"I need these investors, Rae. My campaign depends on it."

*Consequences.* Every decision had consequences, and I'd face these like I had the others. Usually, I faced them on my terms, but taking in my father's disheveled hair and discarded tie, I knew I'd have to put myself aside and face them his way.

"What do you need me to do?"

He froze, as if in shock that I'd so readily lay down my sword and let him take the lead. Austin's words from this morning came back. Was I selfish? Was it so shocking I'd help without caveats? Watching Dad process my answer, I grew more and more determined to prove I was anything but selfish.

Coming to a decision, he took a deep breath as if preparing for impact. "Play it off."

"What?" My head snapped back like he'd slapped me. Surely, I heard him wrong.

"Play it off," he repeated. Nope. Definitely not hallucinating. "We have the Hamptons trip to Scott's house, and I need his support. Other candidates will be there, so I need to put my best foot forward. Jeremy Scott is a family man and wants us all to come." He paused as if bracing himself, and I held my breath. "I want you to bring Austin—to play it off like you got married because you've always cared for each other. Your friendship is common knowledge, so no one will question it."

It was a solid plan—one I might have come up with on my own if it were for anyone else. There was just one problem.

"I don't think Austin will go for it."

"He's your best friend," my mom said like it was the only explanation needed. "Of course, he'll do it."

"He's not...we're not talking."

"Jesus," my dad muttered.

"It's not like we planned this," I snapped.

He took a deep breath and headed back to the liquor cart to refill his glass. Before turning, he grabbed another and filled that one too. With determination sparking the blue in his eyes back to life, he passed me the glass. "Convince him," he ordered. "We don't really have any other choice. Tell him I'll owe him."

"He doesn't need anything from you."

"Everyone needs something eventually."

I couldn't help but think of Bodie and how he never missed an opportunity to ask for more than he deserved. I doubted Austin would ever accept favors. So, why would he help me? Taking a healthy swallow from the glass, I relished in the stinging heat sliding to my chest. Although, it didn't come close to the sharp jab of pain that had been my constant companion since watching Austin walk away.

Even the thought of reaching out to him hurt. Which Austin would I get? The one I'd known since college or the one I met today? Hell, I didn't even know if he'd pick up, and that caused a whole other slew of gaping wounds to open up.

My father watched me, and I reminded myself it wasn't about me. I could do this for him. "I'll see what I can do."

He finally gave me the nod I'd been waiting for since I walked in. It wasn't much, but it was enough.

My bed called to me, and I wanted nothing more than to go home and sleep for days. I'd made it to the foyer before the click of my mom's heels followed. I sighed, looking longingly at the door before turning.

"Are you okay?" she asked.

Leave it to Mom to always call bullshit on the wall I tried to erect. "Yeah, why?"

"Your breakup? Was there anything else going on?"

She may know that the wall was there, but she didn't always know what hid behind it. She studied my face, and I considered laying it all out there.

*Selfish.*

The word snuck up again and punched me in my chest, forcing me to choke back the words. What I allowed Bodie to continue to do was my burden, and it would be selfish to lay it at my mom's feet. Between that and the shame, I couldn't imagine ever telling anyone.

Rolling my eyes, I gave her my best I-don't-care, bad-bitch strength. "C'mon, Mom. I'm not the serious type, and Bodie was a filler at best. It was amazing I kept him around as long as I did."

At least, that was the truth.

She continued to stare, not appeased with my answer. So, I let my wall down just enough for her to see that maybe I wasn't as okay as I wanted to be.

"I'm just tired. It's been a hell of a long weekend."

Her half-smile mirrored mine, except hers had that iconic Mom concern that always made me feel safer. "We'll get this worked out."

"I know."

Before I could walk away, she snagged my hand, giving it a squeeze. "You know he loves you, right?"

"I've never doubted it," I said, not having to ask which he she was referring to.

Mom and Dad met when I was almost ten, and he'd doted on us from the first second. He worshiped the ground Mom walked on and never failed to dote on me as if I was his own.

With one last hug, I made my escape, climbing back into the black SUV, thankfully alone.

I looked out the window, procrastinating the inevitable.

"Fuck it," I muttered, unlocking my phone to find Austin's messages pinned at the top, marked with a circle holding a picture of us posing as Goose and Maverick from last Halloween. With a deep breath and a sad smile, I typed out my message and hit send.

Here went nothing.

## Chapter Seven

### AUSTIN

**Rae:** Can we talk?
**Rae:** Austin, can you at least message me back?

"Who's that?" King asked.

"Rae." I looked down at the messages. One from a couple days ago and then the one that just came through. I wanted to keep ignoring her—maybe if I did, I could keep ignoring the reality of our situation. Maybe I could try to ignore the bullet wound gaping in my chest.

"Of course, it is. I should have known better with that look you get on your face when she contacts you. Except now, it's got this sad puppy dog look to it."

"Fuck off."

"I would, but then you'd be a lonely, sad puppy dog, and I'm too good of a friend to abandon you. You're welcome. Now, tell me what's up."

He ignored my deadpanned stare, not caring in the least that I didn't find his ramble amusing.

"Well?"

"She wants to talk."

"And…"

"And I don't know," I answered vaguely, dodging his inquisition.

"All right, enough with this closed-off bullshit," he declared, pointing his beer bottle at me. "You're not talking to her. You're not talking to your grandparents, and you've given me grunts in response to my questions. I've learned more about what happened from the tabloids than I have from you. So, unless you want to bottle it up until you explode, I suggest you get over yourself and at least talk to me."

As much as I hated to admit it, he was right. I'd avoided my grandparents like the plague. I hadn't even opened their texts, knowing they'd only serve to increase my guilt. The preview text ranged from surprise to congratulations to asking when I'd bring her up to see them. I almost laughed at the thought of Rae at the farm. She was the complete opposite of the small town and creaky old floors.

Draining my beer, I avoided looking at King for as long as possible, instead studying the few patrons at the pub on their lunch. King tapped the table, letting me know my time was up.

"I don't even know where to start," I ground out. "It's just all a mess. I woke up next to her—naked and married."

"Whoa," King exclaimed. "Did you sleep with her?"

"I...don't think so."

King's brows rose to his hairline, his eyes wide.

"No," I answered with conviction. "We were so drunk, I can't remember anything beyond the party, but I'd remember if I slept with her. I'd have to remember something from that, like flashes or something. She's too important not to."

"Damn, Austin," he muttered softly.

"What?"

"I knew you liked her, but this is more than that."

"Of course, it is. I've wanted her for so long. Being married to her feels like...fate or some shit."

"Except it's not."

His words hit me like a slap to the face. "Damn, King. Way to cut off any hope."

"I'm sorry I'm not pulling up your astrological sign to see what we should do next," he said with a laugh. "You know I'm too practical."

"Yeah. Maybe it's really just a cruel plot twist to give me what I've wanted, only to rip it away because she doesn't want to be married to me."

"Is that what she said? She doesn't want *you*?"

I grimaced, thinking over the argument. Trying to avoid a game of twenty questions, I gave him all the gritty details, including what a dick I was to her.

"Whew, boy. We're going to need another round," he said, gesturing for more drinks. "At least, I'm going to need another round. You, my friend, are going to need a miracle to make up for what you said."

"Yeah. I fucking know it," I grumbled. "I was just so angry, and I couldn't help but feel slighted. Every time she laughed over it, I felt like she was laughing at me—laughing at the idea of being married to *me*."

"From what I know, Rae doesn't want to be married to anyone."

"Then why did she marry me?"

"If I had to guess, I'd blame it on the vodka."

"Still, even drunk, something had to spur her on. What's the saying? There's always some truth to what you say and do when drunk."

"Maybe," King conceded but looked unconvinced. "But maybe you need to take a step back and be objective about it all—not take it so personally."

"How can I not take it personally when it's marriage."

"People get divorced all the time."

"I didn't want to be one of them."

He gave me a sad smile. King was one of the few people who knew my past and how it affected me. "I know."

My phone vibrated again, becoming an ominous tremor across the table. When I looked at the screen, it opened the message automatically.

**Rae:** Listen, I know I shouldn't ask, but I need your help.
**Rae:** Can you just talk to me?
**Rae:** Please.

"The bottom line is that you need to go talk to her," King said, reading the message with me. "No matter the outcome, you can't do shit until you've at least talked."

"Yeah," I agreed, already dreading it.

"And you need to distance yourself from this idea of fate and stop taking Rae's choices so personally. It's not like she's fantasizing about her wedding day and just not wanting it with you. This has something to do with her. And for what it's worth, you've told me enough about the shit she does for you that I have no doubt your friendship matters to her. Try not to take it all down because you can't separate what you feel from the facts of what happened. There's not an easy answer, but you can at least direct the outcome."

"Jesus, when did you get so insightful?"

"It's my superpower—one that only works with other people and not myself."

"That explains your dating life."

"Ha. He's got jokes," King laughed. "Now, stop being a big fucking baby and text her back."

With a glare and dread rolling through my stomach like a tidal wave, I did as he ordered.

**Me**: Yeah.
**Me**: Meet me at our spot.

King gave me a slap on the back and a promise that it would all work out when we parted ways, but my nerves clung to me the rest of the afternoon. For the first time ever, I'd rather have stayed at work than go meet Rae, but not knowing what I'd walk into weighed on me.

What did she need help with? It had to be something important for her to keep reaching out. Or was it an excuse to meet up and talk? Or was it…?

I ran through all the options, each one not quite sitting right, making me want to avoid it altogether. But King's words about controlling the outcome pushed me to make my way to the ice cream shop we both loved. I'd never move forward past all the what-ifs unless I dealt with the reality.

Walking up, her beauty hit me so hard I almost stumbled. The shop window backlit her simple ponytail, jeans, and T-shirt that looked anything but simple. She stared off in the distance as she leaned against the window, licking the sides of her Black Sabbath ice cream.

The cup with an upside-down cone in her other hand let me know that maybe we weren't so far off track, that maybe King was right, and we could recover from this.

"Hey," I greeted.

Her eyes jerked to mine and froze. I waited for the smile she always had for me, but it never came. In its place was wariness tinged with sadness. The seconds stretched, and I took in the dark circles under her eyes that she tried to cover with makeup, but I knew her too well to not see them.

"Hey," she finally said, offering me my ice cream. Cardamom and black pepper—my favorite.

We'd stumbled upon this place one drunken night when I'd come to New York City with her on break. They were known for their odd flavors, and with the flair only alcohol could induce, we dubbed it our spot.

"I'll cut right to the chase," she started. "Our Vegas marriage has caused a lot of issues for my dad's campaign. We have this upcoming trip to the Hamptons with some investors, and he wants us to put on a show."

I blinked more than a few times, wincing as I tried to arrange all the too big pieces that statement entailed. Just that one sentence created approximately a million other obstacles.

"A show?" I asked. That seemed the easiest place to start.

"He wants you to come to the Hamptons and act like the wedding was planned. That we're in love, and we're a happy little family."

It was on the tip of my tongue to let her know we didn't have to pretend when my phone vibrated with an incoming call—probably saving me from making a bigger mistake.

*Gma.*

Grimacing, I hit ignore and focused back on Rae.

My first instinct was to agree because when did I ever turn her down. Another part of me whispered that this had disaster written all over it. We could barely be cordial right now. How were we supposed to act in love? Then what would happen when we were alone? Would she push me away? Would we still be friends? I couldn't even begin to paint the picture, and it all started to feel like I was standing on a cliff with nothing but a black void stretched out beneath me.

I tried to read her—tried to figure out how she felt about it, but she'd had days with this idea, leaving her plenty of time to remove any emotion from her face.

"Was this your idea?" Rae often acted as her dad's marketing manager of sorts. She had the skill with social media, and maybe this was one of her grand schemes.

"God, no," she scoffed.

I grit my teeth, trying to detach myself from her reaction like King suggested, but all I could think was how laughable she found being married to me. At least her dad didn't have such a hard time believing we could be together. He had a hell of a lot more confidence than Rae that we could pull off pretending our marriage was real.

"I get it if you don't want to be around me—especially now that I know what you think of me."

Her words, mixed with her lack of eye contact, hit me like a bat to the stomach, simmering any building anger. I *hated* my temper. It'd flared up as a teen, and I'd taken huge strides to control it. While I'd stopped causing fights in school, my mouth still got the best of me sometimes.

"Listen, Rae, maybe we both said things we didn't mean."

Her eyes snapped to mine and flared with the fire that was all Rae. "I've never said anything different than what I said that morning. I've always been honest, but maybe there's a side of you that I don't know very well. Maybe there's a side that comes out when provoked—an angry side."

Closing my eyes didn't help me ignore the knife to the chest. I still saw the damage I'd caused. I still saw the way she curled her lip and took a step back as if I scared her.

"I'm sorry," I breathed.

Standing on the sidewalk of New York, with melting ice cream and regret stretched between us, neither one of us knew what to say.

Finally, she broke the stare, dropping her chin. "Don't be. I just need your help."

"How am I supposed to help you when you won't even look at me?"

"I don't know," she muttered, peeking up from under her lashes. "I just know we have to do it."

My phone vibrated again—this time, a message opened when I pulled it from my pocket.

**Gma:** Hey, Austin, I know Raelynn is a city girl and may not want to come to the farm. Maybe Grandpa and I could make a trip to you.

My heart pinched, unable to avoid the words anymore—hating what my avoidance had pushed them to believe. I wanted to growl in frustration, to shout at the night sky to give me a fucking break. But it wasn't anyone but me that I had to blame. Which meant I had to fix it.

Maybe Rae's offer was the answer to fixing both. Maybe if I agreed, I could ask for something in return. Maybe I could use that time in the Hamptons to repair what was broken. Maybe we'd pretend so well she'd realize she never wanted to stop.

"Okay."

"Really?" she asked, hopeful.

"Yes. But I need you to do something for me in return."

Her eyes narrowed. "What?"

Doubts bombarded my decision, but I shoved on and pushed them aside. This had to work.

"If I go to the Hamptons, then you need to come to my grandparents and pretend to be my wife. Marriage is important to them, and I just…I can't break it to them yet. I want to give them something before I tell them."

She hesitated, chewing on her full pink lip like she always did when deep in thought. I held my breath for so long, waiting for her to tell me to fuck off, that black dots popped up in my vision before she finally put me out of my misery.

"Fine."

"Fine?" I confirmed, blowing out my relieved breath.

"Yes. I'll go."

"Thank you."

She gave a short nod before turning to dump her mostly melted ice cream. "The trip is next weekend. I'll message you with the details."

"We'll do my grandparents after the Hamptons."

"Okay," she agreed, closing the conversation. With another nod, she turned to go but stopped at the last minute to turn back. "For what it's worth, I miss you."

She didn't give me time to respond before leaving.

*I miss you.*

The words didn't help. If anything, they only made the ache worse.

None of that mattered. I had two trips with Raelynn, my best friend—*my wife*—to fix everything.

I didn't have a plan yet, but I'd create a damn good one.

All I knew was that I needed to keep her in my life.

Preferably as my *wife*.

## Chapter Eight

### RAELYNN

"You're doing what now?" Nova practically screeched through the screen.

It'd been a couple days since Austin agreed to this crazy plan, and I still felt just as shocked as Nova looked.

"Uhh, I'm not sure how good of an idea this is," Vera said beside me.

We sat on the couch at her apartment with Nova on FaceTime from her honeymoon. I'd called an emergency meeting because there was no way I could process this on my own anymore. At the very least, I needed them to join me in my crazy for a bit.

"There isn't really any other idea to replace it."

"I can't believe your dad even suggested it," Nova said.

"Dad's expect crazy things," Vera muttered, referencing her own experience.

"So, how do *you* feel about it?" Nova asked.

The question took me back because I hadn't given space to any feelings that didn't revolve around me believing I was doing the right thing for my dad. But with two sets of eyes waiting for an answer, I peeked behind the curtain I kept everything behind.

"I don't know," I answered honestly, not quite sure how to explain the tight band of tension around my chest. The harder I thought about it, the tighter it squeezed. "Trapped?"

"Yeah, no one puts Rae in a corner," Vera joked.

"It's just that…" I paused, trying to decipher what caused the most discomfort, but it wasn't some*thing*. It was some*one*, and that hurt the most. "For the first time, I feel uncomfortable with Austin. Especially after our fight. He said some mean things—maybe we both did."

"You never told us the details," Vera reminded me. "What did he say?"

Bracing myself, I recapped the argument, watching their jaws slowly drop with each new detail.

"Ex-fucking-cuse me?" Nova demanded.

"Ohhhh. Naughty Nova has come out with her big girl words," I joked.

"Yeah, I'm about to go Supernova on him."

Vera snorted, and I winced.

"Yeah, I know it's corny," Nova confessed. "I'm not as good at threatening as you are."

"I appreciate the effort," I said.

She blew me a kiss through the screen.

"I can't believe he said those things to you," Vera said.

"Yeah," I breathed. "I'd never heard him be so mean before. It was like he was so mad he changed into someone I didn't recognize."

Recalling the layer of ice that fell over his eyes when he flayed me with his words had my chest caving in on itself all over again. Austin had been frustrated with me many times before but never so angry I didn't even recognize him. It…scared me.

Watching him shift from my friend to a version I never knew existed hit every button I had—reminded me of every reason I never wanted to get married in the first place. Just because you thought you knew someone—you never really knew what hid in the depths of them. You never knew what would come out when push came to shove until it was too late, and I never wanted to be trapped in a corner with a monster.

That morning played out like a perfectly curated nightmare just for me.

"I just—I don't get it. We could have easily got it annulled, and he turned into this immovable brick wall. I mean, why would he not want to get it annulled?" *Because marriage was apparently this huge sacrament to him—a vow that couldn't be broken, and you didn't even take him seriously.* "Maybe he's not completely wrong. I didn't even know how much marriage meant to him," I conceded, dropping my gaze to my wine swirling in my glass. "Or how little he thought of me."

"We all say things we don't mean in anger," Nova said, speaking from experience.

"Not that it makes it right," Vera added sternly before conceding. "But I'm sure Austin was hurting, too."

"Why? Because his friend won't stay married to him? Wouldn't he want to be married to someone he loved?" When the girls didn't say anything, I looked up to find them having their own silent conversation. "What?"

When they watched me with wide eyes, I waved my hand, urging them to just spit it out.

"It's just that Austin cares for you as more than a friend, and if marriage meant so much to him, maybe the combination created a possibility in his mind," Nova explained.

I huffed a laugh. "Please. We're friends."

"Yeah, but if you ever wanted more, Austin would have jumped all over it."

I gave Nova a doubtful look.

"And if you ever pulled your head out of your stubborn ass, you could admit how much you care for him, too," Vera added. I tried to respond, but she held up her hand. "As more than a friend."

I held her challenging gaze. They always brought it up, but we laughed it off. She wasn't laughing now.

A flare of warmth bloomed in my chest whenever I was with Austin, but I always shoved it aside, refusing to think on it. I explained it away as a feeling of friendship—even though I never had the same feeling with Nova and Vera. If I didn't study it too closely, I wouldn't have to think about it, and nothing would change.

I almost laughed because now, everything had changed.

Austin had changed.

"I can't be with someone I don't recognize."

"Does that mean with everything—friendship too?" Vera asked.

A fist reached in my chest and squeezed, stealing my breath and forcing the golf ball up my throat. I barely swallowed it down before choking out, "I do—I don't know."

The thought of marriage terrified me on levels I'd thought I'd moved past.

But the thought of losing Austin completely shook me to my very core, leaving a mass of emotional chaos I didn't know where to begin to unravel.

"Just take some time," Nova said softly.

"Maybe this time will force you to stop hiding from your feelings," Vera said, not holding back any punches.

I huffed a laugh because no amount of time would change my mind.

"It's not that simple. I made a promise to myself when I was young—I would never be married. I would never trap myself with someone, only for them to end up changing into a monster." As if to ensure that promise stayed intact, life sent me Bodie as the perfect reminder of why I made it in the first place.

"If it helps, I think Austin is the good man he's been since we've known him," Vera said. "I don't think anyone can claim to be completely rational in anger."

Nova pointed through the screen, nodding her head in agreement. "But he still has to make it up to you so you can feel good around him again. Maybe this will be the time you need to at least restore your friendship."

"Maybe," I agreed, but it lacked commitment.

I took a sip of my red wine, wishing it was something stronger.

"Is that what happened to Bodie?" Vera asked, and I almost spit the wine back out.

*Oh, my god. They know.*

My heart thundered, and I kept my head down, eyes glued to the liquid that matched my cheeks. Shame washed over me like a tidal wave threatening to pull me under. I wished it would. I wished I could vanish from this moment rather than face these two women who thought I was so strong, only to admit how weak I really was.

"Did he change too much? I know he got insanely clingy in the end," she finished, making me realize that she didn't actually know.

"Remember when he wouldn't even come to New Year's Eve with us?" Nova recalled. "Now, I think he'd try to come in the ladies' room if he could just so he didn't have to part with you. Talk about stage five clinger."

"More like stage eighty," Vera joked.

I focused on calming my breaths. Digging for the calm strength I used to always have, I managed to laugh with them, adding an eye roll for effect. "That's exactly what happened."

"Ugh," they both groaned.

"Like I said, fucking trapped."

"You look happier," Vera said, smiling like a proud mama.

"I am." Even if things weren't perfect, I was at least free from Bodie.

The front door opened, and Vera and I groaned in unison over the delicious smell of Chinese that came with it.

"I guess I should probably get going. Parker will be getting up soon," Nova said, wagging her brows.

"Naughty Nova," I cat-called. "While you're taking care of Parker, I'll be taking care of that fat, delicious baby."

Nova pouted. "Give her kisses from Auntie Nova."

"Okay, give Parker kisses from me."

We laughed and hung up, and I raced to the door to drown my worries in the squirming ball of joy that Vera had obviously made on her own since Nico was too much of an ominous creature to create something so perfect.

"Hey, my sweet little Camila. Let me take you from that mean ole daddy."

Nico gave me a side-eye while greeting his wife. "Hopefully, girl talk went well. And is over."

"You just missed it," Vera said. "It was a titillating conversation about how marriage is a trap."

He pursed his lips and studied his wife with narrowed eyes. "Hopefully, a good one for you."

"The best. I'd let you catch me again and again."

Watching them almost made me wonder if being trapped by Austin could be good. But then I remembered watching my mom crawl us out of hell and knew it was a risk I couldn't take.

After getting my baby snuggles in, I finally headed home, feeling better about my plan. It wasn't perfect, but maybe it would help Austin and me salvage our friendship. I was so lost in thinking of ways to keep Austin as my friend that I missed the man standing at my door until his dark shadow loomed over me.

I lurched back, my heart in my throat, looking up into cold, blue eyes glazed from too much drinking.

"What are you doing here, Bodie?" I tried to sound irritated, but the shock left me breathless.

"I always knew there was more going on between you two," he sneered.

It was on the tip of my tongue to correct him, but it was none of his business. "Fuck off, Bodie. You have no right to be here."

I moved to unlock my door, trying to hide my desperation to get inside, when suddenly, a rough hand gripped my shoulder and spun my back to the door. He towered over me, but I refused to drop my chin and look away.

"I have every right to be here," he ground out through his clenched jaw. "A fucking year with you. For what? To be dumped over some stupid argument? I don't fucking think so."

"Bullshit," I spat back. "You're an abusive asshole who gets off on hurting me."

"I never hurt you," he denied like I was crazy.

A haze of red tinted my vision, and my head swam. Rage so intense like I'd never felt before consumed me, and I clenched my fists by my side, afraid I would rip his fucking face off if I let loose. "I *still* have bruises from last week. I have spent the last year skipping events to hide them. I have spent the last year perfecting covering up where you'd 'grip too hard' or 'accidentally push me.' Don't you dare pretend you are anything but a conniving pussy who needs to abuse women to feel better about yourself."

He bared his teeth and raised his fist. I flinched before I could stop myself and held my breath, only to let out a yelp when it collided with the door beside my head. I waited for someone to come out and check on the noise—they had before. Except this time, I wouldn't lie and pretend we were two lovers against the door to keep any gossip out of the newspaper. No, this time, I'd throw Bodie under the bus.

"It's not me," he bit out inches from my face. "It's your bitchy attitude and that fucking mouth of yours. Maybe that's what Austin likes. Or maybe he just fucks your face with his tiny cock to make you shut up. You always did suck on my cock like a filthy whore."

"Fuck you."

He glowered, but I refused to relent. "It should have been me."

"It was never going to be you. Now get the fuck away from me before I call my husband. And once he's done pummeling you, I'll call the cops."

Time stood still, and I counted the seconds until finally, he backed off with a growl.

"I'm not fucking done with you."

I watched him until he disappeared behind the elevator doors. Only when I knew he was really gone did I unlock the door with shaky hands and fumble inside. As soon as I turned the locks, I dropped my bags and stood in the middle of my living room, sucking in deep breath after deep breath. The adrenaline fled, leaving me tense and shaking. I ripped my ponytail free and dug my nails into my hair, relieving the pressure.

Soon everything slowed down, and instead of the crash that usually plagued me after leaving Bodie, elation and joy flooded my veins. I smiled, proud of myself for standing up—for being the strong woman I knew I was. I smiled because I realized that Bodie hadn't taken that from me—he hadn't won.

I replayed the words I used to cut him like a knife as if I was re-watching my favorite part of a movie. Each time felt better than the last until the reel skipped and blurred over a certain part.

The part when I called Austin my husband and hadn't hated the sound of it.

## Chapter Nine

### AUSTIN

Neither one of us moved to get out of the car. We both sat there, as silent as the rest of the drive had been, looking up at the white beach house mansion. Other cars lined the driveway, and I knew as soon as we stepped through those doors, we'd have to become the happy couple we promised to be. I'd hoped we'd have a few minutes to get situated before meeting everyone, but I had a project meeting I couldn't miss, making us not so fashionably late.

Subtly, I shifted my gaze from the house to her. Her long lashes curled up to the perfect arch of her brow. My fingers tingled with the urge to run them down the curve of her cheek to her full lips, bare of the rosy lipstick she wore when I picked her up. She'd spent the entire drive biting her lips —a sure sign of her nerves. She hated having a tell, but I loved the way the lush curve of her bottom lip gave way under her straight teeth. The best part was when she followed it up with a quick swipe of her tongue to soothe the bite.

She sat straight as a board, her shoulders already by her ears, and I couldn't remember a time I'd ever seen her look so tense, and we hadn't even started yet.

"If we want to make this believable, we probably shouldn't be so stiff."

She swallowed, forcibly relaxing into the seat, rolling her shoulders and neck. "I know."

"I'm a little worried right now that even if I rest my hand on your back when we walk in, you'll jump." It was such a normal touch I'd done a million times with her that I wouldn't even think twice until it was too late. Unless… "I mean, I'm assuming we'll have to have some contact. Is it okay if I touch you?"

She snorted. The tight line of her lips relaxed into a smile as she laughed like she couldn't hold it in. I wasn't even sure what she was laughing at, but I missed her smile so much that I couldn't help but smile too. "I mean, I've only been trying to get you to touch me for years," she explained, her voice playful.

She finally looked at me, one brow cocked high, and something loosened in my chest. Taking a deeper breath than I'd taken since Vegas, I slipped into our playful banter. "Well, then, today is your lucky day."

We both laughed, enjoying the easy moment. It was… nice. Actually, it was fantastic, and I tried to stay in that moment right there rather than think of what would happen next.

"You ready?" I asked.

"Let's do it."

I got out and rounded the car. Being the gentleman I'd be with my wife, I opened her door and offered my hand. She hesitated for a second that stretched on for an eternity, and I held my breath, waiting for her to set the tone. Would she continue on the path we started in the car, or would she get out on her own and set us back two steps?

Her elegant fingers slid across the palm of my hand, sending shots of electricity up my arm to my chest, leaving a hum of warmth in its wake. The satin of her skin brushed the callous roughness of mine. We'd held hands a thousand times before—on planes, walking through a crowd, finding comfort in a friend when we needed it—but this was so much more. Pretend or not, she was my wife, and having her hand in mine as she exited the car like a revelation filled me with pride.

Even if it wasn't for forever, for now, Raelynn Vos was mine.

As if they were waiting, a staff member greeted us at the door, Mr. Scott close behind.

"Welcome, I'm Jeremy Scott," he greeted, his smile just as big and bright as his Hawaiian shirt. "I'm so happy to have such a beautiful couple as my guests."

"We're happy to be here, Mr. Scott," I responded, shaking his hand.

"Call me Jeremy."

Rae's dad appeared behind him in a much more demure cream linen button up, his eyes bouncing between us as if waiting for us to give up the shindig and admit the truth.

"Thank you for having us," Rae said. "Dad talks so highly of you, so I, of course, had to see if you lived up to all the hype."

Jeremy barked a laugh. "I'll do my best," he promised her. Then he leaned toward me, covering his mouth for a stage whisper. "She's a firecracker, this one."

"The best kind of woman," I agreed.

On instinct, I coasted my hand up her back to her shoulder. She stepped to my side as if it came naturally and wrapped her arms around my waist, leaning her head against my shoulder. Each touch, move, and hug sent small sparks flying as if it was the first time. I couldn't help but give in to the role and let this mean more.

"Well, we'll get you shown to your room and let you freshen up for dinner in a couple hours. Sound good?"

"Sounds perfect," Rae answered.

"Austin," Rae's dad called before I could follow her up the

stairs. "Do you have a minute?"

"Yes, sir."

"And he's got manners, too," Jeremy crowed. "Rae, you found yourself a good man."

"He's okay," she joked, winking at me.

Jeremy gave another bark of laughter before facing Rae's dad. "Go ahead and use my office to chat, Kenneth. I'll be outside with the ladies."

"Thank you," Kenneth said.

"I'm going to head on up," Rae let me know.

I followed Kenneth to the smaller room. He shut the door, and I looked around at the dark wood shelves and desk, lightened by the white and blue decor. Not that I took any of it in because my mind was too consumed with what the hell he wanted to talk about. He moved to the bar cart in the corner and filled two glasses. Each second he didn't talk screwed my muscles so tight I was surprised I could move my arm and accept the glass when he offered it.

He didn't look away with his sip, and I mirrored him, feeling like a kid about to get reamed for getting caught with his hand in the cookie jar.

"I paid off your grandparents' house."

The bourbon went down the wrong pipe, and I sputtered. "What? Why?" I asked once I got my coughing under control. Of all the things I expected him to say, that hadn't even registered in the same universe as my list.

"I owe you," he answered simply.

"No. I'm doing this for Rae—and you. I like you guys. Besides, we had a plan to pay it off. I didn't need you to step in." My grandpa's health had hit a few bumps over the last few years, and they struggled with the medical bills, but we were figuring it out. We didn't need a handout.

"I have no doubt that you were able to take care of it. It's the kind of man you are, and they're obviously good people who raised you well. So, I paid because I can."

I stood a little taller as if making sure to meet the standards of the man he saw me as.

"I know this situation isn't ideal for you, so I appreciate you doing it. Whether it's for me or for Rae. You're a good friend to her, and we're all lucky she has someone like you in her life."

"Thank you, sir."

He nodded, taking another drink.

Kenneth was a good man. He'd accepted me with a smile and a firm handshake the first time Rae brought me home from school. He'd taken the time to ask me about my intentions with Rae, but when I told him we were just friends, he never doubted me. My own father had been paranoid and never took the time to trust anyone—which led to his multiple marriages. So, meeting Rae's dad had been refreshing. Other than my grandpa, he was one of the few men I looked up to. I didn't want him to think I needed anything from him or give him a reason to doubt why I was friends with Rae.

"I'll be paying you back," I announced, leaving no room for argument.

"Interest-free if you have to," he rebutted.

"Fine."

Another nod. "If there's ever anything else you need, you just ask us. You're family, no matter what happens."

"Thank you, sir."

"Unless you hurt her," he added. "Then I'll break all your bones one at a time."

My brows shot up at the serious threat, and I huffed a soft laugh. "Now I see where Rae gets her ability to threaten from."

Kenneth smiled, shaking his head. "Oh, no. That's one hundred percent her mom. She taught me the skill when we got married like she had Rae. Except my wife is scarier, so I'd be more afraid of her than me if you hurt Rae."

*What about if I get hurt?* I wanted to ask. I was at a much higher risk of being crushed to dust at the end of this than Rae. "I'm not sure anyone could hurt Rae and live long enough for anyone else to defend her."

"Very true," he admitted, smiling softly. I went to leave when his smile grew pinched. "She's a hard shell to crack, but the shell is there for a reason. She's been through a lot."

Confusion pulled my brows tight, but I hid it behind a nod of understanding. I assumed Rae lived an idyllic life. Maybe I assumed wrong, taking her silence as nothing to talk about when instead I should have been asking questions to find out what shaped her.

"I'll see you at dinner, Austin."

He patted my back outside the door and left me to go find my wife.

Our room was better than any hotel suite. Across from the white bed was a balcony showcasing the stunning views of the ocean beyond. I was so distracted by the scenery I almost missed the running shower. A standing mirror in the corner of the room reflected perfectly, showcasing the wide-open bathroom door and direct line of sight to the shower. My body froze while simultaneously combusting, sending wave after wave of heat through my veins.

The frosted glass door hid the details of her body, creating a torturous shadowy display of all her curves and every move. My cock hardened, taking in the swell of her breasts, remembering the rosy hardened tips I'd glanced in Vegas. She turned, lifting her arms to wash her hair. It was like some kind of erotic peep show I never wanted to look away from.

On instinct, my hand pushed against my length, and I groaned at the contact. The sound snapped me out of my daze, and I blinked, forcing myself to look away and focus. I needed to get ready and get out of there. I glanced around for my bag, finding it tucked away in the closet, already half unpacked and missing my toiletries.

Already knowing where I'd find them, I closed my eyes

and inhaled, trying to prepare myself for having to actually go in to get them—trying to brace myself to be within touching distance of her naked body and not rip the glass door off the wall to get to her.

"Hey, you're here," she greeted as soon as I walked in, almost like she'd been waiting for me. "I left the door open so you could still get ready. I just needed to wash the drive off me."

"Thank you. I just need to brush my teeth, and I'll finish getting ready in the room."

"'Kay."

Then as if I wasn't already barely clinging to my self-control, she cracked the door and popped her head out. Drops of water slid down her neck to hidden places behind the edge of the glass, and I desperately wanted to chase it with my tongue.

"Hopefully, Dad didn't bother you."

I swallowed, forcing my attention to putting toothpaste along my brush. "Nah. He just asked how my project meeting went," I lied. I didn't want Rae to think I was only there because I was paid. I meant what I told Kenneth—I was there for Rae. I didn't need any incentives.

"Good." She thankfully closed the door and went back to showering. "How was the meeting, by the way?"

"Successful," I answered once I rinsed my mouth.

"Of course. You're so damn talented, how could it be anything else."

Her confidence hit me in my chest, and this time when I looked at her silhouette in the mirror, the warmth wasn't sexual but pride. King always gave me shit about the silly things I did for Rae, like taking pictures and rescuing her from sticky situations, but she did so much for me too. She believed in my art and shoved confidence down my throat. I had no choice but to believe her and have the same confidence in myself. She gave up parts of herself to build others up.

"Thanks," I said softly.

"Just being honest."

With a smile in place, I left the room, making sure to shut the door behind me.

My mind swirled with thoughts of Rae as I got ready. Emotions mixed, fighting for dominance. Warmth from her compliment. Love for my friend. Heat when I remembered the naked shape of each curve. Desire for how much I wanted to taste every inch.

I rarely let myself think of Rae in a sexual way. I loved her, but I could convince myself that that love was purely for my friend if I didn't think of her sexually. It mostly worked.

I fought it as much as possible, but there were times when my barriers were down, and I lost myself in my lust, growing unbearably hard until I worried I'd snap if I didn't relieve it. Only in those moments did I imagine pushing inside her heat as I stroked myself. Only then did I allow myself the pleasure of fantasizing about her skin beneath my touch until I came with her name on my lips.

By the time she came out, I'd gotten myself under control and ready for dinner.

"You look nice," she complimented my cream pants and light blue shirt.

"I'd tell you the same, but that's nothing new. You always look amazing."

She smiled and preened, spinning in a circle to show off every angle. The dress wasn't even revealing, covering her from her full cleavage to the top of her knees. But the buttons all the way down the front allowed room for illicit thoughts.

"Stunning," I breathed.

"Thank you." She brushed her long wavy hair behind her ear, smiling at my compliment. "Will you take a picture?"

On cue, I rolled my eyes and groaned. "I guess."

"Ugh. Such a baby," she joked, slapping my shoulder on the way to the balcony.

I found comfort in the role of taking photos as she moved fluidly from pose to pose. The past week, I'd struggled with the fracture in our friendship, unsure if the foundation would hold long enough for us to repair. But complaining about having to take pictures we both knew I didn't mind taking, making funny faces behind the camera to make her laugh, and letting her pull me into a selfie slid a missing piece in place, healing what was broken.

"Should we take a serious one together?" she asked me. "You know, as a married couple."

"Sure." My heart skipped a beat, stumbling over the mere idea of it. As if it wanted to take flight and soar.

"It would be good for my dad's brand if everyone thought this was real."

And just like that, the stumble quickly turned to falling back to reality. Of course, it was just for show—at least for her.

Before she could stage the pose, I remembered the package my grandma sent me. "Hang on one second." I rummaged through my bag and pulled out the velvet box hidden away. Despite the reminder of it all being a ruse, my palms still sweat as I made my way back out. The sun shined on her brown hair like a halo, casting a glow over her smiling face. When I held out the box on my palm, her smile slipped, and her eyes bounced between me and the box as if it was a possible bomb.

"It's my great grandma's ring. My grandma sent it to me before I left. I figured it would add to the reality if you had an actual ring."

She opened the box and gasped.

"I know it's not much, but—"

"It's perfect."

"You like it?" I asked, unable to hold the smile back.

"I love it."

She removed the simple gold band, but I grabbed the ring

before she could put it on, wanting to slide it on her finger myself. Something inside me urged me to have this moment, even if it wasn't real. I held her hand softly and placed my ring all the way to her knuckle, loving the way the small pink stone shined against her tan skin.

"Let me grab mine. I kept the one from Vegas."

"Actually," she said, stopping me from walking away. "I got you one."

"Really?" There went my skipping heartbeat again.

"Yeah. You know, same thing you said. Add to the reality," she explained, a little less believable this time. Like maybe that was what she wanted it to mean, but maybe it meant more.

She came back with her own box but opened it for me, not waiting for my reaction before grabbing my rough palm in hers and sliding it on. The black band shined differently at each angle under the fading sun.

"I got it because it looked like layers of paint bleeding together. It reminded me of the artist in you."

While she studied the ring, I studied her, trying to hold on to the piece of me she was tugging away. I could have sworn she had all of me before, but it was nothing compared to the chunk she just claimed as hers.

"Thank you," I barely choked out.

She looked at me from under her lashes and something shined in their depths, warmer than ever before, and I wanted to snatch it, but it was gone before I could even get close. "It's no big deal."

It was a lie.

A lie so obvious it shook the ground we stood on, forming a new rift. But instead of the fissure that almost broke us in Vegas, it shifted, locking something stronger in place.

We both knew it.

But neither of us knew what it meant.

## Chapter Ten

### RAELYNN

As promised, Austin rested his hand on my back, guiding me into the living room, where everyone mingled before dinner. He'd placed his hand there before, and I'd always noticed it through the years, but when I imagined what it would feel like tonight while getting ready, I assumed it would feel different. I assumed it would weigh on me like a chain trapping me in place.

Instead, his fingers laid like a weighted blanket, noticeable but offering comfort—the same as always. Except this time, they caressed lower, just above my ass, sending warmth up my spine and down to my core. The soft touch had never felt so erotic.

Between that and the weight of his family's ring on my finger, there was no denying that Austin and I were husband and wife. And I couldn't tell if that thought filled me with anxiety because it terrified me or because it didn't.

Thankfully, the party was in full swing when we arrived, distracting me from my inner turmoil. However, each time I lifted my glass for a sip of champagne, the ring glinted under the light, reminding me that I didn't hate the way it felt.

"Raelynn, you look gorgeous." My mom pulled me in for a hug and more praise.

"You don't look too bad yourself."

"Like mother, like daughter," Jeremy praised. "You're lucky men."

"I'm very lucky to have Rae," Austin agreed. "She's one of a kind."

The other men in the circle introduced themselves, shaking hands with Austin and giving us their congratulations. Some I had met before, while others were new.

"I was just explaining to everyone about the Virago Foundation and how you've been helping out," Dad explained.

"Yes, Mom and Dad started the charity a few years ago, and I'm excited to help where I can. Domestic abuse is a serious issue I'm passionate about. Helping women become strong and find their footing after everything they've endured is something my parents taught me. Dad is an incredible advocate for women." I wanted to take every opportunity to push my dad's campaign while we were here. I didn't want a single person leaving without knowing how valuable he could be in the Senate and that he was the right candidate to back in the campaigns.

Not that it mattered because no one heard me anyway. These men were older and came from traditional families that stuck with outdated societal norms.

"Are you helping by featuring them on your social media?" one of them joked.

"Nonsense," another cut in, laughing. "She'll be giving them makeovers and taking them to clubs."

My jaw clenched tight, the strain reaching around my neck. The tension twisted the muscles in my shoulders, creeping down my spine until it collided with the strong fingers tensing as much as me, gripping my hip as if it was his last shred of patience.

Out of the corner of my eye, I saw him stand taller, taking a deep breath, and I knew he was about to cut these condescending men down. As much as I wanted to watch him do it—as much as I could do it myself—it could be detrimental to us being there.

I stepped to his side, sliding my arm along his back to glide along the thick, flexing muscles. He relaxed, only to tense again under my exploring touch. Usually, hugs with Austin were quick or about comfort, but we were acting as newlyweds in love, so I stroked along his side, gliding my fingers over the muscles I'd thought of exploring more than once.

I was so focused on trying to read Austin's every reaction to my touch that I almost forgot to respond to their comments. But I needed to do something because if I didn't, I knew my mom or dad would. I didn't have to look over to know they were equally as annoyed while trying to remain diplomatic.

Thankfully, Jeremy, obviously as uncomfortable with the comments as everyone else, saved us all by cutting in to change the subject. "So, how did you two meet?"

We glanced at each other, both of us remembering the moment I approached him. As if on cue, we started laughing, and I knew he was imagining us telling them exactly how it went, if for no other reason than to watch their jaws drop.

Getting myself together, I explained the watered-down version without looking away from Austin. "We met at a party in college, and he swept me away, winning me over with waffles at midnight." I wanted to read every reaction that flashed in those green depths when I talked about us. I wanted to take the time to study the way they darkened when my hand continued holding onto him tight.

Austin's lips tipped into the tiniest of smirks, making me smile harder.

"And you were friends when you first met?" Jeremy asked.

"Yes," he answered. His smirk shifted, changing into something softer—something I couldn't remember seeing before. Something different than the darkening my touch caused.

"But I loved her from the moment I saw her. I was just biding my time until I could snag her as mine."

He softly brushed my hair back from my cheek, only adding to the scene. Because it was a scene…right?

My nipples pebbled, and my heart fluttered under the waves of electricity fluttering in my chest.

It *had* to be a scene.

*It was a scene*, I reminded myself.

*Not real.*

Even if it was real, I wouldn't want it to be.

No way.

The end.

Then why wouldn't my body stop trying to light itself on fire?

"Dinner's ready," someone announced, but I barely heard. I was too busy trying to collect myself and shove away the crazy-ass fog that drifted over me.

His hand fell away, and the moment was gone, but the words lingered.

*Loved me?*

Maybe he meant as a friend. I mean, I loved Austin. He was my best friend. But something about the way he said it, the way he touched me with such care, felt like so much more than friendship.

*Loved me.*

My thoughts consumed me so much that I missed the woman dashing into the dining room just before we sat.

"Sorry, I'm late. I had a meeting for that freelance job, and it ran late," the blonde bombshell explained with a small wince and laugh.

She glanced around the room, offering everyone an apologetic, radiant smile, but froze when her eyes landed on us. No, not us—Austin.

"Austin?" she breathed, the smile fading.

"Aubrey. Hey," he responded, his words slow and uncertain.

However, she was certain enough for both of them because she used her Amazonian legs to cross the room, and the next thing I knew, Austin's hand slid from mine to wrap around this woman.

Something pierced my chest, almost like a sharp jab. There and gone so quick I couldn't place it. All I did know was that I didn't like it.

Thankfully, she pulled back. "Wow, it's been so long."

"Yeah, a few years." Austin pushed his hand through his hair. Like my dad, it was his tell-tale sign of discomfort.

"Excuse my manners, I'm Aubrey," she said, finally addressing the woman by his side. "I'm William Dawson's daughter."

"This is Raelynn Vos," Austin introduced me.

I studied her, trying to find what had Austin so on edge. She stood there—regal, stunning, confident, polite, like she would save babies in a war zone and still look like a supermodel even though she hadn't showered for five weeks.

She looked like a blonde version of Vera with her pearls and well-groomed manners.

None of that shook me. I loved seeing another woman confident in herself. No, what bothered me was how she looked at Austin like he was the best steak she'd ever had, and she'd give her left tit to have it again but was also too polite to act on it.

Which was the only excuse I had for what came out of my mouth next.

"His wife," I explained, offering my hand.

Austin's attention jerked to me, and I could only imagine the confusion hitting him. But I couldn't look because I was too busy trying to hold my smile in place to hide the confusion currently bitch-slapping me.

"Wife?" Her hand moved to mine just as slowly as the

words struggling to leave her lips. "You're married?" she asked Austin.

"Recently," he explained.

For someone so eager to keep this marriage going, he didn't sound like it. Something else lingered in the background of the conversation—something only they could see.

Before I could ask any questions, my mom came up behind us. "We can talk at the table. Let's grab a seat."

With a polite smile to Aubrey, I moved past her to find our nametags at the long table. Lucky me had Aubrey right across the low flickering candles. Small talk ensued while we ate the delicious meal. At least, I assumed it was delicious. I barely tasted any of it, my mind too consumed with thoughts of what lingered between Austin and Aubrey and why he stopped giving me small touches each chance he could get. Or why he wouldn't look my way.

Was he avoiding me, or was I being paranoid, and he was just focused on his meal? I couldn't help but think his reaction was because she had been someone special. If so, then why hadn't I ever seen her before? I knew everyone Austin dated.

The real question was why I cared.

I'd watched Austin go through almost as many partners as I had, and never had I ever felt this burning need to know more. Not even about the few he'd dated for a few months. So, why now? Why her?

"Oh, wow. That's amazing, Aubrey," a voice said, bringing me out of my ruminations. One of the men who'd insulted me earlier smiled at Aubrey like she'd discovered world peace.

"It's nothing much. I have some time, so why not donate it to the underprivileged. It's a relatively simple bioinformatics app that we make for bigger companies all the time. I ran into Candace, the pediatrician from the hospital, at a conference, and we hit it off. She told me her story, and I offered to help."

That sharp jab from earlier landed more like a fierce blow as I watched everyone fall over her every word. My teeth clamped shut so hard I was worried they'd snap as I remembered the way they laughed at my involvement with my parents' charity.

I didn't like this feeling. Aubrey hadn't done anything to me, yet I wouldn't mind tripping her on our way out. I didn't like the petty urge to see her fall. It wasn't me. I was a woman who prided myself on supporting others' wins.

"Did I hear correctly that you know Austin?" Jeremy asked.

She glanced his way with a small smile. "Yes, we met our senior year at college. We had a computer science class together."

"Really?" The question popped out before I could stop it. I looked to Austin, but his eyes focused on the fork he dragged through the leftover cheesecake on his plate.

"What a small world. Did you know you both would be here?" Jeremy asked before Aubrey could answer my outburst.

"Oh, no." She waved it away like it was silly. "We lost touch a while ago after dating for a while."

"Dating?" Again, the word slipped without permission. The last thing I wanted was to encourage this conversation, and yet, I couldn't shut up. "I thought I knew everyone you dated," I said to Austin, who still wouldn't quite meet my eyes.

"Well, we were actually engaged after college, but you know…sometimes things just don't work out."

"Oh." The word slipped so quietly I was surprised she heard it.

The fierce blow in my chest was now like a train knocking the wind from my lungs. It hit so hard I couldn't even figure out where it came from. What was this?

"Sorry," she winced, somehow still looking stunning. "This is probably weird."

Digging myself up off the ground, I used the etiquette ingrained in me to hold myself upright and force a smile. "Not at all. We all have pasts."

"You can say that again," one of the wives muttered, eliciting a round of laughter.

It was enough to break the attention from the three of us, and conversation moved on to nothing worth paying attention to. I couldn't have paid attention even if I tried. A storm of unknown thoughts and feelings raged through me, and I hated it. I liked relationships cut and dry. I liked my friendships honest and loyal, and this felt like a betrayal.

But it wasn't really, and I didn't know how to merge the feeling with the facts. It was as if a piece of the puzzle was missing. I knew I had it, but it stayed hidden from me, and it only served to make my frustration grow.

So, by the time we said our goodbyes and headed to bed, I stood on the precipice of snapping, and I couldn't explain why.

All I knew was that exhaustion pulled at my bones, and I didn't want to look for the missing piece anymore. I didn't want explanations. I didn't want to talk. I didn't want to understand this feeling. I just wanted it gone.

"It was the year after college. When you were traveling."

It was the first words he'd given me since dinner started, and if anything, they only added fuel to the fire. Why? Because it was a one-hundred-percent valid explanation. I'd traveled Europe for over six months after school, and between the time change and life, we kept missing each other. It was the most time we spent apart, but it hadn't mattered because each time we got back together, it was like no time had passed at all.

It would make sense that he had someone in his life that I hadn't known about.

So why didn't it make me feel better?

"Rae—"

"I'm tired, Austin. We have a full day tomorrow, so let's just go to bed. Please."

He wanted to push. I could see it written all over his

pained face. But I desperately needed him to let me shove this away with a night of sleep, and he could see that.

After the long day of unknowns, one thing went as I knew it would.

Austin saw what I needed and gave it to me.

With a nod, he pulled the covers back and climbed in the bed.

As if the day hadn't messed with my emotions enough, when he rolled over with his back to me, instead of the relief I should have felt—I hated it.

## Chapter Eleven

### AUSTIN

Unfortunately, the hope and prayer I gave last night didn't work. Rae rolled out of bed and didn't speak to me. She barely made eye contact at breakfast, and if she didn't stop, everyone was going to question what the hell was going on.

Fate granted me one small reprieve when Aubrey didn't make an appearance for breakfast. Not that I didn't like her or anything, she just threw me for a loop.

Aubrey had been a whimsical relationship—fast-paced and consuming. It ignited and gave me the perfect distraction from hating that Rae was gone. One night, Aubrey threw out the idea of marriage, and I blindly agreed, but when it came time to pick out the ring, I bailed.

I couldn't marry someone when all I did was compare them to Rae.

But how the hell did I explain that to Rae?

I didn't, which led to Rae not talking to me.

On the flip side, watching her shut down when confronted with one of my exes had me intrigued—hopeful.

Was Raelynn Vos—the girl who claimed she'd never care for any man enough to give a shit if he fucked another woman—jealous? As much as I hated the never-ending dinner, I hadn't hated that. Amongst the dread and constant reel of 'holy fuck' running through my head last night, a spark flickered under it all, only growing with each forced smile and unguarded reaction she let slip free.

While I couldn't quite find my words to soothe the situation last night, all my other senses had been on high alert—including the one that took in everything Raelynn since I met her. Each smile, each laugh, each response to Aubrey had carried a tinge of fakeness I hadn't known Rae capable of possessing.

She'd been anything but fine, and after mulling over every option of why, I kept coming back to the same one—Raelynn Vos was jealous that I asked another woman to marry me.

And when someone was jealous, they cared. Right?

Right.

Needing proof, I promised myself to take the first opportunity to push the envelope. I'd avoided ever pushing against the friendship boundaries before, but I'd never been married to her with obvious evidence of jealousy. Desperate times called for desperate measures, and I'd happily flip the switch from friendship to more if it meant getting an answer. Because I was desperate to know the truth. Could Raelynn care about me as more than a friend? Could she want more?

My chance came when she stepped onto the patio to take a phone call. I followed, and as soon as she hung up, I snapped into action.

She gasped when I gripped her arm and gently tugged her aside. Her eyes flicked over my face, her mouth agape as I maneuvered us to the corner, blocked by the curtains. Guests still lingered inside, and the wall of glass doors barely provided any privacy, but some of the curtains weren't completely open, giving me the perfect spot.

"What the hell, Austin? What? I won't fall at your feet like Aubrey, so you have to go all caveman?"

She crossed her arms and probably rolled her eyes, but I

was too distracted by the way the deep vee of her little yellow summer dress showcased her full breasts resting over her arms. Fuck, what I wouldn't give to lick my way from one curve to the next.

Usually, I cut those thoughts off, hid them behind a wall, but I reminded myself of desperate measures. So, when her tapping foot let me know she was waiting, I let her read the desire in my eyes.

The tapping stopped.

"Why are you jealous of Aubrey?"

She scoffed, looking away. "Puh-lease. I am not jealous. Why would I be? You can marry whoever you want."

I waited for her to meet my stare again before responding. "And here I am, married to you."

"I just don't understand why you didn't tell me."

I wanted to call her on ignoring my comment, but as soon as the words left her mouth, her teeth clamped down on her full lip. It bothered her that I hadn't told her, and this was her way of asking, with forced nonchalance that carried a depth of meaning.

"Because you were busy, and when you got back, it just seemed irrelevant."

The *tap, tap, tap* of her shoe returned, and she released her lip, looking out at the ocean beyond the pool and vibrant green yard. I watched her think and waited, wondering if she was planning her escape—not that I'd let her. I wasn't done yet.

"Did you give her the same ring?" she demanded, her eyes snapping back to mine.

"Would you care if I did?"

"Pft. No," she huffed with an eye roll you could have seen from Pluto. "I just don't like sloppy seconds."

"Oh, Rae." I took my time looking her up and down, taking a step forward. She took a step back but hit the wall with nowhere to go. "You're not anyone's sloppy seconds."

"I'm aware. Trust me."

"So, what has you so mad?"

"I'm not."

Somehow, I managed to hold back my bark of laughter, but my brows shot high with doubt. "Really?"

"Yes, really," she assured with a curled lip and sassy tone.

"It doesn't bother you to be here as my wife with the only serious person I've ever been with?"

"As a real wife, maybe I would care."

"You are my real wife." She could call us fake all she wanted, but legally, she was my wife, and I'd make her own up to it as long as I could. "Does that mean you do care?"

"No."

"Could've fooled me."

Another eye roll, but it only served to encourage me more. I was getting too close to something she didn't want to acknowledge. Rae was eloquent in her arguments, but in her need to push me away, she turned to petulance and immature rudeness.

Damn, she was so stubborn, but so was I.

Adding more slack to the reins around my desire, I took another step, closing the gap to almost nothing. Her head tipped back, staring me down, but what she found in my gaze halted any snarky comment.

"So, it doesn't bother you that she knows what it feels like when I do this to you?" I gently brushed her hair behind her ear, skimming my thumb along the outer shell and down her jaw. Her lips parted, and I rested one hand on the wall by her head and took the final step, removing all space between us. "Or how about when I get close to you like this? Does it bother you that she can place herself in your shoes because she knows what I feel like?"

"I—I don't care."

We stood on a precipice, and she clung to the edge of her denial, but it was time to let go. Maybe like me, Rae buried any attraction or feelings beneath our friendship. I assumed it had only been me—that my attraction was unrequited, but I was wrong. I didn't know why she'd denied anything more than friendship when so much heat simmered under the surface, but our Vegas wedding blew the cover off, and I planned to dig in and find out.

I just needed to push a little harder to make her let go.

Her skin pebbled under where I ran my finger down her neck to her shoulder, toying with the edge of her dress. Her eyes darkened to almost black. Her soft breaths brushed my chin, and I knew then I'd give anything to hear her pant for me.

Opening the gates to my fantasies, I let her see every ounce of want and need that had been caged inside me since the first moment I laid eyes on her and played my final card. "You're not jealous that she knows how I like to fuck, and you don't? Because a wife should know how her husband likes to fuck her."

"No," she breathed.

So fucking stubborn, and I loved it.

She could be as stubborn as she wanted, but we both knew the truth.

My lips tipped the slightest bit in victory, refueling Rae's fight. I should've known better than to gloat. She only took it as a challenge, and she thrived on a good challenge.

"Arrogance doesn't look good on you."

"It looks great on me." Despite a renewed spark, her insult was weak at best. So, I kept my arrogance in place, wanting to get her riled up. Maybe then she'd get flustered and do something crazy—like admit the truth. "And jealousy looks good on you."

Her eyes flared. "I am not—"

"There you are," Jeremy called from the doorway. "Whoops. Sorry to interrupt." He started backtracking when he took us in.

"No, no worries," I said, taking my time to back up with a wink to Rae. "We were just taking a moment alone."

"Young love. You can never have enough of each other."

"I think I've had enough of you," Rae muttered for only me to hear.

I barely choked back the laugh. "What did you need?"

"We are getting ready for a game of croquet. Would you two like to play?"

"I'd love to," Rae answered.

"Great. I'll see you out there."

Once he headed toward the yard, Rae made a break for it.

I let her get all the way to the door. "By the way, you're the only woman to wear that ring."

She stopped and turned just enough to look over her shoulder. I held my breath, waiting for her to roll her eyes and tell me how much she didn't care. Instead, she surprised me by lifting her chin and giving me a single word that admitted so much more.

"Good."

She left before she could see my smile, but it buoyed my spirits. I smiled all the way out to the lush green lawn for croquet, only for it to fade when Rae apparently shored up her defenses inside and came out colder than at breakfast.

She laughed with Jeremy and her dad. Shared a glass of lemonade with her mom. Greeted each person with a warm smile as they came to join us. Somehow, she managed to be this perfect social queen while treating me like I didn't exist and never making it obvious to anyone but me. I'd be impressed if it wasn't undoing the progress I'd made.

As we waited for the game to start, I watched her, scrolling my mind for any ideas to knock down the wall she'd erected in record time. In the end, I didn't need to think at all because before we started, Aubrey came in like a wrecking ball.

"Aubrey, I'm so glad you could join us," Jeremy greeted.

"Of course. I've only played a handful of times, so go easy on me."

Playing with fire, I added, "You'll do great. It's just like mini-golf."

As I hoped, Aubrey laughed and brought up our past. "Oh, my gosh. We played so many rounds that summer after college. It's probably a good thing we're not on a team; otherwise, no one would stand a chance."

"Such a shame," Rae tsked with a smile. Like magic, she appeared, sliding her hands around my bicep. Chills chased her touch, my skin rising to get more.

I almost got whiplash with how fast Raelynn switched from ignoring me to not leaving my side. She swayed like a pendulum, and if I could help her swing further in the direction of claiming me, then I'd do it. Even if it meant getting singed in the process.

We lined up and started taking shots. Aubrey stood close, bringing up the different mini-golf courses we went to. I laughed but barely heard her, my mind too focused on Rae's ire bubbling close to the surface.

"Austin, will you help me with the first shot? I want to make sure I line it up right," Rae asked.

Barely biting back my smile, I obliged, wrapping my big body around her small frame. Not looking a gift horse in the mouth, I ran my nose through her hair and inhaled the sweet floral scent.

"Austin is such a great teacher," Aubrey said. "He helped me when we went to the driving range, too."

"Great," Rae said before shoving her ass back against my groin.

I kept my grunt as quiet as possible but couldn't quite choke it back completely. She huffed a laugh as if she'd won, but while Rae was stubborn, so was I.

"Careful, Raelynn. Your brown eyes are looking a little green," I taunted.

She took control of the swing and knocked the ball through the metal arch, sending it flying too far.

"So, close," I laughed, backing up. She turned with a subtle glare, only making me smile harder.

I barely paid attention the rest of the game, fully enthralled with Raelynn not wanting to prove me right but also wanting to show Aubrey that I was off-limits. She didn't ask for any more help but continued with subtle touches that drove me wild.

At the end of the game, when she asked me to take a picture with her, I would have agreed to anything. I even forgot to do my usual groan.

"How are we doing this?" I asked.

"Let me check. I did a poll asking them what they wanted to see," she explained, pulling out her phone. "Of course, they want to see more of you."

"I mean, who wouldn't." I laughed at her deadpan stare. "Anything specific?"

"Umm…" Her pursed lips and hesitation set off warning bells. "They want to see us kiss."

"Oh, okay." I tried to answer as nonchalantly as possible. People still lingered around, listening and watching. I was her husband, so why wouldn't we kiss. It was perfectly natural.

Except we'd never kissed.

I'd imagined it about a thousand different times, and doing it for an Instagram photo op in front of a group of people hadn't come close to a single one. While I should have gladly pulled her in my arms and taken my chance, a ball of dread grew when I pictured the lack of intimacy—the lack of emotion.

"Do you want me to take it?" Aubrey offered, because she was the kind of girl who happily offered to take a picture of her ex-fiancé kissing his new wife and not think another thing of it.

"That'd be perfect," Rae answered, passing the phone off before turning to me. "Ready?"

"Are you?"

"I've been waiting to show that mouth who's boss since day one."

I barked a laugh, loving the way she bobbed her brows. "Bring it on," I challenged.

"Okay." She looked around, analyzing all our options. "Here." She grabbed my hand, tugging me to where the sparkling ocean sat as our backdrop. "Now dip me and lay it on me."

Pulling her close, I wrapped my arms around her tight and dipped.

Except there was no anticipation, only that growing ball of dread threatening to choke me.

This wasn't how it was supposed to be.

Everything screamed how wrong this was, and I fought every tense muscle that urged me to stop. Especially when at the last moment, I met her eyes, and I didn't find the playful Rae smiling back. Instead, I found a matching nervousness.

Before my lips could land on hers, I shifted and landed just outside her lips, kissing the petal soft skin of her cheek. I held myself steady to make sure we got the picture and held her tighter when her nails dragged up my neck and into my hair.

Fuck, I wished we were alone.

"Looks perfect," Aubrey announced.

I lifted Rae up and waited for her approval.

"You guys look great," Aubrey complimented.

"Thank you. You take an amazing picture," Rae said.

"Will you be at the party tonight?" Aubrey asked us.

"Of course. I can't wait," Rae answered.

"Great. I'll see you there."

The walk back to our room was silent but filled with unspoken words. It wasn't until I'd closed our door that she finally spoke.

"Why didn't you kiss me?"

I considered my options, weighing the pros and cons of how honest I wanted to be. With a deep breath, I turned to face her, figuring why the hell not be completely honest. What did I have to lose?

"I didn't want my first kiss with my wife to only be done for a picture. It's not how I imagined it."

"You're so traditional. It's just a kiss," she joked, but curiosity lingered behind the brush-off.

"There's not just anything with you, Raelynn."

Her smile faded.

One second.

Two seconds.

"So, how did you picture it?" she finally asked.

I could've used words and easily explained something inconsequential. I could have said something crude and joked my way out of it. But I didn't. I wanted her to see what I wanted. I wanted her to see me as a man who desired her—not just the friend who would do anything for her.

I needed her to see that I was passion and friendship all rolled in one. I needed her to see that I could be the perfect man for her if only she'd let me.

I wasn't missing this chance to show her.

Closing my eyes, I plucked one of the many fantasies, letting it wash over me. When I looked at her again, I made sure she saw it all.

She didn't say anything as I slowly closed the gap. She didn't say anything as she retreated until her back hit the wall. She didn't utter a single word when I towered over her and used my finger to lift her chin so she couldn't look away.

"I imagined us being around people all day, unable to find a second alone. I imagined us both knowing how much the other wanted it. I imagined watching your mouth, letting the need grow and expand inside me with each swipe of your tongue across your lips until I'm consumed by it."

As if she couldn't help it, her tongue made a pass, and I stroked my thumb across her lip to smooth the dampness into the plump skin.

"I imagined us so desperate to be alone because we know any kiss we share would be savage and indecent. Our passion would take over, and it would only be for us—it'd be ours alone. We'd need time."

"For what?" she pleaded with barely a whisper.

"Mmmmm," I hummed, just the thought of it enough to bring me to the edge. "To feel. I want to know the give of your lip under my teeth, to know the exact spot your lips seal to mine. I'd need time to taste." Giving in just a fraction, I snaked my tongue out to briefly brush the edge of her lips. Her whimper almost had me going back for more, but I held strong. "I want to taste every inch. Your lips, your tongue. Every part of your mouth inside and out. I want to devour you whole."

Her eyes slid closed as if picturing every word. We were so close her soft, short breaths brushed my lips, begging me to do it. And like the weak man I was, I did. Just a taste. Just the softest graze of skin that left her chasing me when I pulled back.

"That's what I imagined."

"Austin," she whispered.

Redness stained her cheeks, but I wanted to see what it looked like when it stretched its way down her chest. I didn't want just a stolen kiss right now. I wanted it all, and to get it, I needed to be patient. I needed to make her want it as much as I did.

"You should probably get ready," I said, inching back.

Her eyes snapped open, hazy as if coming out of a dream.

"The party," I clarified. "You said you wanted to get ready. You can have the shower first. I'll respond to some emails while I wait."

She blinked, and I watched her, enjoying the way she

floundered for her composure. I couldn't remember a time I hadn't seen Rae immediately snap back. I marked this moment as a win and was kind enough to wait to smile until she closed the bathroom door.

I'd been dreading the black and white party when she told me, but something about tonight felt different than any other formal we'd attended.

Something about tonight felt like each win I'd earned today would come to a tipping point. I just had to make sure it tipped toward winning the war and not losing it.

## Chapter Twelve

### RAELYNN

IF I THOUGHT I was going to make Austin pay for calling me jealous all day with my sexy-ass dress, I was right.

Watching his jaw drop when I strutted out of the room in the silky white dress, flooded me with satisfaction. A satisfaction that evaporated as soon as he stood from the chair in the corner.

I wasn't the only one using my body as a weapon tonight.

His white pants, jacket, and shirt with a few buttons undone fit him like a second skin, and all I wanted to do was peel it off one delicious layer at a time.

Tracking up his body to find a gloating smirk, only pissed me off more.

"Ready?" he asked.

I matched his arrogance with my own, forcing an unaffected tone. "Of course."

He held the door open, and I did my best to ignore the rich vanilla and sandalwood cologne that made my mouth water as I walked past.

I'd smelled the scent a thousand times, but after today, after the way Austin knocked down some barrier in my mind firmly caging him in the friend-zone, it permeated differently.

It reached different, deeper, and sparked my imagination in ways I never considered to think of Austin. Of course, I flirted with him, but never seriously. I never closed my eyes, trying to picture what it would be like to be with him.

Now, I couldn't stop.

Not after that kiss.

God, that kiss. It was nothing—barely a fraction of skin touching. Yet, it consumed me like an inferno. Hell, hours later, and it still left me hot. I tried to rub my thighs together to ease the ache and ended up stumbling.

"You okay?" he asked, gripping my arms.

I met his green eyes and wanted to beg for more. The words climbed up my throat, and I barely swallowed them back down.

*Jesus, Rae,* I reprimanded myself. I needed to get it together. "Yeah. I just need to run back and get my lipstick. I'll meet you down there."

I dashed back to the room, not waiting for a response. In the bathroom, I ran cold water over my wrists, staring in the mirror at wild eyes. Leaning in, I searched for any green that Austin claimed was there but only found the usual brown. I almost laughed at my lunacy.

I prided myself on being bold and honest. Yet, there I was hiding. The least I could do was be honest with myself.

Maybe I *was* jealous.

What did Aubrey have that I didn't? Was it her demure personality? Was I *too* bold? Did he think I was a slut, and that was why he turned me down that first night? I'd never thought about it, but after being confronted with Aubrey, I couldn't stop wondering.

"Ugh," I groaned in frustration. "I'm going fucking insane."

I needed help, and I knew just where to get it. I dug through my purse for my phone and hit call.

"Daaaaaaaamn," Vera greeted.

But I didn't have time for pleasantries. The car would be leaving soon, and I needed to get my head straight. "I don't care what men think of me."

Her eyes widened comically wide. "What?"

"And I'm not jealous."

"Okay. Wait. What are we talking about? What do you need? Fill me in."

God, I loved her for knowing exactly what I needed. I gave the cliff notes version, managing not to laugh at the full gamut of facial expressions.

"And now I'm in a bathroom, trying to get myself to be honest, but I feel like I'm on the edge of losing it."

"So, be honest. Say it," she ordered like it was nothing. "Say it out loud."

My jaw clamped tight, and she met my stubbornness with her determined stare. She knew she was right, and dammit, I knew it, too.

"I—I'm *jealous* of Aubrey."

"Why?" she asked, not holding any punches.

"Because…" I swallowed and bit my lip, not wanting to say the words but needing to. "Because she knows Austin in a way I never will."

"And…"

"What do you mean, and?"

She stared harder, and if I had to guess, she was probably tapping her foot on the other side of the screen. She knew there was more. *I* knew there was more. It stood there in front of me, and I didn't want to face it. Dropping my gaze, I studied the sink. Glitter caught my eyes, and I looked over to where the golden band sparkled on my ring finger—my wedding band.

A wedding band that could have been hers.

Closing my eyes, I started chipping away at the root of what really bothered me. "He almost married her."

"And what if he had?" Vera asked.

I snapped my gaze back. "I would have come back from overseas to my best friend married—without me."

"So?"

"What if she hated me? What if she made him choose between her and me, and I lost my friend? Because, of course, he'd choose her, she'd be his wife. She would be more important."

My heart throbbed painfully, racing toward—or maybe away from—the truth.

"But you're his wife now."

"Not really."

Vere did a very unladylike eye roll I knew she had to have learned from me. "No matter what your intentions are in the future, you did marry him. So, that does, in fact, make you his wife. The question is, how does it make you feel?"

"Trapped," I answered without thinking.

"Thanks for that rote response," she deadpanned. "Now, let's get the real answer. When you spent time with him today, flirting and acting married, how did that make you feel?"

I ran through the moments we interacted and kept coming back to when he first accused me of being jealous. He'd cornered me, but that feeling lingered for the rest of the day.

"Cornered."

"But not trapped?"

"No," I answered, shocking myself.

"Why cornered?"

"Because I didn't want to answer his stupid question," I said without thinking.

"Why?"

"I didn't want to admit I was jealous."

"Why?" she repeated again as if prodding a tender spot, pushing and pushing until I broke.

And break I did.

"Because I freaking care about him."

"Holy Halleluiah." She raised her hands in the air. "The

heavens have parted. It's about fucking time. Nico," she shouted past the screen. "You owe me a hundred bucks and a back massage. I told you guys she wouldn't make it home before admitting it."

"Dammit," Nico muttered in the background.

"You had a bet?" I screeched.

"Yeah. Hang on. I need to message Nova. She thought you wouldn't admit it until at least his grandparents' house. Way too much faith in your stubbornness."

"What the hell?" I wanted to say more—ask more questions—but my mind scrambled to keep up with its own thoughts, let alone the bet I had no clue about.

Vera finally focused her attention back on me, changing her victorious smile to one of concerned friend. "Listen, you can give us shit later. We need to focus on your feelings for Austin."

"What? No. No." Hearing it laid out so bluntly had me backing away from my phone.

"Why?"

"Because I don't want to have feelings for him. I can't. I don't do relationships."

"You could try," she offered.

"I don't want to because if I do, I know how it will go. We'll fall apart, and then everything will change."

"It's already changed, Rae." Her softly spoken truth hit me more like a two-by-four, and the panicked feeling that had me calling her in the first place only increased.

"You're not helping, and I have to go."

"Listen," she snapped.

Her voice hit like a splash of cold water, calming me down enough to do exactly as she ordered.

"I don't have an easy answer, no matter how much I wish I did."

"I know," I whined.

"The bottom line is that you have feelings for Austin, and

it's up to you to decide what you want to do with them. Don't let fear of change keep you from doing something about it because things have already changed. The best you can do is guide it to the best outcome."

And with those not so helpful final words, we got off the phone, leaving me to face everyone at the party as Austin's wife—not feeling any better than before I had the bright idea to be honest with myself.

Thankfully, I didn't get the opportunity to be alone with my thoughts—or Austin. We shared a limo with my parents and the Scotts' to the party at a much larger mansion. As soon as we walked in, the crowd of partygoers, decked out in their best black and white, greeted us. They offered their congratulations and asked to see my ring, concerned about the small size, and then gushing over the fact that it was a family heirloom. When they were done ogling my ring, they moved on to ogle Austin.

Not that it bothered him. He'd been my plus one to so many events I'd lost count. At first, he'd been alarmed but quickly mastered the polite smile while creating distance. The first time he came home to a Christmas charity gala over a school break, I'd been in tears watching him flounder under all the forward advances. Now, laughing was the furthest thing from my mind. I wanted to bare my teeth and pull him close.

*I care about him.*

Dammit. Just hearing the admission in my head had me wincing as if the memory actually slapped me.

"You okay?" Austin asked.

"Yeah," I answered, quickly smoothing my face to a smile. "Just thirsty."

"Ladies, if you'll excuse me, my wife needs a drink." He pulled us away with a smile as they awed over how romantic it was that this big, strong man guided me away like a little girl who couldn't find her way to the bar all alone.

It was eye roll-inducing.

*I* should have been eye-rolling.

Yet, part of me awed right along with them.

*I care about him.*

God, I was screwed.

Austin grabbed two glasses and found a small standing table in the back corner, offering a modicum of reprieve from the noisy crowd. Just as I was taking a sip, the crowd parted, giving the perfect view of Aubrey in a white, single-long sleeve dress. Part of me wished she had bad taste, but I had to admit she looked stunning, and her dress was straight amazing. *Dammit.* I never held back from appreciating a woman and her style—even if I was jealous.

"What made you want to marry Aubrey?" I blurted.

"Uhh," he stuttered, as surprised as me by the question. "I don't know. I liked her at the time."

"Yeah, but you liked a lot of girls. Why her?"

He set his glass down and rubbed at the furrow growing between his brows. I probably should have pulled back. The middle of a party might not have been the top pick of places to play twenty questions, but Pandora's box had been opened.

"I guess it was just life at the time. My brother had recently gotten married and maybe that, mixed with the small panic of the seriousness of life after college, had me on edge. I mean, we got along well."

With herculean effort, I kept a passive look locked in place, despite wondering if he heard how absurd it was that he wanted to marry her because they 'got along well.'

"Was she right for you? Was she the kind of woman you imagined your life with?"

His eyes, which had been watching the crowd, snapped to me. The deep green bored into mine—intense and holding me captive. "No, she wasn't the kind of woman I imagined," he finally answered. Something lingered behind those words, but he blinked before I could study it. "And the timing was all off."

"What do you mean?"

I wanted to grip his jacket lapels and shake him, scream the question, and demand he answer. My mind reeled like a flashing slideshow of options. Did he think the timing now would be better? Would he keep in touch after this? Oh, my god, what if they kept in touch? What if it worked out this time? What if he ended up marrying her now? Time stretched into an endless wait, pushing me closer to the edge. Realistically, I knew maybe half a breath of space came between one question and the next.

"Are you guys going to keep in touch when you leave here?" The question spewed out. Between the fast-paced questions and the barely masked, high-pitched, panicked tone, his mood shifted. Suddenly, this didn't feel like two friends talking off in a corner. In all honesty, I wasn't sure it ever had, but now it shifted to something more.

His shoulders relaxed as if figuring out the game and preparing to play, while mine tightened, preparing for a challenge.

Oh, yeah. Just like before, Austin watched me with a challenging look. It coiled around my muscles, pulling tight. It sunk low to my core when his tongue glided across his lips before shifting to an arrogant smirk I wanted to hate but kind of loved.

"Would it bother you if I did?"

Not trusting my voice, I rolled my eyes and took a drink, trying to come up with a question to throw him off as much as he derailed me.

"Do you miss fucking her?" I finally asked, realizing too late that my question revealed more than it shocked. His smile grew, and I rushed to speak so he couldn't. "Just curious…" I shrugged. "I mean, maybe there's more behind those pearls that can keep up with you."

"Why do you say that?" he asked, his head tipping to study me.

"You had a pretty descriptive mouth earlier. Makes me think that maybe you crave more in the bedroom than you portray."

*I'd want to devour you whole.*

Remembering those words whispered like a promise against my lips fired bolts of electricity through my body. It was the only excuse I had for not just shutting up.

"Not that I would know since you never wanted to fuck me."

His loud burst of laughter drew people's attention, who laughed as if they were part of the conversation and got the joke. I wanted to ask them what the hell was so funny, but they quickly went back to their own group.

"Oh, Rae." Austin shook his head and pulled himself together. "Just because I never fucked you didn't mean I didn't *want* to."

The way he drew out the word *want* should have been illicit—illegal—against the rules. It wasn't fair how just a word could suck the air from my lungs and make my heart skip a beat, only to thunder back to life a second later.

It wasn't fair how just hearing him say he wanted to sleep with me caused a thrilling jolt to harden my nipples. It wasn't fair that he could all of a sudden make me want him so damn much.

*The best you can do is guide the change to the best possible outcome.*

Vera's advice replayed, bolstering me to act. "Then do it."

His smirk dropped. "What?"

"Why not?" I asked. He studied me, probably looking for the joke he wouldn't find. I'd offered to sleep with Austin about a million times since I met him, but other than that first night, they were all in jest to watch him look away and blush. Nothing about this was funny. "We're away from everything—in our own reality of sorts."

The idea sounded better and better the more I thought about it.

"Rae," he breathed.

It didn't sound like a protest, but I added more reasons why he shouldn't fight this just in case. "And we're married. Why not consummate the marriage?"

He studied me, his chest rising slow and steady. Meanwhile, I couldn't regulate my breathing if I tried. I dug my teeth into my lip, locking down any more ideas that tried to escape.

The crowd and music and drinks and laughter muffled until all I heard was the pulsing thunder of my own heart. I curled my fingers into my palm, desperate to distract myself from the endless seconds of silence. All the while, I never looked away. I wanted to read every thought rolling across the face I knew so well but also looked so different.

As if someone pulled the plug, his chest sunk with a deep exhale, and I knew then, his decision was made.

Slowly, his lips quirked back up in the smile that I will forever blame as my downfall. "Consummate isn't the word I'd use."

His words rumbled across the space between us, stroking my skin, pulling me into a side of Austin I decided I needed to know. Ignoring the fraction of shock that this was actually happening, I finally figured out the game too, and I was ready to play.

With a quirk of a brow, I guided us to the change I wanted. "What word would you use?"

"More than one."

"Tell me," I almost pleaded.

"Can I have your attention, please? It's time to reveal some of the auction winners," a man announced over the microphone.

The overwhelming boom of his voice through the speakers barely permeated our bubble. Austin held my gaze as he drained his glass, setting it aside before slowly edging his way around the small tabletop. Every muscle pulled tight, waiting for his next move—except my heart. My heart galloped along, racing toward whatever he had planned.

He turned me to face the pseudo stage, coming behind me. I gasped at the contact of his suit jacket abrading the bare skin of my back, but no one noticed. We stood behind everyone else, who was too busy watching the stage. We didn't exist to anyone but ourselves.

One hand crept around my hip, pulling my ass into him while the other brushed my hair aside, making room to graze his nose along my ear. "You sure?"

Was I sure I wanted him to tell me all the words he'd use to describe fucking me? Without hesitation, I nodded.

Both hands framed my hips, his long fingers playing with the slits that ended just below my hipbones. His rough fingers abraded my skin, sending bolts of electricity up my spine and back down to my core.

"I'd fuck you soft," he whispered, his words caressing my ear. "I'd push my cock in slowly so I could memorize the feel of every inch inside your pussy. I'd hold your legs wide, so I could watch your swollen, wet cunt stretch to take all of me while I eased in and out. You'd beg me for more, but I'd barely touch your clit—just enough to drive you wild but not let you come. And when you thought you had the torturous rhythm figured out—when you thought you found a way to come—I'd fuck you so hard, so deep, you wouldn't know who you were anymore. I wouldn't stop until you lost control—screaming my name, your pussy squeezing my dick, begging for my cum." The sharp sting of his teeth against my ear contrasted deliciously with his soft tone. "And I'd give it to you. I'd fuck every drop so deep inside you, you'd never get rid of me."

"Austin." I didn't recognize the whimpering plea that begged for more with just his name.

"Do you want it?"

*Who was I?*

Who was this girl melting at his feet? I didn't know her, but in all of this new chaotic lust ravaging me, I knew one thing— I wanted to. I wanted to discover more about the girl who allowed her best friend to set her on fire. "Yes. Please."

"Say it," he ordered.

Turning my head enough to meet his heated gaze, I did something I never thought I'd do. I obeyed. "I want you to fuck me."

As if his eyes weren't dark enough, his pupils dilated, leaving the barest hint of green. "Good. Let's go."

Without waiting, he grabbed my hand and started walking, barely giving the few people we passed a polite nod. In record time, the valet had a car to take us home.

Every sense rose to high alert. The cool leather of the seat chilled my heated skin. The slam of the door reverberated through my body, matching the thudding pulse inside. The roll of the tires across the gravel created a vibration that only intensified the sensation already bringing my skin to life.

Austin shifted his large frame into the corner and watched me do my best to sit with etiquette, hiding the needy desire from our driver. Austin had no such qualms about keeping anything private.

"You have no idea what it does to me to see your nipples hard, begging me to play with them."

As if wanting more attention, they pulled painfully tight, sensitive to even the slightest movement against the silk of my dress. God, I ached.

I peeked in the rearview mirror, finding the driver's eyes glued to the road. Usually, I wouldn't care, but this whole scenario was specifically for my father, and it made me pause before acting. But I could barely think beyond the live wire that was my body.

"Probably the same thing it does to me to see your cock so hard," I said, pointedly looking at the large bulge against his pants.

He shifted, widening his legs, and my mouth watered. "Then do something about it."

Any other time, I would've laughed in the face of any man who gave such an order. I would've mimicked their pose and told them that maybe I'd suck their cock if they ate my pussy well enough. But again, I didn't recognize this side of myself, and I didn't hate it. I didn't hate the way I wanted to fall to my knees for him.

Still, I lifted my chin like I was too good for him, casting a look toward the driver. "Maybe I will when we get home. If you're lucky."

"I'll give you five hundred dollars if you keep your eyes on the road and never speak a word of this," Austin offered the driver, never looking away from me.

"Yes, sir," the driver answered.

"Well?" Austin asked me. "What are you waiting for?"

That damn smirk—so different from my best friend. But the challenging glint in his eyes was also familiar. It reminded me that, while I usually never let a man boss me around because I was in control, this was Austin—my best friend, and the truth was that I trusted him.

So, I let myself admit how much I liked his bossy side.

I let myself give in and got on my knees.

## Chapter Thirteen

### AUSTIN

As if my own personal fantasy played out in slow motion, I watched Raelynn Vos slide off the seat to her knees.

She never took her gaze from mine.

Not when her fingers caressed my knees, pushing them apart.

Not when she painfully, achingly, slowly dragged her palms up my thighs, hesitating only a fraction of a centimeter from my dick. In that moment, I studied her and saw the flash of unsurety in her decision. I held my breath, waiting for her to pull back—to tell me to fuck off. With each step I took tonight, bringing us closer to the edge, I waited for her to jerk away. With each revealed layer to what I really wanted—*the pleasure, the command*—I waited for her to laugh in my face.

Yet, there she knelt, looking unsure but so fucking strong.

As if I couldn't love her more, I watched her cede control. I watched her give in to me. I watched her enjoy it.

That half of a second stretched on and on until my lungs screamed for relief. Her lip barely twitched—the only warning before her palm continued, firmly stroking over my length.

"Oh, fuck," I groaned through my exhale.

Her tongue slid across her crimson lips before digging her

teeth into the lush flesh. Unable to keep my hands at my side any longer, I pushed into dangerous territory. I slid my hand along her neck, forcing her chin up with my thumb before dragging it across her lip, pulling it from her punishing bite.

"I can't wait to make a mess of your mouth."

She nipped my thumb playfully before focusing on freeing my cock. Just as eager, I lifted, helping her tug my pants down far enough to reach me.

"Holy shit," she breathed.

She eyed me like a kid in a candy shop, and I grew even harder. Blood pumped harder through my veins, pulsing along my cock until I feared I'd come just from a soft puff of air.

"Put it in your mouth."

Her eyes flashed, a fiery blaze almost burning me alive. I didn't know if it was her dominance fighting back or her desire from my command.

I didn't know, and I didn't care because, in the next instant, her hand gripped the base of my cock, and her warm, wet mouth slid over my head, continuing down, down, down until I pushed against the back of her throat.

*Fuck me.* It took everything I had not to grip the sides of her head and force her to keep going—to push past the resistance and slide into her tight throat.

Not yet. Not now. Pushing her with my words was one thing. Pushing her physically would take time and more room than this luxury car had. I'd waited years for this. I could wait a bit more to ensure we had an experience we couldn't ever say no to again.

I collected her hair from her face, so I could watch her red lips stretch around me. Up and down, up and down, her breasts brushing my knees, driving me wild in a way I hadn't even considered. As if she could read my mind, she grabbed my hand, pulling it to her chest.

Thank god she was too focused on the task of dragging her tongue up the back of my length to notice the way my hand trembled with eagerness to feel her. Just as I slid my hand under the edge of her dress, her soft, warm, full tits filling my palm, she dipped her tongue into the slit along my head, ripping a moan from deep in my chest.

When she smirked like she'd won a battle, I retaliated, finding her nipple and pinching hard enough to hurt but also hard enough to play. She gasped into a moan, and it was my turn to smile.

"You have the most perfect tits. All night, I couldn't take my eyes off you, imagining ripping that dress down and covering your pale skin with my cum."

Another moan, but this time, with her mouth around me, sending shockwaves straight to my balls. I was seconds from coming, and I couldn't tell if I wanted this to last forever or if I wanted to hurry and finish just so I could watch her take my cum.

*But how?* My mind reeled with possibilities.

Twisting her nipple softly with the occasional brush of my thumb, I teased her. "Would you let me come on your tits? Would you hold them up for me to spill all over?"

Dragging her tongue up again, holding my gaze the entire way, she nodded. Fuck me. Her submission shocked me, turning me on even more.

"Later," I promised. "I'll paint you with my cum later. Now, I want you to taste me. I want to watch my cum fill your mouth and spill from your pretty little lips while you struggle to swallow every last drop."

As if I issued a challenge, she resumed bathing my cock with her mouth, sucking harder on each pull, pushing deeper on each descent.

Darkness crept in on the edges of my vision. My heart thundered like a racehorse toward the finish. My body vibrated, vibrated, vibrated until it finally exploded. I slammed my head back against the seat and came. Her soft palm rolled my balls, prolonging the pleasure until I thought I'd blackout.

When the world stopped humming around me, I lifted my head to her wiping a drop of my seed from her lips, sucking it off her finger. "Good girl," I praised, rubbing my thumb over the same spot.

The car rolled to a stop, and as if she hadn't just had a cock in her throat, she pushed back up to the seat and pulled out her mirror. I quickly adjusted my pants, barely fastening them because I knew I'd have them off as soon as we walked in. I passed the promised cash to the driver and turned back to her just in time to grab her wrist, stopping her from touching up her lipstick.

She looked to where I gently held her in place, then back to me with a *what the fuck* look.

"Don't bother. I'm just gonna take it off all over again," I promised.

Again, she hesitated. Again, I held my breath. Had I gone too far?

But this was Rae. Even if I was revealing the sexual side of myself, she'd always been open. She may be willing to cede some control, but if at any point, she didn't? She would have no qualms about telling me so.

"I fucking hope so." With that, she exited the car, and I raced to follow.

I stalked behind her, letting her make it through the door before making my move. My finger down the length of her back was her only warning before I whirled her around to face me. She stared up with wild eyes—so dark, yet bright with a fire I wanted to burn in.

Our heavy breaths echoed around the dark empty foyer. The whole house was quiet. Everyone gone for the night, including staff. Thank god, because I'd waited long enough and didn't want to wait a second more.

Like an animal cornering its prey, I loomed over her,

letting every filthy fantasy play across my face. Each step I took forward, she took one back until she bumped into the round table. Still, I didn't stop. I rested both hands on the dark wood, staring down her body as she arched back to hold my gaze.

Her tongue slicked across her lip, and my mouth watered to do the same. Not yet. Pressing my forehead to hers, I closed my eyes and inhaled, losing myself in her scent—in the way she trembled against me.

"Austin," she breathed, inches from my mouth.

"I need to taste you," I said, my desperation bleeding through. Dropping down her body, my hands skated over her curves, not trusting myself enough to let my mouth play. I knew that once I put my mouth on her full tits, I'd be there until she came from that alone.

"Make sure you watch," I ordered, nodding toward the mirror behind me. "I want you to know what it looks like with my head between your thighs."

"Oh, god," she whimpered.

Her sweet aroma permeated the air and fueled the animal I barely kept on a leash. I kneeled before her, wild and on the edge of losing control. Two high slits bared her strong legs. Starting at her knee, I dragged my tongue up one thigh, shoving the silky material aside. The daintiest scrap of white lace barely covered her. Such a virginal juxtaposition to the filth I was going to do. I fisted the material and delivered a sharp bite to her inner thigh as I ripped the panties off her.

She gasped, and finally seeing her swollen, wet lips bared to me was the final straw. The chain around my control snapped.

I wedged a shoulder under her leg and dove in like a man starved. She yelped, falling forward, digging her hands into my hair to hold herself up.

The sweet, tangy flavor burst on my tongue, only urging

me to get more, more, more. I shoved my tongue between her folds and dragged it from her opening to her swollen clit.

"Oh, my god. Fuck. Fuck," she whimpered. "Austin. Please."

Her begging shot straight down my spine, bringing my cock back to life. I wanted to stay there forever with my face between her thighs, but I needed inside her.

Gripping her ass, I pinned her where I wanted and feasted, sucking on her clit with quick fast flicks of my tongue, losing myself in the way she rocked against my mouth, in the way her cum dripped down my chin.

"Shit. Yes. I'm coming."

Her hands fisted painfully in my hair, only adding to the pulsing beat of need between us. Her whimpers and moans would follow me to the grave. I wanted to record them and play them every night. I was a man obsessed, and I needed more.

Her pussy throbbed against my lips, and I didn't bother waiting for her to completely come down before I rose to my feet, hoisting her over my shoulder on the way.

"Austin," she shrieked.

I smacked her ass, earning another shout. "I need inside you. So, unless you want people to start coming back to find me wedged deep inside your cunt, I suggest you stop wriggling."

"You're barbaric."

"Oh, Rae," I laughed softly, "I'm desperate. But if you want barbaric, I'll happily throw you down right here on these steps and rut against you like the goddamn animal you've turned me into."

"You wouldn't."

I stopped, setting her on a step above me so I could meet her gaze. "I would, and I wouldn't stop, even when they came in. I'd happily let them watch until I spilled everything I had deep inside you."

She swallowed, the only sign that she wasn't as unaffected as her mulish silence wanted me to believe.

"Would you like that, Raelynn?" I asked with a slow smile. "Would you like for everyone to watch you take me?"

Still, she didn't say a word. She didn't need to.

My smile grew. "I'll have to keep that in mind. But for now, I need more than a set of stairs for what I have in mind."

"And what do you have in mind?" she asked, her voice needy.

Without answering, I hoisted her back over my shoulder again, running to our room. I kicked the door shut behind us and stood her at the foot of the bed.

Her mouth parted, begging me to kiss her.

Not yet. Something held me back. Something told me that this kiss would be more important than anything else I did to her tonight. I needed to make sure it was monumental.

Her breasts rose and fell. I couldn't wait a second longer. I needed to see them—to see all of her. I dragged my palms down her neck, over her shoulders, taking the straps with me. The silky material caught on her hard nipples before I tugged it free.

"Years," I muttered, pushing her dress down past her hips. "Years, I wondered what color your nipples were, what size. The glimpse in Vegas wasn't enough." She stood still, letting me look, letting me strip her, each of her needy breaths bringing the rosy pink tips closer to my mouth. "I wondered what they tasted like."

"Do it," she whispered.

I waited, dragging out the anticipation, huffing my breath across the tender bud, sending chills along her pale curves.

"Austin, godda—"

I flicked my tongue across the tip before nipping softly. Her shocked cry softened to a moan of pleasure when I gripped her hips. I held her still, dragging my tongue around one nipple, through her cleavage, to suck on the other.

"Yes. More."

I released her nipple, promising to come back, and stood tall and in control.

"Get on the bed."

As if she wore a suit of armor instead of nothing at all, she lifted her chin and a single brow. "What if I don't want to."

I raised my own brow with a soft laugh. "We both know you want to. Now get on the bed," I ordered harder this time. "And spread your legs."

A war between her natural dominance and doing what we both knew she wanted played out behind her eyes while I was seconds away from falling to my knees and begging her to keep going.

"Fine."

I thought I would collapse in relief but was too consumed with each sway of her perfect tits, each flex of her muscles as she inched back against the pillows. She waited until she was stretched out like a Playboy model to comply with my last order and spread her legs.

Taking my time, I dragged my eyes up her body. "I'm going to fuck you so hard you'll scream until they hear you across the ocean."

"Promises, promises."

Her usual taunting voice was replaced by a breathy plea. I stripped my clothes with zero finesse, tossing them aside after grabbing a condom, growing harder and harder under her awed gaze. I knew I was attractive, but having the woman of your dreams look at you like that blew my confidence sky-high.

She trembled against the fluffy white comforter, like a nervous virgin sacrifice all laid out for me. It was time to claim my prize. "Do you remember what I said?" I asked, climbing up the bed between her spread thighs.

She nodded jerkily, her mouth falling open over a gasp

when I swiped my fingers through her folds before shoving inside. "You're so wet. That's good because you'll need to be to take all of me."

Her hand snapped around my wrist, halting the teasing twist and turns. "Get inside me. Now," she issued her own order through clenched teeth.

"My pleasure." I straddled her hips and lined the head of my cock up with her opening, brushing it back and forth. "Watch," I demanded, waiting for her to push to her elbows and see where the head of my dick pressed against her. "I want you to remember every detail of what it looks like, feels like, to have me push inside you. Watch me take you—*claim* you."

Just like I promised, I slid in one agonizing inch at a time, watching her swollen cunt spread wide to accommodate all of me. I inched back out, groaning over the sight of her cum smeared along my cock before sliding all the way until my balls pressed to her ass. Pressing my hands on her thighs, I held her open wide, gliding in and out at a painstaking pace.

"Look at you. Such a good girl, taking my cock so well. Your little cunt is stretched so tight around me, I have to force myself in."

"Yes," she gasped, "I want you. I want more—faster."

She squirmed, and I'd probably leave bruises from where I held her so tightly, but she never once told me to stop.

Sweat dripped down my temples, and I struggled not to rut into her like she wanted. I slid my thumb to the swollen clit between her legs, barely grazing it.

"Oh, fuck," she exclaimed with a guttural cry.

"You're a mess," I moaned, gliding across her slippery bud. "Your pussy's so wet, I can hear it sucking me back in."

"Because I want more. I want you to fuck me," she begged.

I brushed her clit faster, bringing her to the edge. Her hips writhed, and her head dug back into the pillow, her mouth open.

And I stopped.

I pulled out, so just my head sat inside her opening and held her wide again, keeping her from moving.

"Are you fucking kidding me?" she screamed like a wild woman.

I loved it so much I almost laughed. The truth was, not many women were strong enough to fuck the way I wanted to, but Rae was. Which was why I didn't hesitate to fall over and give her what she wanted.

She wrapped around me, and I gripped her shoulders, holding her steady through my brutal thrusts. With each push, I went deeper, leaving a piece of myself behind.

"Fuck, Austin. It shouldn't feel this good," she cried, her words almost incoherent and lost in pleasure. "It hurts, but god, I want more. I want it harder."

I was too far gone to give her anything other than what she wanted. I dug my hands in her hair, holding her, so she had nowhere to look but at me. I drove into her, our skin slapping together faster and faster, both of us racing to finish.

And not once did we look away.

In that instant, everything lined up, and I knew I was exactly where I was supposed to be. I knew it, and with her eyes on mine, I saw she knew it too.

I ground against her clit with each thrust and sent her over the edge, where she pulled me with her. We held tight and fell together through an abyss of heaven.

Enveloped in each other, cries of pleasure falling from our lips, I kissed her. Without hesitation, she held me as tightly as I held her and fed from my lips, feasting on my groans. We kissed like savages, nothing but nerve endings of need. Nothing but live wires setting off sparks each time our tongues brushed.

Wave after wave washed over us until I lost track of space and time. Nothing mattered but this—but her. But us.

Slowly, the ocean waves permeated the room through the open balcony door, mixing with our gasping breaths, and I slowed our kisses to soft drinking pecks.

With a groan, I slipped free. She buried her hands in my hair and held me close as I kissed down her neck until I could rest my head on her chest.

Her heart thudded, and I knew I should say something. Make sure she was okay. Make sure *we* were okay. But I didn't know where to start, and I wasn't ready to face what happened next. I knew what I wanted to happen, but I also knew there was no guarantee.

So, instead of talking, I lost myself to the heat of her skin wrapped around me. I lost myself to the feel of her nails scratching along my scalp and let it lull me to sleep.

Tomorrow.

We'd face it all tomorrow.

Maybe after another round.

Then we could talk.

It would be fine.

## Chapter Fourteen

### RAELYNN

WAVES CRASHING against the beach tugged me from my sleep just enough to notice the heat against my back and deep breaths coming from behind me.

For a moment, I was back in the hotel in Vegas. Except this time, I knew exactly who I'd find behind me. I knew exactly what I'd done. My body ached in ways I didn't even know were possible. Each movement I made reminded me of how thoroughly Austin used my body, how he bent me to his will, how he stretched me to my max.

Rolling over, I knew to expect my friend. I knew I'd find the same nose with the slight bend from a break in football in college. I knew I'd find the same dark blond scruff and sleep-ruffled hair. I knew I'd find the same sharp jawline and perfectly-shaped lips. Except, when I took him in under the early morning light, I didn't find that.

I found so much more.

Instead of sleep-ruffled hair, I found hair I'd dug my hands into to hold him in place because I hadn't ever wanted him to stop. Instead of the familiar mouth I'd noticed and dismissed since his very first rejection, I found the lush lips I'd watched devour every inch of me. Instead of rolling over and finding comfort in my friend next to me, I found an unfamiliar pressure wrapping around my chest and a skipping heartbeat.

The more I studied him, the more the intense pressure grew. It was like last night had ripped a veil down between us, and something new pressed in on me, but I wasn't ready to look. So, I stood there squeezing my eyes shut while tentatively reaching out to touch it, but I jerked back as soon as I grazed whatever last night had revealed.

It was too much.

I needed space.

As quietly and quickly as possible, I rolled out of bed and did the bare minimum to be presentable enough to go downstairs. I hadn't even looked at the time in my mad dash and didn't realize how early it was until I got downstairs to an empty kitchen.

I was in the middle of studying the ridiculously fancy coffee machine when one of the chefs popped around the corner like I'd willed them there.

"Sorry, miss. I wasn't expecting anyone awake just yet. Can I get you anything?" she asked.

"Just a coffee, please. Unfortunately, my coffee machine knowledge stops at a Keurig."

She laughed with me at my joke as I stepped back so she could work her magic.

In minutes, she had a cup prepared for me with the promise of a spread in about an hour. "Can I get you a croissant or anything?"

"No, thank you. This coffee is perfect."

The pressure still squeezed tight, and I wasn't sure I'd be able to get much down past it. I found a quiet spot out on the patio tucked away in the corner so I could watch the rising sun sparkle against the pool and listen to the waves crashing against the shore.

I thought it would help.

It didn't.

Every time I saw a glint in the water, I imagined the same spark in Austin's eyes when he stared up at me from between my thighs. Each lap of the wave reminded me of how it played as background music to our groans of pleasure. The band tightened as my body swelled against it with burning memories.

I'd had lots of sex before, with all kinds of partners and an entire sex book worth of locations and positions. But *never* had I experienced the intensity of last night. *Never* had anyone ever looked at me like they could see inside my soul. *Never* had anyone made me bend to their will. *Never* had anyone made me like being under their control. *Never* had anyone kissed me so intensely, like they'd waited their whole life for just a taste.

How had I never experienced any of it before?

Was it me? Was it Austin?

Or was it us? Was it something we created—something *only* we could create?

I clutched my coffee, studying the green grass and white décor like maybe I'd find answers for what it all meant.

Unfortunately, none came.

Over the next hour, more and more people filtered downstairs. Thankfully, no one noticed me outside. I enjoyed sitting back and watching instead of everyone always watching me. I loved the brand I'd created through social media, but sometimes I just wanted…to be.

A flash of blonde hair caught my attention, and I found Aubrey laughing with a group of friends that must have stayed here after the party. Unbidden, I wondered if Austin fucked her the way he had me. A sharp knife pierced my chest, almost stealing my breath, and I didn't bother to call it anything other than what it was: jealousy.

The feeling rarely plagued me. I never gave it the time of day, but this pain stole my breath and dug in before I could stop it.

*No.*

With more strength than I imagined I'd need, I shoved the pain aside, only managing to ease it rather than remove it completely. In the end, it only made room for more questions, but one kept hammering like a woodpecker.

Why was I jealous?

I almost wanted to focus on the jealousy rather than even consider where it came from.

Instead, I shoved both aside and watched the crowd again. I watched them grab their coffees and pastries, stocking up on carbs and social gossip before heading back to their normal lives.

I almost laughed out loud when I thought of Austin and me leaving to head back to normal. Because what the hell was normal? Did we sleep together again? Did we go back to friends? Pretend it didn't happen? I'd never lacked so many answers in my life, and rather than too many options creating chaos around me, I felt like I stood in a vast desert with nothing in sight, completely unaware of which direction to go in.

But then he appeared down the stairs, and instead of nothing, two forces slammed into me out of nowhere—both saying the same thing.

*Run.*

To him.

Away from him.

My head struggled, jerking back and forth between the two urges. My heart jolted into fight or flight mode, ready for either option. My lungs squeezed in around the rampant muscle while my stomach dropped straight down to my core as flash after flash of the night before joined the party.

*"Swallow every last drop."*

*"Spread your legs."*

*"Watch."*

*"Such a good girl."*

I stood on shaky legs, not knowing which way they would carry me.

When they ended up carrying me straight to him, I should have been concerned. I should have fought it. Instead, I couldn't look away from his tall frame as he stood in the middle of the room, looking side-to-side—looking for me.

I made it within five feet when his eyes finally landed on me. While his shoulders dropped like he'd been holding his breath, his deep green eyes still held their own load of tension —like he was just as unsure about what happened next as me.

My mind may not have a clue what was next, but my body sure did. I walked right up to him, ignoring the man who had been trying to talk to him since Austin came down, and wrapped my arms around his neck, laying a playful nip and gentle kiss to his mouth.

"Good morning," I muttered.

Who the hell was I?

It didn't matter. My brain could take a vacation any time because his beautiful, radiant smile was worth it.

"Did you two love birds enjoy last night?" The old man's voice barely permeated our bubble.

"Very much," Austin answered, not looking away from me.

"Young love," the old man muttered and laughed. "I'll leave you two alone. Got to grab breakfast before it's all gone."

"Yeah, we'll be right in," I said absently.

My heart beat so hard I was sure he'd be able to hear it in the silence between us.

One.

Two.

"Listen, Rae—"

"Did you see Raelynn Vos and her husband last night?" A high-pitched voice carried from around the corner.

"Who?" another one asked.

"Kenneth Vos's daughter. Bless him," she cooed. "He's running for Senate, and he has her gallivanting around social media making a fool of herself."

I peeked over my shoulder and took the smallest step back to glimpse who was talking. A tall plant blocked most of my view, but I was able to see it was the same girls that Aubrey had been with earlier, but she wasn't there anymore. They all looked the same, perfectly put together with fake, bitchy smiles.

"Oh, yes. God, her husband is so hot. I'd give at least half my trust fund to fuck him."

I snapped my attention back to Austin to find a thundercloud brewing over his features. When he cringed at the comment, I couldn't help but breathe a small laugh.

"He's in marketing for some elite company. Poor man will probably end up cheating intellectually because he's married to such an airhead."

"Don't worry, he'll come home to bang her. She's got more experience than all the women put together at the party last night."

A gaggle of laughter spilled around the corner and sank into my chest. Warmth bloomed into something fragile—not like a delicate flower, more like a bomb. Women spewed vile words all the time, and they never bothered me. I knew my worth, and their opinions didn't change that—but maybe they could change Austin's.

I couldn't help but think of his angry words in Vegas. He apologized, and I was sure he didn't mean them, but maybe they came from somewhere, and these girls' words only reminded him of it.

Heat spread into my cheeks—through my veins until it almost took on a life of its own.

"This is bullshit," Austin growled.

The deep rumble of his voice forced my attention to him. The thundercloud grew to apocalyptic size, and the sight of it was enough to cut off the spread of my own anger. He took two steps around me before I snagged his arm.

He looked to my hand and back to me, ready to go to war...for me. It was enough. I didn't need him to defend me—just knowing he would was enough to make their words disappear.

"Don't worry about it. They're just bitches with nothing better to talk about."

"But what they said was wrong."

"Who cares. It doesn't change anything about me, and I sure as hell don't need their approval for anything. I'm fucking awesome."

He studied me for a moment before the tension fled his body and the skies parted over his soft laugh. He shook his head and hooked his arm around my shoulders like he had a million times before.

And just like before, I tucked into his side and wrapped my arms around his broad back. Except this time was different. It wasn't like the times before at all. This time, he pressed a gentle kiss to the crown of my head. This time, our hands held tighter, and they didn't remain still without any thought. No, they roamed every ridge of his back as he stroked mine, exploring every dip and curve, remembering what it felt like when there wasn't anything between us.

I pressed my cheek into his chest, closed my eyes, and inhaled his woodsy scent. It was the same cologne I bought him after our first Christmas together, but now it sank into my veins and reminded me of how it smelled mixed with sweat and sex.

I sat on the edge of begging him to fuck breakfast and take me back upstairs when a group walked by and greeted us on their way to the kitchen. Pulling back, I attempted to push the thought from my head and failed because when I met his gaze, the same want and need burned behind his green eyes.

Another group walked through.

More greetings.

With a laugh, I shook my head. "We better get something to eat before it's all gone."

"Yeah," he agreed, though it looked painful for him to do so. We made it to the entrance of the kitchen when he added, "Someone wore me the fuck out."

My smile came too quick for me to hide it, no matter how much I tried. With a mock gasp, I pressed a hand to my chest and gave my best shocked stare. "I would never."

"Mmmhmm," he hummed. "The least you could do is feed me."

"If you say so," I joked back.

Despite everyone's warning, the table still overflowed with platters of every fruit and pastry available. When I saw a pastry labeled with dragon fruit jam, I grabbed two for Austin. I'd mocked him for liking something that lacked so much flavor, but he'd merely told me I brought enough flavor to his life to make up for it.

We moved down the line, and he grabbed a banana—my favorite fruit.

I added a cup of blueberry yogurt next to the pastries because I knew he loved blueberries.

He added a whole wheat biscuit next to the banana even though he hated whole wheat.

We continued down the line adding the other person's favorites. When we got to the end, we swapped plates—continuing the tradition we started years ago at the college cafeteria.

They'd had buffet-style eating, and we'd gone to different ends. I would find something I knew he liked and didn't want him to miss out on, so I'd add it to my plate only to end up with it full of his favorites. When we'd met back at the table, he'd done the same. So, we swapped plates as if it was completely normal. Nova and Vera had looked at us like we were insane, but we laughed and didn't think anything of it. We just clicked—figuring the other person out with ease.

I hadn't considered our connection abnormal, but after last night, I overthought everything. I felt everything differently, so when I looked down at my plate and saw a cinnamon roll I wouldn't usually add, I couldn't help but smile.

We grabbed a seat at one of the round tables, mingling and talking with other guests between bites—staying on the edge of conversations. It went perfectly until the spotlight shifted to us.

"You know, Raelynn, when I heard of your Vegas wedding, I assumed it was a publicity stunt. Especially to such an outstanding man," one of the men who'd made dumbass comments the first night joked, giving a commiserating look to Austin. "So, just between us men, did she trap you for publicity? You're an accomplished man for such a young age. It boosts her—" his eyes flicked to me, or more importantly, my chest, and back to Austin before finishing, "—personal reputation."

Having someone talk dumb shit with a bunch of girls was fine, but to have a man say bullshit right to my face like I was too dumb to even notice the blatant insult pissed me off.

*Rein it in, Rae. Rein it in.*

I took deep breaths, reminding myself of my father's campaign and the important sponsors watching around us.

The man laughed at his own joke until others slowly joined in. What I wouldn't give to shove that chocolate stuffed crescent roll down his wrinkly, old throat.

I was midway through finding a socially acceptable response when Austin's deep voice cut through the laughter.

"No," he stated coldly. He waited for everyone to stop, the twitching muscle in his sharp jaw the only hint he may not be as calm as he appeared. When the asshole's eyes finally met Austin's, he continued. "She's my *wife* because I couldn't have imagined her as anything else since I first laid eyes on her. I'm lucky to have her. Especially since she kicked my ass in school, graduating top of our marketing class. She's actually highly sought after by various companies who appreciate the wealth of knowledge and experience she has in such a fast-paced and always-changing digital market. Unfortunately for them, she's too busy assisting her father's campaign, filling in at their family company, and helping to build their charity to take on anything else." He faced me, and I was too shocked by his speech to question how it looked when he cradled my jaw and stroked his thumb along my cheekbone. As if I was something precious. "I'm the lucky one and grateful that she makes time for me."

Silence fell, but I was too busy basking in the warmth of his fingers to care. I leaned into his touch, placing a barely-there kiss of thanks against his palm.

"I had no idea." The man tried to backtrack uncomfortably.

I faced him, holding his stare, enjoying the way he floundered. Too often, these gatherings were filled with generations that refused to acknowledge we weren't in the good 'ole boy days where women were just trophy wives to have dinner ready when they got home. We had minds and the skills to deserve our own trophy, but also confident enough to accept ourselves as our own trophy. It wasn't until someone else spoke up that I finally gave the asshole a reprieve and looked away.

"My marketing has gone a little stagnant. We're halfway through the year and not making the same profit increases as before. Do you have any suggestions on who or what I should look in to?"

I froze for one second—a second I wanted to commit to memory forever. I'd been the life of the party, the silly one, the one that allowed you to assume I only cared about social media and my appearance. I was so much more and didn't usually care if people saw it or not because I knew it was there. But maybe after the last year with Bodie, maybe because Austin was by my side, and maybe after last night, I wanted to be seen as something more. I didn't know, but having the men around the table, laughing seconds ago, now lean in as if I was about to spill the most scandalous secret had me sitting a little taller.

"It depends," I answered, barely dipping my toe into this new role amongst the men.

"On what?" he pushed.

"Where you're at with your marketing now and how flexible you're willing to be to adapt to an unconventional approach. It's not just about your ad design anymore. You need more than a picture that lures people in. You need to explore every option of advertising, from billboards to finding influencers to mention you in a TikTok. You need to get to know your customer."

"We know our clients," someone objected.

"I'm sure your general market, but with the technology available, you can get to know them better—their purchase trends, their search trends—and apply that to your marketing in a more detailed way. Also, make your marketing more social. With the availability of connecting, people want to feel like they're the only one you're marketing to."

"That's ridiculous," he scoffed. "We can't market to each individual."

"Of course not," I agreed. "But that is what Artificial Intelligence optimization, predictive analytics, and quantum computing are for."

"Quantum what? Do you know what she's talking about?" he asked Austin.

I looked for his reaction to find him leaned back in his chair with a big-ass smile. "It's all you, babe," he said with a shrug before shoving half a donut in his face.

Everyone at the table waited for me to speak. I wasn't one to ever let down a rapt audience, so without any more interruptions or insults, I set about revealing just how wrong they all were about me being nothing but a dumb girl.

After over an hour of questions, I was finally able to pry myself free without any promises of being available for the future. It served them right for doubting me in the first place. I may be wicked smart under all this style, but I still enjoyed being a petty bitch when I could—especially to a bunch of men who needed another man to help them pull their heads out of their asses.

---

I WAS BEAT, on the verge of sleep on the car ride home. Austin drove with music playing in the background, and I looked out the window, replaying his words.

*She's my wife because I couldn't have imagined her as anything else since I first laid eyes on her.*

*I'm lucky to have her.*

*Grateful that she makes time for me.*

"Did you mean everything you said to them?"

"Of course," he answered without missing a beat.

When I didn't follow up with anything else, he glanced over and winced, reading the question I wasn't asking written on my face.

*Then why did you say everything you did in Vegas?*

As much as I wanted to blindly accept his compliments, his insults in Vegas left a mark I couldn't ignore.

His hands flexed around the wheel, and he took a deep breath. "Listen, Rae, I said a lot of shit when I was mad—a bunch of bullshit. But what I told them about you was one hundred percent the truth."

"Thank you," I said softly.

His knuckles remained white, and I knew he had so much more going on in his head, so I waited him out.

"I—I had a temper growing up."

My heart dropped to my stomach. Of all the things I wanted to hear, that was the last. *A temper?* Before my mind could spiral into a yawning hole around my chest, he continued.

"Not that I started the fights. Other than that one time the school bully was picking on a girl for her pigtails. Or that one time in high school I caught a guy trying to fool around with a drunk girl. Or that time in college when…" He laughed nervously glancing my way. "I'm not helping myself." One of his hands released its death grip and dragged through his hair.

I almost laughed with him because while he thought he was incriminating himself, he only confirmed that I had been right about him all along—that my gut instinct about Austin Caldwell hadn't been wrong like it had with Bodie. Relief buoyed my heart back where it belonged, and for the first time since that morning in Vegas, I could breathe easy.

"Either way," he continued, "I had a temper with my words. I'd use someone's biggest issue with themselves and twist it into a weapon to defend myself. The problem is that I'd lose control, and I'd go too far. I hated it—hated myself every time I did it. So, I did anger management and studied ways to control it. I didn't want to be that kind of person. And I know it's a shit-poor excuse, but that morning in Vegas, I was shocked, and triggers I hadn't even thought to look for were flipped, and I reacted. It was shitty and not something you ever, ever deserved."

His Adam's apple bobbed as he kept stealing the occasional look to gauge my reaction. If he hadn't been driving, I would have hugged him. Instead, I offered him my own apology. He hadn't been the only one wrong that morning, and I was the one that pushed him too far.

"I'm sorry, too. I shouldn't have said all the shitty things that made you so mad."

His head snapped, doing a double-take with pinched brows. "It's not your fault," he declared, his voice firm.

"You're not responsible for my actions. I am. No matter what you do, I am accountable for how I act, and I acted like a dick."

Fire burned a path up my throat to the backs of my eyes. When was the last time I hadn't been blamed? It wasn't until just then that I realized that somewhere in the past year, Bodie molded me into a person who apologized for making someone mad.

How many nights had my mother told me that I am not responsible for other people's actions, no matter what they say? I *knew* that. *I knew it.* But Bodie had whittled away at that confidence in the most subtle way, and I hadn't even noticed until now—until Austin reminded me of how it was supposed to be. Until he reminded me of who he really was.

"Raelynn," he said when I still hadn't responded. "How we ended up there was both of us, but that never gives me the right to lose my temper. It never gives me the right to hurt you. I *never* want to hurt you."

"I know." And I did. I knew Austin. I knew him like the back of my hand, and regaining the confidence in my gut meant more than his apology. "Thank you, Austin."

He gave me a soft smile before turning his attention back to the road.

I studied his strong profile and considered bringing up what was next for us. Now would be a perfect time, stuck in a car. But no other conversation mattered right then. A weight I hadn't realized was so heavy lifted. I wanted to bask in the relief, not turn right around and face another one.

Especially one that could snatch it all away and end horribly—one that could end everything.

## Chapter Fifteen

### AUSTIN

**Rae:** Thanks for this weekend.

I LAUGHED at the selfie she must have taken when I didn't notice. Her brown eyes were wide and obviously laughing as she caught me mid-headbang in the background. When I held the picture down, it went live to her face, scrunching into a laugh. She sent it to embarrass me, but I couldn't stop rewatching her face break out into the most beautiful smile.

I'd dropped her off at her apartment yesterday after our karaoke drive home. She'd invited me in, and it had physically hurt to say no, but I did. I *had* to.

Rae always talked about how she never wanted to be smothered, and after the perfection of the weekend, the last thing I wanted to do was push my luck. I needed to show her that she could still have her life and be her own person while also being my wife. I loved her. I loved her as the beautiful woman she was, and I didn't want to change that.

I wanted her to be the wild and free girl I met in college. I just wanted her to be wild and free with me by her side.

So, I said no and went home to suffer through my blue-balls the rest of the night. Even jacking off in the shower to images permanently imprinted in my mind hadn't helped.

**Me:** It was fun.

Instead of telling her how I'd happily repeat the weekend forever, I kept it simple and added a photo of my own—one I snuck when she had passed out with her mouth open and possibly drooling if you zoomed in close enough.

**Me:** Also, I like this one better. Totally Instagram-worthy.
**Rae:** OMG! Where did you get that?
**Me:** I snuck it.
**Rae:** That is horrible.
**Me:** Nah. I like it.

I almost joked about how it reminded me of her mouth being wide around other things, but again, decided to keep it simple. Especially over text. Somehow, we managed to avoid the conversation on our drive home, and now we lingered in ill-fitted limbo.

**Rae:** Fuck it. I'm posting it. We can have the whole Ryan Reynolds and Blake Lively thing where we post bad photos of each other.
**Me:** Good luck getting one of me. I don't take bad photos.
**Rae:** My eyes actually rolled all the way back.

Besides, not talking about it came easy when our bantering friendship still remained the same. Now I just knew what she tasted like—what she felt like. Days later, I still couldn't get the taste of her cum out of my mouth—and I hoped it never left.

"What has you smiling like that?" King asked the next day.

I looked up from the screenshot Rae just sent of a comment on her Instagram post about us being a fun couple.

"I'm just happy," I answered easily.

"I take it the weekend went well."

"Yup."

"And? Spill, bro," King demanded.

He'd messaged me the night we got back, but I told him we'd talk over lunch instead.

"What are you? Some kind of gossipmonger? Do you need me to spill the tea?"

The waiter delivered our food just then, and King stared me down the entire time, apparently not appreciating my Valley girl voice.

"Ha! No," he said as soon as we were alone. "I just need to know if things are blowing up in your face yet."

"Yeah, right."

"Okay. So, what's happening then?"

I bought myself some time with a bite of my burger, earning me another knowing stare from King. For a moment, I considered not telling him—keeping these moments to myself, but honestly, other than Rae, all I had was King. I wasn't close with my brother, and I was the kind of guy that had quality over quantity with my friendships.

And this whole experience left me feeling like I was guessing the right move at every turn. I needed someone to hear me out. I sure as shit knew Rae had probably already gone on and on to the girls. So, as soon as I swallowed, I spilled.

"We slept together."

"It's about fucking time." He slapped the table before throwing his hands up, drawing more than a few stares.

"Dude," I reprimanded.

He didn't care. He patted his chest and smiled like a dad

proud of his son losing his V-card or some shit. "Well, was she everything you imagined?" he asked.

"So much fucking more. She's…" I struggled to find the words to describe our night.

"Oh, fuck."

"What?"

The smile vanished from King's face. "You're so fucked."

"So, you've told me before," I deadpanned.

"No, that was just me bullshitting about being pussy-whipped. Now, you're truly and genuinely fucked."

"I don't understand."

He took his time studying me, shaking his head like I'd told him I had two weeks to live unless I could produce a billion dollars, and he knew I was a goner.

"What the fuck, man?" I pushed again.

"She's going to break you."

"What? No."

"C'mon, Austin. Have you guys even agreed to be together for real? Did you guys end up planning some future this weekend? Is she as happy as you, or is she being typical Rae and looking for an exit?"

"I…I don't know what we are right now."

His face screwed up. "How do you not know?"

I looked down at the scarred wood of the table, bracing to receive more shit than ever and searching for my own exit, knowing damn well there wasn't one. "We haven't really talked about it," I muttered.

"I'm sorry, what?"

I rolled my eyes, knowing he heard me.

"Jesus Christ." He fell back in his seat. "Seriously?"

"Listen, it just didn't come up."

His jaw dropped as he continued to stare.

"I know. Okay? I know," I defended. I should have just kept it to myself. Now, I had to sit there under his incredulous reaction and face all the plot holes around me. "I just…I don't know what she thinks, and I…I don't want it to be a one-off."

"Austin, Rae doesn't do relationships."

His softened tone had my hackles rising. It was like he was already counting me out and preparing for my downfall without even hearing the details.

"She doesn't like to be chained down," I corrected. "I can show her a life without boundaries. I can show her how good a marriage can be without her feeling trapped."

"Bro, what are you doing?" he asked softly.

"I'm trying."

"To get your heart ripped out?"

"No, of course not." I took a deep breath and rubbed a hand over my forehead where the beginning of a headache pulsed. "I know it sounds crazy right now, but this weekend was crazy. Things changed. I saw a side of her I don't think she even knew existed."

"What does that even mean?"

"She was jealous. She saw Aubrey and—"

"Your ex-fiancée was there?" King shook his head like he was trying to rattle all the pieces into place. "What the fuck?"

I huffed a laugh. "Yeah. Like I said, crazy."

"Okay, start from the beginning."

By the time I reached our apologies in the car on the way home, King had switched from water to beer, and his eyebrows were about to become one with his hairline.

"That's a whole fucking lot," he surmised, draining his glass.

"I know," I laughed. "It's just not as simple as before. I let a part of myself out that I didn't usually share with her, and she let me in. Something happened this weekend. Something changed, and if ever there was a chance to make it work, this is it."

"And if it doesn't?"

Only four words. A simple enough question. One I didn't

want to think about yet. "Then I'll deal with it if it comes to that."

"Are you willing to bet your friendship on it?"

"I already have," I said truthfully. "I can't—I can't go back to being just friends. I didn't think I could even before we got to the house. I've been wearing thin for a while now—seeing her with Bodie. Vegas just pushed me too hard."

"Yeah, a drunken marriage will do that," he deadpanned.

I flipped him off just as my phone buzzed. My screen lit up with her name, and the dread from the conversation ebbed away.

**Rae:** Wanna come over? Bachelor is on.

King saw the message and shook his head. "Is that some booty call?"

"No. Maybe? I mean, I don't know."

"Jesus," he groaned, rolling his eyes.

"It doesn't matter what tonight is. I need this to be different. I need to show her that we have something different. I'm not going to be some guy that just fucks her and lets her walk away."

"So, you're going to go but not sleep with her?"

I tried to imagine Rae in front of me and not ravaging her —not going in for another taste—and hated it. But I needed to show her all sides of us, of what we could be, so I ground my teeth and met King's eyes with a decisive nod.

"Good fucking luck, bro," he laughed.

"It'll be fine. I've gone years without sleeping with her."

He hummed doubtfully before turning serious. "Eventually, you're going to have to talk about what comes next."

"I know."

"If you go, you'll probably end up talking tonight."

I swallowed the ball of nerves trying to choke me. "Yeah. I know."

"And if it doesn't go well?"

Taking a deep breath, I remembered the other half of our deal. "No matter what, she still owes me a trip to my family, and if it all goes to shit, then I'll make the best of what I have left. I'm not going down without a fight."

King huffed a laugh, knowing when to stop pushing. He knew what a stubborn fucker I could be. So, he shook his head and smiled. "Good fucking luck, dude."

I was gonna need it.

**Me:** I'll see you then.

## Chapter Sixteen

### RAELYNN

"Are you... are you dressed up?" Nova asked, moving closer like she'd be able to study me through the computer screen.

"I'm always dressed up," I defended with nonchalance.

Vera gave me a dubious stare from her square of the screen. "Not for an episode of *The Bachelor*, you're not."

"It's different. I always put in at least a little extra effort when I have someone coming over."

Vera laughed, earning a glare.

"Not for Austin," Nova declared.

"Since when?" I scoffed.

"Since never," Nova said. "I've legit seen you look like a hobo almost every time he comes over."

I rolled my eyes, trying to remember what I usually wore. The problem was, usually, I hadn't just slept with my best friend and now overthought how I looked around him. Usually, it was just another Monday night that he came over and vegged out just like he was one of the girls. After the weekend, I could one-hundred-percent vouch that Austin was *not* one of the girls.

But I still wasn't ready to admit that maybe—*just maybe*—I put in a little, tiniest bit of extra effort getting ready. Maybe.

Not that they would let me get away with it.

"One day, your sweatpants had a hole in them," Vera accused.

"They're my favorite and lucky."

"They had a hole over your ass cheek. And not a little one," she kept going.

"God, I thought Austin was going to have an aneurism when you bent over," Nova said. Both women broke into laughter while I scrambled through my brain for a memory of Austin checking me out.

"What?" I asked, coming up empty. Sure, maybe he looked at me but nothing compared to the way he did this past weekend. I would've remembered that. Hell, I was sure I'd remember the feel of his eyes burning me alive on my death bed.

"Oh, yeah," Nova mused. "That's when you were in denial that Austin is attracted to you."

My face screwed up in denial, but no actual words passed through my mouth, opening and closing like a fish out of water. They'd harped on the same thing for years, but I always brushed it off. The man had straight-up turned down a chance to sleep with me. How the hell could he have wanted me when he could have had me?

Despite not being as easy to deny anymore when he had clearly been more than attracted this weekend, I didn't want to admit it because I didn't know what it meant. So, scoffing, eye-rolling, and head shaking, it was.

"Oh, are we still denying?" Vera asked.

"I thought you said she admitted to caring about him," Nova said.

"She did," Vera defended. "Which is why I figured she was wearing the crop top."

"And makeup," Nova added.

They went back and forth like they were the only two on the call. "Hey bitches, I'm right freaking here."

"Yeah," Vera agreed. "So, explain what's going on. What changed to put you all back in your denial? What happened?"

"I'm not…" My weak denial faded, leaving me in silence. They continued to stare with expectant looks until I couldn't stand it anymore. "What?" I snapped.

"We're waiting for the rest of it," Vera said with a wave of her hand to continue.

"Rest of what?"

*Deny. Deny. Deny.*

*Nothing to see here.*

*Nothing to admit.*

*Nope.*

*Look away.*

They didn't look away. In fact, Nova actually began humming the Jeopardy song, and Vera leaned back in her chair like she had all day.

Assholes.

The best assholes in the world and ones I knew I shouldn't have even bothered hiding from. I knew that facing them meant facing me and everything inside I tried to keep hidden under a blanket, shoved in a corner, duct-taped, and chained into a tight ball, so I didn't have to look at it.

I didn't *want* to look at it.

But the more they stared, the more it rattled until the jangling took over every inch of my body, filling up more and more, crawling its way up my throat until it exploded.

"FINE!" I shouted. "Oh, my god! We slept together, and it was the best sex I've ever had, okay?" Their eyes widened comically large at my outburst, but I wasn't done. Now that I'd started, it was all coming out. "And oh, my fucking god. He's just as big as I imagined. And his mouth. Holy fuck. It says the filthiest things like he's talking directly to my pussy before he does even dirtier things to it."

"Yes," someone shouted off-screen. "Fuck yeah! Fucking told you."

"Is that Parker?" I asked. "What the hell is going on over there?"

"Dammit," Nova hissed. Next thing I knew, she had her wallet in hand, digging out a bill.

"I fucking told you they'd fuck," Parker said, appearing to snatch the hundred from Nova before looking at the screen. "You can tell Nico he can pay me next time we're together."

"Are you fucking kidding me?" I shrieked. "Another bet?"

Vera rolled her eyes and released an exaggerated sigh. "You used to take bets on everything."

"Like when?"

"How about how many shots of tequila it would take for Nova to dance on a bar?"

"Not many," I muttered before shaking my head to focus. "But this is different."

"Oh, please," Vera exclaimed. "It isn't, and you know it. You're just pouty because all of a sudden, you're the one with boy woes."

I sputtered like I had at every other proclamation in this conversation. "I'm Raelynn fucking Vos. I don't do boy woes."

"Yet, here you are," Vera said with a little too much gloating.

"Speaking of, what's next?" Nova asked. "Are you together now?"

I snorted just to switch up my sounds of denial. "No."

"Ummm… okay," she said slowly. "So, what are you going to do now?"

This time I couldn't produce a single sound—not a scoff or a snort or an eek of anything because wasn't that the million-dollar question. I swallowed as their faces shifted from expectant to knowing.

"We haven't talked about it," I admitted with a wince.

My two best friends gasped in unison, slapping their hands to their chests. "I'm shocked," Nova proclaimed.

"Me, too," Vera added with a bland tone. "I never would have guessed."

"You're not fucking funny," I deadpanned.

"We're hilarious," Nova said.

"And we know you," Vera explained. "Of course, you'd avoid all conversation with Austin about how you had sex and needed to decide what the next step was."

"So why did you ask?"

"We didn't," Vera said. "We asked what *you* are going to do now."

"What do *you* want to happen next?" Nova clarified. "Are you going to give the marriage thing a try?"

"No. No," I objected immediately. "I don't want to be married. I can't be."

"I mean, you can," Nova mused.

"I said I would never get married. It's not who I am."

"People change," she said softly.

"Not with this!" I snapped. "I just—I can't. And I don't know what's next, and I don't know how to talk about it, and I don't want to because I don't know what that looks like, so I'm avoiding it like a little bitch. Okay? I'm a big fat scaredy-cat."

"Raelynn…" Vera said softly, but I couldn't handle that right now. I didn't want to handle any of it.

"All I do know is that I just had the best sex of my life with my best friend and that I have to go visit his grandparents next weekend, so why not just enjoy the time we have to stay married. What's the point of talking about it now and possibly creating a shit show? At least more than it already is. Especially if we don't have to."

"Okay," Vera said, throwing me off. I expected at least another five minutes of battle.

"Okay?"

## Blame it on the Vodka

"Yeah, okay. If that's where you're at, then that's where you're at," Nova said.

"We'll allow you to bury your head in the sand—for now," Vera explained. "But because we're your friends, we also get to tell you that you're only pushing off what you'll have to face at some point, and the more you push it off, the worse it will get."

"It's like turning up the heat, but only holding the lid on tighter—eventually it's going to release," Nova added.

"Maybe it won't," I suggested hopefully. "Maybe we'll get it out of our systems, and it will be fine."

Their forced smiles did *not* fill me with hope. They may allow me to bury my head, but they weren't going to pretend to believe the lies I told myself.

"Listen," I sighed. "You can hound me later. Austin's going to be here any minute, and I just can't find a better answer than that right now."

Vera held up her hands in surrender. "We'll set a formal date for more hounding."

"For now, we'll be in the group text to chat about if Layla finally goes home tonight," Nova said, directing the conversation back to safer topics like Monday night television.

I latched on to the branch to pull myself free of the deep conversation. "God, I hope so. She may be the worst one in all the seasons ever."

"Homegirl is cra-ay-zee," Vera agreed, making us laugh. When we sobered, she gave me a soft smile. "You really do look stunning tonight."

"I know," I said, preening.

Vera rolled her eyes but laughed. "Tell Austin we said hi."

"Also, one more thing," Nova said before we hung up. She leaned in close to the screen and muttered, "How big are we talking?"

"NOVA!" Parker shouted from the background.

She whipped her head to the side. "I'm just curious. Damn. You know I only want you."

"Whew," Vera catcalled. "Parker has turned you into a slut. You would have blushed at the first mention of a penis."

"My baby girl is growing up," I said, wiping a fake tear away.

"She doesn't need to know," Parker declared.

"Of course not, Rock star," Nova soothed before turning back to the camera just to mouth *how big?*

I held my hands apart, studied them, and then moved them even further, mouthing *so big.*

Both women gave me a thumbs up before ending the call.

Realizing Austin would be there any minute, I ran to the bathroom to apply one more coat of lipstick. I laughed as I fluffed my hair. The girls were right—as they usually were. Maybe I was going over the top with Austin coming over. Maybe I did pick out the crop top that laced over my cleavage because I wanted his eyes to eat me up again.

So what? It wasn't like it meant I wanted to stay married or anything.

I met the deep brown eyes in the mirror—so familiar, but also so new, alight with an excited glow I hadn't seen before. I did my best to face life head-on, whether it be easy or hard, but lately, I did exactly as they accused me of—burying my head in the sand. Because the truth was, I knew the outcome of the game Austin and I were playing would be rough. I just didn't know what the outcome looked like exactly.

What I did know was that I couldn't be married. I just *couldn't.*

I knew I didn't want to lose Austin as my friend either.

I knew we had to pretend to be married for at least another week.

I knew I wanted to take that week to explore his body like my own personal playground.

I knew I needed to have him inside me again.

I knew I needed to have him own my body with the intensity I'd only ever found with him.

I knew that even thinking about it filled me with an unknown warmth I'd never felt before.

And I also knew that I didn't want to know what that warmth was.

So, before I found something that I couldn't turn back from, I blinked, looking away.

Just in time for a knock at the door.

My heart skipped over itself in as much of a rush to get to him as my feet. Taking one last deep breath, I did my best to look aloof and opened the door. "Hey, stranger."

"Special delivery."

His jovial greeting faded slowly, his eyes dropping to the strip of cleavage bared by the laces holding the two sides of my shirt together. My nipples pebbled under his gaze, and I bit my lip, trying to hold back the smile, knowing he could see them.

The girls might have been right about a lot, but they weren't right about me not noticing how Austin looked at me. There was no way in hell I could have missed the physical caress of his eyes on me. It stroked my skin like a match, setting fire wherever it touched.

I just needed to get him inside so he could do something about it.

"You coming in, or did you want to watch from the hall?"

He blinked, shaking his head. "Sorry. Where do you want me to put this?"

"Where you always do," I laughed.

Austin and I had done about a million pizza nights. There was no reason, other than maybe all the blood rushing south, for him to not know where to put things.

"Yeah, yeah." He brushed past me and headed to the kitchen.

I hadn't been sure what to expect tonight, but I'd braced

for it all. Would we kiss? Not that we had since the morning I walked up to him, but a girl could dream. Would we act normal? Did we know what normal was? Neither option seemed more possible than the other. Especially since he hadn't given me any hints to what was on his mind since that night.

Hell, I'd even asked him to come up when he dropped me off, only for him to turn me down. Part of me wondered if I was the only one hoping for more, even if I wouldn't say it. I shoved the possibility aside, ignoring the way it sank to the pit of my stomach.

Instead, I opted for business as usual. Just like any other time we hung out. Sure. Super easy.

"So, how was work?" I asked, following behind, already failing my plan when I stared at his ass.

He set the pizza down and grabbed a wine glass from the top shelf. "Good. Just wrapping up a project."

I grabbed the beer mug I kept in the freezer for him and a beer from the fridge. "The focus app?"

He pulled out the bottle opener and opened the bottle of wine and beer. "Yeah. It's pretty cool. They offer up monetary rewards for accomplishing tasks."

I poured the beer and wine while he got the plates. "Oh, that is fun. What kind of design did they go with?"

He put a slice of meat lovers and a slice of veggie on my plate and piled an obscene amount of meat lovers slices on his own. "A really unique design. I got to have some artistic freedom with it."

I added one more slice to his pile because I knew he would want more eventually. He always did. "That's amazing. I bet they loved it. Do you have a picture?"

He took the napkins and plates over to the couch, and I grabbed the glasses. "Yeah. Let me pull it up."

He tugged his phone free before plopping back. I curled up in the corner and stretched my legs out just enough to tuck my feet under his warm thigh.

My jaw dropped when he passed me his phone. "Wow, Austin. That's amazing."

A black and white blend of geometric shapes formed a mountain range with the company's name written across the front in white. The real treat was when you looked closer and saw each shape held an image of a usual day-to-day task.

"I thought it represented how the app creates a way for you to focus on the big picture even with everything going on in the background. It just quiets it all down."

"It's perfect." I handed his phone back, giving him a proud smile.

"Thanks."

"You're so cute when you blush."

"Whatever. Let's get this chick show going."

"Oh, please. You love it."

He gave a noncommittal shrug and stuffed a huge bite in his mouth, but I could still see the smile twitching his cheeks.

I spent about half the show watching him, looking for any hint of something more. Then berating myself because more sex probably wasn't the best answer to fixing our situation. Even though it sure as hell felt like the right answer. Then I'd wondered what it could hurt since we'd already slept together. Then I wondered if his head was as much a mess as mine or if he was really into which one of these girls was getting picked for the one-on-one. That thought—along with the other seven-hundred-seventy-two million—made me nauseous.

"Could you imagine being one of these contestants?" he asked, pulling me out of the tornado of thoughts.

I took in the girls mingling and glaring with champagne in their sparkling gowns. "I'd walk in, and they'd take one look at me and know I was the winner."

"Really?" he deadpanned.

"Oh, yeah. I'm just that awesome. But they'd all concede because they'd want to be my friend. Except Layla," I sneered at the leggy brunette with crazy eyes on the screen. "She sucks. No one wants a fake, bitchy friend."

He nodded sagely. "I'd just keep them all—like a harem."

I poked him with my foot, laughing. "Slut."

He laughed. "Nah. I'm just a total giver."

"That you are," I said before thinking of the consequences.

He was mid-drink and coughed, sputtering some of the golden liquid back into the glass.

A spark ignited in my chest. Maybe Austin wasn't as composed as he seemed. Once he got his drink under control, I pushed a little more. "And you sure have *a lot* to give," I said, looking pointedly at his crotch.

"Raelynn…" he said, his cheeks turning ruddy.

"Oh, looky there," I teased. "Are you going back to blushing when I flirt with you?"

He huffed a breath and rubbed at his brow.

"I mean… You already know how much *I* have to give." I arched up just enough to test the strength of the strings holding my shirt closed and lightly dragged a finger through my cleavage. His eyes burned so intensely that I feared my shirt would singe away completely.

His jaw ticked, and his muscles bunched against the black T-shirt pulled tight against his thick arms. I held my breath, bracing for the attack, already feeling his hands and mouth consuming me.

Except…it never came.

## Chapter Seventeen

### RAELYNN

In the next instant, Austin stood and walked away, leaving me there to stare at his retreating back, my jaw on the floor.

What the hell?

I blinked like it would bring him back to sitting in front of me, like it would make his reaction make sense.

I didn't get it.

Shaking my head, I shoved enough of my confusion aside to go after him. The last thing I expected was to find his hands braced on the kitchen counter, his head hanging low between his hunched shoulders.

My heart lurched, jumping toward my friend, who looked in pain. Rarely had I ever seen Austin so distraught, and I didn't understand anything other than wanting to make it better. Slowly, I approached, my hand reaching to gently press against his shoulder. The muscles flexed, but he didn't pull away.

"Austin, are you okay?"

"Do you know how hard it was," he started, his voice guttural, "to not take you as soon as you opened the door? To not pick you up and pin you to the wall. To not rip away that scrap of a shirt and feast on your tits."

His words shot like electrical currents through my body, lighting up my nipples and core even before my brain could process it all. He stole my breath when he lifted his head just enough to level me with his burning gaze. "Goddamn it, Raelynn. I've spent the entire episode imagining pushing my cock deep between the valley of your breasts—gripping each full curve and wrapping it around my cock until I come."

"I—I don't understand." The words escaped between panting breaths. The image he painted clouded my brain, leaving me confused. Why hadn't he done it? Why hadn't he taken me?

He looked down at the counter. "I have no idea what the fuck is going on between us, Rae. I don't know the rules. I don't know what's next, what you want, or what it means."

My needy pants tinged with panic.

*Shit. Shit. Shit. Shit.* How did I answer that?

Doing my best to slow down, I considered my options. Maybe...Maybe I didn't have to have an exact answer. Maybe *not knowing* was the answer itself.

Latching on to that, I closed the gap and ducked under his arms, pinning myself between the counter and his big body, forcing him to meet my gaze. "I don't know either." I studied the curve of his lips, the line of his jaw, and the faint lines around his eyes. With a shaking hand, I touched each feature, connecting myself to him. "What I do know is that I need you inside me again. I need to feel you," I confessed. I couldn't look in his eyes—I couldn't watch him turn me away. So, instead, I stroked my thumb along his plush lips and uttered a word only he could make me say. "Please."

As if taking scissors to a thin cord around his control, he snapped. Standing to his full height, gripping my jaw, he held me in place and kissed me.

But this was no simple kiss. Austin controlled me. Ravaged me. Claimed me.

It should have scared me how rough he was. Alarms *did*

sound at the way his thumb dug between my jaw to force my mouth open, but all I had to do was breathe in his familiar scent and remember who held me. One breath, and I relaxed into his hold, letting myself go enough to realize how much I liked it.

I liked the way he held me.

I liked the ache in my jaw.

I liked it all.

Like savages, we attacked, hungry and desperate for one another. His hands gripped my top and carelessly tugged until the strings gave way enough to bare my breasts. His mouth crested down my neck to bite across my chest to my nipples. All the while, our hands moved frantically to unfasten the other's pants.

I'd just pushed his cock free, ready to stroke him—to fall to my knees and taste him when the world spun.

He jerked me around, his palm pressing against my back until my chest pressed against the cold counter. He held me there and shoved my pants down enough to spread my legs.

"Austin," I whimpered. I didn't know what I was pleading for. I just needed his name on my lips—a reminder that it was him.

"I need more room. Need inside you. Stay," he commanded, dragging his hand down my back to grip my hip. He lifted me to my toes, holding me in place.

The fat head of his cock stroking across my entrance was the only warning I had before he shoved inside. I cried out, pressing my forehead to the counter as my body split in two in the most delicious way.

There was no slow tease—no sweet warm-up—no filthy words to make me wetter.

They weren't needed.

The sounds of him fucking his cock into my soaking cunt blended with my cries and his grunts of pleasure. The sharp smack of my hand on the counter before squeezing into a tight fist matched the sound of his hips snapping against my ass.

He hovered over me, caging me in—but not to trap me. He caged me in so I didn't fly away when he shattered me. I smacked the counter again, crazed and out of control. Animal sounds pouring from us both.

It hurt but so, so, so good.

Somewhere between my guttural cries, I managed pleas for more. His hand snaked into my hair and jerked me back against his chest. Reaching back, I gripped his ass and worked my hips to take more of him. Lips pressed against my neck. Fingers slid between my slit, stroking my clit. Hands palmed my breasts.

All of it a perfect symphony of us.

All of it too much to hold off.

Like a rising fire, it started at my feet and consumed me in a quick rush, sucking the air from my lungs. Not a single inch of my body didn't tremble—didn't snap apart just to come back together anew. Wave after wave of fire burned me, blotting out the vibrations of his own pleasure.

His hips snapped a few more times before finally slowing, both of us floating back to the present. We stayed connected, catching our breath until he slid free—a rush of liquid following.

"Shit," he hissed. "I forgot a condom. Fuck, Rae. I'm sorry."

The sticky fluid dripped between my thighs, and all I wanted to do was drag my fingers through it—rub it in, keep it forever. "I'm on the pill. I'm safe."

"Me, too."

"Oh, you're on the pill, too. That's good to know," I joked.

He nipped at my ear.

"You know what I mean." A sharp smack landed against my ass before his hand shifted. I gasped and jerked when he dug into the particular spot where the bruise Bodie gave me when he left hadn't quite healed.

"Did I hurt you?" he asked, already pulling back.

"A little."

"Shit. Rae… Fuck," he hissed, pulling away enough to inspect my back. "You have a brui—"

Before he could finish that thought and think too much about it, I whipped around in his arms and looked up through my lashes to get lost in the green depths of his eyes. "That's not what I meant. I meant it hurt when you pushed inside so fast and hard."

His mouth parted, the apology written all over his face, but I pressed my fingers to his lips.

"It felt good," I confessed. "It feels so good when you stretch me too wide."

With a growl, he bent his knees and wrapped his hands around my thighs, hoisting me up to wrap around his waist.

"Good. Now let me kiss it better."

## Chapter Eighteen

AUSTIN

I'd meant it when I said I hadn't planned on fucking her again, but I knew it was a losing battle when she opened the door in that scrap of a shirt. I spent the entirety of the show putting up a valiant effort to resist, but when Raelynn set her sights on something, she got it.

Not that it took too much for me to give in.

And now that I've had her, I sure as hell didn't plan to stop until she made me.

Thankfully, I knew her apartment like the back of my hand because I spent the walk to her bedroom sucking and biting every inch of skin from her nipples to her neck. My knees bumped into the edge of her bed, and without warning, I tossed her back, almost falling to my knees at the sight of her full breasts bouncing.

"I could fucking live between your tits," I groaned.

"I could live with you between my thighs," she countered, inching her way back on the bed.

She had no idea how much I wanted to take her up on that offer—how much I wanted those words to actually be true, but I kept it to myself and left them as the playful parry she meant them as.

Instead, my gaze raked over her body, landing between her legs. She rested back on her hands, her shirt falling off her shoulders and her pants lost somewhere in the kitchen. She gently dug her heels into the mattress, bending her knees and spreading her thighs, giving me the most perfect view of her core—wet and creamy from my cum.

"I do not have words for what it does to me to see my cum spilling from your pussy."

She arched her hips, rolling them side to side like a red flag to a bull, and as she assumed, I charged. I shackled an ankle and jerked her back to the edge of the bed, where I fell to my knees and shoved her thighs wide. Not once did she complain about my roughness.

My heart sank to the pits of hell when she admitted I hurt her, but then she'd admitted how much she liked it, and I knew right then and there, Rae was made for me. She was strong and stubborn and fought me, making her submission all the sweeter.

Latching onto her thigh just inside her knee, I tongued and bit my way closer to heaven. I'd almost made it when a hand in my hair stopped me.

"Your cum," she explained.

I peered over her mound, meeting her worried eyes with a devilish glint of my own as I tugged her hand free.

"I know, and mixed with yours will be the best fucking thing I've ever tasted."

Holding her gaze, I circled her opening with my tongue before dragging it up to do the same with her clit. Salt and musk exploded on my tongue, only making me want more. Again and again, I dipped low only to always go back up to tease her where she most wanted me.

Crimson colored her cheeks all the way to the tops of her breasts, which heaved with each desperate pant. Not once did I look away until she finally dropped her head back with a moan. She dug her heels into the mattress, thrusting her pussy against my lips.

Her hips worked faster and faster, her cries growing, and just when she was on the edge of tipping over, I wrapped my arms under her thighs and gripped her hips, halting all movement.

"No," she cried. "Please. More."

"I'm not ready yet."

"Dammit, Austin. I swear to g—"

Her words choked off when I dipped lower than before, slipping between the cheeks of her ass. Her muscles tensed, but she didn't say anything to stop me, so I did it again, pushing further. I pushed her thighs back and wide and circled her tight hole.

She cried out and jerked up as much as she could with a shocked face.

"Do you like that?"

"I—I—" she stumbled, her blush deepening.

"Ohhhh." Realization dawned. "Has *the* Raelynn Vos, conqueror of men, never had anyone play with her here?" I asked before swiping low again.

"N—No."

Like a feral animal, I bared my teeth and growled. I might as well have stood over her and beat my chest. Knowing I found a piece of Rae that no one had claimed felt like finding the rarest gem. It brought out my inner caveman, desperate to throw her over my shoulder and drag her off to claim my prize.

I pressed my fingers into her pussy, twisting and curling to coat them in our cum before dragging them out to play at her tight asshole. She tensed for a moment, but I took my time, circling and pressing in the smallest increments until she was back to thrusting—searching—for more.

"I'm going to fuck you here," I said.

She tensed again, and I groaned at how tight it was around my finger.

"Not today," I assured, causing her to relax again. "I need time to get you ready for me, but it will happen." I added my tongue to the mix, pushing deeper. "There will be a day that you will take my fat cock up your little virgin asshole, and you'll like it." Another lick. "You'll never want me to leave."

Her whimpers urged me on, and I used my other hand to play with her clit as I continued to torture her with my tongue and words.

"Can you do it, Rae? Can you take me?"

"Yes," she hissed.

I added another finger to the first, pushing harder. "It's going to be hard to squeeze in. You're so small here—so tight."

"I can do it."

"It will hurt at first."

"Good. I still want it."

"Me too, baby. I want to know I'm the only man to take you here. I want it to be mine."

"Me too," she moaned.

Fuck. Me. I almost came right then and there when she agreed so readily. "Soon," I promised. "For now, let me eat your cunt and play."

My length throbbed between my thighs, each pulse a reminder of how much I wanted to be inside her again. Desperate to feel her warmth around me, I fell over and worked both hands and my mouth in tandem to bring her to a screaming orgasm in record time.

Before she even came down from her high, I climbed up the bed, shoving her back to where I wanted her. I gripped my cock, lining up with her entrance, when the world spun.

With more strength than I was ready for, Rae flipped me to my back so she could crawl over me. "My turn."

Her dark hair fell around her like a lioness, and I gladly yielded my control—at least some of it.

"Atta girl," I encouraged, gripping her hips and lifting her enough to get my cock at her entrance. "Ride me."

She braced her hands on my chest, her nails digging into my pecs, giving me the perfect view down her body.

"Goddamn," I grunted. "Look at you, taking me even though you're so swollen and so tight."

Her breasts swayed with her nipples pulled tight, and then I watched her pussy slowly work its way down my length with each rock of her hips. It took everything I had to let her take her time.

"You're so big," she whimpered.

"Tell me, Rae. Am I too big for that little pussy?" I challenged.

"No," she gasped. "God, no. You're just right."

"Show me. Show me how good I fit."

"Help me."

I didn't need to be told twice. My hips snapped up at the same time I forced her down.

Her scream slammed into my chest, sinking into my body just like her nails. As if forcing myself inside her was all she needed, she took over.

She rocked back and forth before hoisting herself upright and rolling her hips. Her breasts bounced with each move, and I thought I could die the happiest man—with her wet heat stroking me into oblivion and her naked body above me like a goddess chasing her pleasure.

Fire ignited down my spine to my balls, and I knew I couldn't last much longer. Especially when she reached behind her and began rolling them in her small hand.

"Holy fuck," I grunted.

She smiled like a minx, only adding to the pleasure. Giving as good as I got, I slid my thumb between her folds and rubbed hard across her clit until she lost her rhythm and came. The tight pulses of her cunt pulled me right along with her.

Every cell in my body exploded with a euphoric high I wasn't sure I'd ever recover from. The pleasure stretched on and on until I finally floated back to earth. Just in time for Rae to collapse over me and roll to her side.

I moved to wrap myself around her but stopped at the last minute. "I should wash real quick."

Without opening her eyes, she pointed toward her bedside table. "I have wet wipes in my drawer."

"Always prepared," I joked, doing my best to blot out the sting of why she would need to always be prepared.

"Nah," she said through a yawn. "I don't bring guys here. This is my bed—my sanctuary. I keep the wipes there for when I masturbate."

A lump lodged in my throat at her confession. I never had any issues with Rae's sexuality. Sure, there had been times I'd been jealous, but she was so open about her sex life that it was what it was—it was part of her. I guess I just hadn't expected to find this feeling with her—this unique place carved out just for us, which made it all the more emotional—not that I'd say anything.

"There's a sight I'd love to see," I said playfully instead.

She gave me a lazy smile, curling into my side as soon as I'd settled again. "I'd love to show it to you."

"I'll hold you to it," I promised. Her eyes slid closed again, and her breathing evened out on the edge of sleep. "Do you want to clean up?"

"No. I've never let anyone come inside me, and I kind of like the feel of your cum between my legs."

*Fuck. Me.*

If I thought I was happy before, that was nothing compared to this. Hell, she was so tired, I wasn't even sure it counted or if she'd remember in the morning. But I didn't care. I'd die with those words playing on repeat in my head.

Swallowing past the ever-growing lump in my throat, I pushed her hair off her forehead so I could look down at her lying against my chest.

"I'll happily put more there any time you want."

"Later," she murmured. "For now, we need rest."

"Yes, ma'am."

## Chapter Nineteen

### RAELYNN

"How did I not know you grew up on a cattle farm?"

He laughed from the driver's seat, giving me a brief glance that created flutters in my chest I'd been trying to ignore over the past week.

The last week had been different but also so much the same.

We still messaged and joked and poked fun at each other. He continued to roll his eyes every time I asked him to take a picture for social media. I still pushed him to step out of his comfort zone and do wild things with me.

Except now, we did all those things between the hottest sex of my life. And in those moments, *he* was the one that pushed me to do wild things. I was still waiting for him to follow through on his promise to fuck my ass. Every time we touched, I held my breath, anticipating him letting me know it was time. I was surprised by how much I wanted it as I never had before. But I hadn't ever trusted anyone enough before.

I trusted Austin, and that did crazy things to the intensity behind all our fucking. We were almost desperate, falling on each other every chance we got. Which had me intrigued about how we would be this weekend at his grandparents.

"Yup. And apples."

"Austin the apple-picker."

"And cow-milker."

"No wonder you're so good with breasts," I teased.

His dirty smile created havoc between my legs. It always did, and each time it blew me away that I never knew Austin was so capable of that kind of smile.

Actually, in the last few hours, I'd realized how little I knew about him. How had I missed so much? Despite both of us apologizing for our hurtful words in Vegas that morning, sometimes it still crept back in. Sometimes, it made me doubt.

Maybe there was some truth behind them. He called me selfish, and here I was with my best friend, and I didn't even know he grew up picking apples and milking cows.

"What's your favorite apple," I asked, determined to know everything there was.

"Granny Smith or McIntosh."

"Ohmygaaaaahd," I groaned. "Granny Smith is so good. Especially when it's with—"

"Peanut butter," Austin finished.

"Exactly."

"My grandpa will love you."

"I mean, who wouldn't?" I flipped my hair and batted my lashes.

"So modest," he said, laughing.

"Okay, so your grandma and grandpa ran the farm, but your grandma went to college and was the accountant?"

"Yup. He said she was the brains to keep it all going."

"Most women are," I said with a wink before scrolling my mind for any more facts I should know. "I know all the basics. You were the high school football star, worked on the yearbook staff, and were voted most popular. Wait," I gasped. "Were you prom king?"

"Runner up."

I gasped again with my hand to my chest. "Those fools."

"I know. Assholes."

"So, is there anything else I should know?"

"Rae, you've known me for years. We'll be fine. Don't stress."

It was easy for him to say. He knew everything about me because he was an unselfish friend that listened to me ramble on and on about myself and gave in to my whims of facials and shows I liked.

"Besides, we're here." The crunch of the tires against gravel pulled me out of my self-loathing and doubt.

I wasn't quite sure what to expect. I'd lived most of my life in the city and traveled the world, but the knowledge I had about a farm came from movies at best.

The small house in front of me didn't disappoint. It was a two-story farmhouse, all white, with the cutest front porch and swing. It was worn but well-loved and adorned with the most beautiful pink flowers hanging in pots. What I hadn't seen in movies or expected was the rolling hills behind the house with a few mountains rising up in the distance.

"This is beautiful," I breathed.

"It's home."

Austin parked the car, but neither of us moved. We sat there, taking in the house and all the land beyond it.

"It was my great-great—probably few more greats—grandpa's home. It'd only been a cattle farm for years until my grandma came along and suggested apples."

"Smart woman."

"Yeah, it sure kept them afloat."

"What do you mean?"

He heaved a sigh. "Until recently, I wasn't sure they'd be able to keep it."

"What? Why?"

"My grandpa had heart issues a few years back, and they needed to take out a loan to cover the costs. At the same time, they expanded the loan to cover repairs. They used the house as collateral, which is totally normal, except their loan got sold to someone who wanted to use the land for commercial use and tried to push them out."

"Why didn't you tell me? I could have helped." Again, guilt that I hadn't known—that he'd carried the stress alone—pricked at my conscience. Had I been so self-absorbed that I missed it?

"I guess it just never came up. But it doesn't matter because it's paid in full now."

"Good, but next time, tell me these things."

"What could you have done, Rae?"

"I could have been there for you. I'm your friend."

He faced me for the first time since we parked, his eyes both bright and dark at the same time. I sat taller under the intensity of his gaze.

"You're my wife."

He wasn't wrong, but the words still managed to compress in on my chest. He said them with so much confidence and determination that I almost nodded, wanting them to be true.

But they weren't, I mean, they were, but they also weren't. We were married, but that was different from being a *wife*.

I was about to correct him when the screen door to the porch slammed, pulling my attention to the house. An older couple stood on the porch until Austin stood from the car, and then the woman quickly made her way over to envelope him in a hug.

"Oh, it's so good to see you," she said, pulling his hulking height down into her hug.

"It's good to see you too, Grandma."

Watching the big, powerful Austin—who I'd seen do one too many keg stands—crouch down and smile like a little boy for this woman had my eyes misting over.

As soon as she let him go, she turned to me with a warm smile only grandmas had, that promised cookies and breaking the rules. "You must be Raelynn."

"You can call me Rae," I said, smiling back.

"Well, it's nice to meet you. I'm Ethel, and that anti-social man on the porch is Sylvester."

"I'm not anti-social; I'm just letting you get all your hugs out first."

I looked to the man, standing just as tall as Austin, and offered another smile and wave before sticking my hand out to greet Ethel.

"None of that," she said, shooing my hand away. "We're a hugging family, and since you're part of the family, you get a hug too."

"I won't turn a hug down." I opened my arms and hid my wince about being part of the family behind her back.

She pulled back but kept her hands on my shoulders as she looked me up and down. "I don't know how my Austin landed you, but he's one lucky man to have such a beautiful wife."

"Oh, thank you." I looked down, hiding how forced my smile turned. Taking Austin to the Hamptons had been a breeze. We'd lied to strangers, almost turning it into a game. But being here was so different. Here we lied to his family, and I hadn't realized how much that would turn me inside out.

"Well, let's get you inside and settled. We'll let Bernie get the bags," she said, looping her arm through mine.

"Bernie?" I asked, coming to a complete stop.

She laughed at my confusion, waving it away. "I've called him that since he was little. It's short for his middle name, Bernard."

My brows rose so high I thought they'd get lost in my hairline as I struggled to hold back a laugh. We'd just made it to the stairs where his grandpa passed us when I looked back to find Austin glaring our way.

I gave him my best what-the-fuck face while mouthing Bernard.

He closed his eyes and shook his head like he was asking

God for patience because he knew I wouldn't let that middle name go for a while.

Once he opened his eyes, I blew him a kiss.

"Young love," his grandma sighed beside me. "It makes separating even for a moment seem impossible. Although, I still blow kisses to Sylvester whenever I can."

"Because you're still young and in love."

She smiled knowingly and patted my arm as we crossed the threshold. "I like you. I like you a lot."

The guys eventually brought the bags in after talking for a while. I wasn't quite sure what people did on a farm, well, other than farm, so my expectations hadn't been very high for this trip. But I was pleasantly surprised by the amount of fun we had for the rest of the night.

Ethel had a quick, sarcastic sense of humor that had Sylvester rolling his eyes. I made sure to continue to call Austin by his nickname and joined Ethel in the jokes when I could. We made a hell of a team.

After dinner, we sat around the table and had a drink while they showed me how to play an intense game of Euchre. It seemed pretty slow, but Austin informed me that they took the game very seriously. We played one round, where I kicked his butt, before Ethel pulled out the baby album, much to Austin's dismay.

Each flip of the page had its own story that had me laughing, and Austin groaning in embarrassment.

"You sure did love those cowboy hats, Bernie," I commented when I saw another picture of him running through a sprinkler while holding a cowboy hat to his head.

"They looked good on me. I had to wear them."

"Oh, my goodness," Ethel exclaimed. "One summer, he would only wear a cowboy hat and boots. And I mean, *only* wear that."

"Hopefully, when he was younger," I surmised, laughing.

"I wish," she groaned. "He did it right before college."

"Grandma!" Austin shouted like he was scandalized.

I just stared wide-eyed at the very serious woman in front of me. My mouth tried to form words, but it was overridden each time I imagined a grown Austin running around the house naked as an adult.

"I'm just yanking your chain," Ethel said, slapping my leg with a laugh.

"Oh, thank god," I sighed.

"He was about three or four when he went through that phase."

"Whew. I mean, I'm all for letting it hang out if that's your jam, but to be running around a farm like that…" I shook my head with fake sincerity. "Those poor people."

"They'd be lucky to see all this," Austin claimed with confidence.

"Oh, boy," Sylvester groaned, rolling his eyes.

"I wonder who he gets his over-confidence from," Ethel asked, pointedly looking at Sylvester.

He held up his hands. "Hey, I'm just an honest man—never overconfident."

"Oh, please," she scoffed.

"Hey, you're lucky," he claimed. "Janice was looking at me the other day like I was water in a desert. I'm a hot commodity."

"We've been married fifty years. No one is looking at you," Ethel deadpanned.

"I'm just saying…like water in a desert."

Austin snorted, and I looked over and watched him watch his grandparents bicker. With every word and action, you could see how much they loved each other. And with every move, I could see how much Austin idolized what they had.

"Wow, fifty years is a long time," I said.

I watched my parents be in love, but fifty years was incomprehensible to me. I struggled to believe that kind of love existed when I'd been introduced to so much destruction that stemmed from love early on.

"Yet, not enough," Sylvester said to Ethel, resting his hand on her leg where she gripped it tight in hers.

"Marriage is such a commitment," Ethel said, looking between Austin and me with glassy eyes. "A commitment to love each other even when it's hard. A commitment to not give up and fight for each other even when the other is acting like they don't deserve it."

"I sure didn't deserve as much as your grandma fought for me." Sylvester smiled at us. "I have no doubt Austin would never marry a woman who wouldn't fight for him just like Ethel did for me, even though I'm sure he'll make it hard," he said with a laugh.

I tried to laugh with him, but a lump lodged itself in my throat, and I struggled to make noise past it.

"I know we didn't get to meet before your spur of the moment wedding," Ethel said. "But even in the short time I've gotten to know you, I can see how amazing of a woman you are, and I know how much Austin values marriage."

"He always claimed he'd only marry once he knew he'd found the one he could spend forever with," Sylvester added.

Each word poked a hole in the bubble of denial I'd built over the last week. We'd spent every minute basking in each other, and I made sure to not look beyond that minute alone. But with Ethel in front of me with her watery smile, it was like looking at every minute before, now, and beyond, all at once.

I remembered Austin's words from the morning in Vegas, his panic when the message from his grandma came through. I remembered his frustration and passion. It started adding up. I didn't think I had all the information but seeing who raised him made a lot more sense.

It's too bad it didn't make it any easier.

"Whew," Ethel breathed, dabbing at her eyes. "I must be getting tired. I always get emotional when I'm tired."

"And when you drink," Sylvester muttered, earning him a smack to the arm.

"One glass of wine is hardly going to make me weepy."

"Thank goodness. You'd be crying every night," he joked.

She rolled her eyes. "Like, I said, love them even when they don't deserve it."

Somehow, I managed a laugh despite the band of guilt pulling tighter and tighter around my chest.

"Well, I'll let you two be for the night. Coffee will be ready in the morning, and I'll be up to make some breakfast."

"Do you need help?" I offered.

"I'm not a woman to turn down help, so if you're up, I'd love it. Then we can make these boys clean up," she joked.

"I like the way you think," I said with a wink.

They said their goodnights and left Austin and me alone. I studied the worn wood exposed where the rug didn't quite meet the edge of the carpet. Anything to avoid looking into the eyes I could feel urging me to look up. The silence stretched on so long I thought maybe he'd fallen asleep. But then he cleared his throat, and I knew he was still waiting me out.

"Rae—"

"They're amazing," I interjected before he could say anything. As bad as the silence had been, I was sure that whatever he planned to say next would be worse.

"Yeah, they're pretty great. I'm lucky I had them."

Finally, finding my vagina, I bucked up and stopped looking at the floor, finding his intense green eyes shining right at me even in the dim lighting of the living room. "You never told me how they ended up raising you."

*You never asked*, my subconscious whispered, hammering home that I was a shit friend.

He exhaled hard, puffing out his cheeks. "It's kind of a long story. I'm not exactly sure where to start."

Tension radiated off him as he dragged his hand through his hair and took his turn to avoid my eyes.

"Give me the cliff notes version," I suggested.

"Well, I never knew my mom. She left as soon as I was born, and my dad passed away when I was thirteen. That's when my grandparents took over."

"I'm sorry." The words were useless, but they were all I could manage because my chest hurt too much. Imagining Austin having lost so much formed a physical ache—like a vise around my heart.

"Don't be. I mean, look at me. I'm kind of awesome," he joked.

God bless the relationship we created with banter and joking our way through anything serious. It made every conflict or tough subject easy to find our way out of. *Almost* every situation. I wasn't sure how we'd find our way out of this marriage.

But that was future me problems, and now that Ethel wasn't there tearing down my denial, I could start putting it back together. Starting with latching on to his olive branch.

"I guess you're not too shabby."

"Not too shabby?" he scoffed. "Did you miss the story about how I was star bagger at the local grocery eight months in a row?"

"If only it was nine."

"And my basketball awards?"

I barked a laugh. "You mean the best effort one they gave you because you sucked?"

"Hey, I was there to make everyone else look better."

"So noble."

He shrugged. "Like I said, I'm awesome."

"Fine. I guess you're okay." He thrust his fist in the air. "Now, take me to bed. I'm exhausted."

"Gladly."

While he got ready in the small hall bath, I took my time

inspecting each picture and poster in his room. Each one revealed a little more about him. Each one shone a light on how little I knew.

I soothed myself with the small things I found that confirmed I at least knew some things. A poster of his favorite band, Nirvana. His walls painted his favorite shade of blue. A geometric shape rendition of the ocean—his favorite place to be.

But it was a hollow effort at best. I had no idea he was Valedictorian or that he apparently won a spelling bee, or that he very obviously went through a horrifying phase of wearing pants that were so wide they looked like they housed a circus.

Okay, that I could have gone on not knowing.

*How about how much he values the commitment of marriage?*

I really wanted to block that one out, but it kept rearing its ugly head, no matter how much I shoved it back.

"Find anything good?"

I whirled around from studying his desk and almost started drooling immediately over his bare chest. Reminding myself his grandparents were right down the hall, I forced my eyes up from mapping each ridge of his abdomen. "Just your porn collection."

He laughed, pulling the covers back for us both.

"*Star Wars?*" I asked, studying the characters all over the sheets.

"Oh, yeah. I totally wanted to be Han Solo when I grew up."

I laughed, climbing in beside him. He turned off the light and laid back, mashed right up against me since we were in a bed barely bigger than a twin. In the dark, with the sounds of the outdoors creeping through the cracked window, my mind whirred with the bombardment of new information about the man next to me.

His breathing evened out, and I assumed he was asleep until his pinky reached out to stroke along mine. I smiled at the contact and shifted my finger to link with his. With the simple touch and the shadows all around us, it was easier to be serious—easier to talk about my guilt.

"I'm sorry I'm not a better friend."

"What do you mean? You're a great friend."

A lump grew in my throat, and I struggled to swallow past it. "I never knew any of these things about you."

"Rae…" Somehow, he managed to soothe me with just my name from his lips. He always had.

"Maybe I am selfish, and that's why I never knew you liked *Star Wars* or that—" I choked off the words, not quite ready to face how I never knew about his marriage beliefs. Instead, I said, "Or that you were a spelling bee champion?"

He huffed a laugh, rolling to his side to face me. "Rae, you know who I am. Maybe not the ins and outs of my past and my forte for spelling at the age of eight," he joked. "But you know me as a person. You make me happy. You make me laugh more than I thought was humanly possible. You're kind and go to art shows even though you find them pretentious—but you go anyway for me."

Each compliment sank deep into my bones, somehow loosening the band while tightening another one. It eased the lump blocking my throat while forming a second. A single tear slid down my temple, and I quickly swiped it away. How I got so lucky to have Austin Caldwell as my friend, I'd never know. I just desperately hoped I never lost him because of all I *didn't* know about him.

"You're a good friend, Raelynn Vos. And frankly, a damn good wife, too."

The words were light—joking, but they hit too close to the mark of what had me so on edge and unusually emotional. And despite how light they were, they were also prodding. I could have pushed back. I could have taken the chance and finally opened up the conversation we'd been avoiding—but I couldn't yet.

I couldn't dismiss the comment either. Something about the way he said it. Something about being in that tiny bed, in the dark, in the small creaky house in upstate New York with a family bursting with love, I could admit that I didn't quite want to push the word wife away.

I couldn't quite accept it either, so I settled on matching his playful tone.

"I know. I'm fucking crushing this wife thing. I may start a blog."

"Or a book," he shot back, not missing a beat.

"It'd be a best seller in days."

"It'd be full of pure genius."

"I'd call it Ain't Austin Lucky."

He grunted a laugh before rolling over top of me.

I sucked in a breath, shocked by the quick move, and immediately turned on by his weight pressing me into the bed. I gripped his sides and stroked the flexing muscles. When he didn't move or say anything, I looked up, and even in the dark, I caught the serious glint in his eyes.

"I am," he admitted softly. "I'm very lucky. I'll never regret the day you came up and asked me to fuck."

I laughed, unable to stop it. "I still can't believe you turned me down."

"It was pretty hard but totally worth the wait." He moved, and I sucked in a breath when his length pressed against my mound.

"Was it?" I asked, shifting my legs open around him.

He thrust against my core. "You know it was."

"Hmmm…Maybe I don't know. Maybe you should prove it."

With his hands and mouth, because the bed was creaky and the walls were thin, he set about doing just that.

## Chapter Twenty

AUSTIN

"So, these are the great bars of upstate New York farm towns?"

"I don't want to say we represent them all, but this is definitely one of the best."

She gave the most doubtful look and laughed, and I couldn't help but join her. I looked at the old brick building with the neon sign hanging out front claiming it as the best in town, and imagined it from her eyes. Rae had attended some of the most high-class bar openings in New York.

Kewpie's was definitely not her usual speed, and watching her small cringe as she peeked inside at the all-wood interior through the open door confirmed it. I would have high-tailed it out of there if I also didn't know she'd bar hopped from one run-down college bar to the next. Hell, I'd picked her up at some bars I didn't even want to go to when she called.

No, I knew Raelynn well enough to know she'd never hide her thoughts, but I also knew her well enough to know she wouldn't really care either. I loved it. The girl who presented herself as all about appearances never let appearances deter her from discovering something new.

God, I loved her.

"I don't see why your grandparents didn't want to come with us," she joked.

"I think we wore them out at the fair."

We'd eaten dinner and spent the past few hours at the county fair I used to look forward to as a kid. I hadn't gone in years; it had lost its sparkle as I got older, but watching Rae experience it for the first time, brought it all back. She'd wanted to ride every ride and play every game. She'd laughed and ate more fair food than I thought was possible for a single human.

I half expected her to collapse at any moment, but when I mentioned the bar, she was all for it.

"Pshhh, they wore me out."

"Yeah, you look super tired," I deadpanned, watching her shift from foot to foot.

"What? I love this song," she explained. "Also, it's totally a sugar high. I'll just burn it off with some dancing. Do they allow dancing on bars?"

"Dear God, have mercy on my soul."

She laughed and tugged me toward the door.

The old bar looked exactly the same as it had when I snuck in as a teenager. Hell, it probably looked the same when it was first built in the seventies—wood-paneled walls and worn red leather seats. A band played a country cover song on the stage, and couples danced around the scuffed wooden floor.

Just as we grabbed seats at the bar, Rae pulled her phone out and ended the incoming call with an eye roll. That was about the seventeenth time she'd done it that day.

"Two beers, please," she ordered before I could ask about it. "I briefly considered vodka, but this feels like a beer kind of place."

"Definitely a beer kind of place," I agreed.

"So, are we going to run into any ex-girlfriends here?" she asked after taking a drink.

I laughed, shaking my head. "Maybe some high school ones, but they're all mostly married now."

"Already?"

Another laugh escaped when her face screwed up like she'd sucked on a lemon. "Not everyone is allergic to the idea of marriage."

"Still…we're only in our mid-twenties."

"It's pretty common here for people to get married by then. Usually, they've known that person their whole life or most of it."

"Is that what you wanted?" she asked seriously.

"It's not that I didn't want it; I just wanted more. More than the farm, the small town, and always knowing the same people. And not to brag, but I was smart." I shrugged, picking at the label on my beer, remembering the guilt I'd carried around with me throughout my last few years of high school because I knew I didn't want to stay. Hell, the first year of college saw guilt clinging to me. It wasn't until I met Rae that I knew I was exactly where I needed to be. The first time she took me on one of her crazy adventures, I knew this was the life I wanted. Leaving my small town was the way to live with the excitement I dreamed up—with the woman I dreamed of.

"Well, we did go to U-Penn."

"Very true. And I loved art. It's not like there's a thriving business here for my goals."

"And you're amazing at it. It would have been a shame to keep your art from the world."

"That's what my grandma said, too. But it's not like I'm Nova, selling my art in galleries."

"Yeah, but you're still sharing it. And who knows, maybe one day you'll branch out and end up having your own showing."

"Maybe," I agreed noncommittally. "I'm not sure I'd want to show everyone my art."

"Well, you can show me any time you want," she proclaimed with a smile.

That was Rae—always so supportive. She'd been one of the first people at college to push me to enter competitions and pursue displaying my art outside of my marketing program. She'd believed in me so much that it caught on until I believed in myself too.

She drained the rest of her beer just as her phone vibrated across the bar top. I fought the urge to lean over and see who it was when she flipped it over, rolled her eyes, and muted the call.

"It's been going off a lot. Are you sure it's not something you need to get?"

"Nah. You know New York City—the city that never sleeps. Hence why I'm always getting notifications at almost midnight."

"Yeah," I said doubtfully.

But she ignored my disbelief with an exaggerated smile and rushed to another topic. "So, is the small-town mentality how you ended up engaged to Aubrey?"

I breathed a laugh, going over all the reasons Aubrey seemed like a good idea at the time. "Maybe it had its part. Like I said, my brother had just got married, and maybe that planted the idea of marriage."

"What else?" she asked.

"I think college ending and you gone kind of left me in this floating in between—a little lost. When I saw Johnathan at graduation, he looked happy with his wife, and I fell back into something familiar."

"I'm sorry I wasn't there," she said softly.

"It's not like we didn't try to talk. Different countries and the chaos of post-college made it hard to keep in touch."

"True. If it makes you feel better, it was hard being without you every day, too. We'd spent all the time in college together that I felt like I left a limb behind," she joked.

"It does make me feel better," I gloated.

"You're welcome," she said with a flourish. "So, I guess the bigger question is, why didn't you follow through?"

My cheeks puffed from my heavy exhale. "It was a pretty spur-of-the-moment engagement anyway. She actually asked me."

"What? How untraditional of her," she mock gasped, making a dig at my traditional views.

"Anyway," I redirected with an eye roll. "She just threw it out there as a why not, and in that moment, I didn't have a good enough reason to say no."

"Was it mid-sex?" she guessed with a smile.

"Not exactly."

"Post sex high then."

"Jesus, Rae."

"I'm totally right."

"*Anyway*."

"Okay. Fine. Focus." She pointed fingers at her narrowed eyes and then back at me. "So, why didn't you follow through?"

"Because it might have been spur-of-the-moment, but when it came time to actually plan anything, it all felt wrong. When I went to buy a ring, I couldn't. I didn't even know where to start, and I realized I didn't know her well enough to know what kind of ring she would want. None of it was right."

I left out the part where I was browsing through rings, and all I could think about was how Rae would love a ring as unique as her. I left out that when I imagined my wife, I never saw Aubrey.

"I picked up on falling back to this town and my past, and I remembered my promise never to do that. I wanted to be different from my family, and agreeing to marry a woman I didn't even know the ring size of hit a little too close to what my dad did all our lives."

"What'd he do?" she asked.

I rubbed a hand over my face, thinking of life before living with my grandparents. "He was a serial husband."

"Better than a serial killer," she joked, easing some of my tension.

"True. But he married and divorced seven times."

"Jesus."

"Yeah. Our house was a revolving door of stepmoms. Some good and some bad. Both of them sucked. The bad ones because, well, they were bad. The good ones because you knew they were going to end up taken advantage of, and that sucked too."

"I'm sorry, Austin." She turned in her stool to face me and wedged her legs between mine, pulling my hands in hers on her lap.

"Between him, watching my brother start doing the same thing, and taking in the example my grandparents set for what marriage should be, I knew I wouldn't marry anyone unless I was serious. Unless I knew they were the one."

"Then I came in." Her smile looked painful. When she tried to pull her hands away from mine, I held tight.

"I'm not seeing a downside to that." I was dead serious but delivered the words lightly.

Her eyes flicked to mine. I knew she saw the truth there, but she clung to my playful tone. We toed the line of facing our consequences but always turned back before we had to talk about them.

"Is it wrong that I'm jealous of missing out on such a big part of your life that obviously had a lot of meaning to you?" she said, pivoting away from my confession.

"I like you jealous," I gloated.

She rolled her eyes. "You know what I mean. We went through almost all of college together—the highs and lows and every adventure in between."

"Most of them led by you," I grumbled.

"You're welcome for that."

"I'm still not over the skydiving experience."

"You loved it."

"I loved when it was over," I deadpanned.

"If you hated it so much, why did you go?"

I studied her. Her sharp cheekbones softened by the full pout of her lips. The deep brown eyes that shined even in the dark. They always held a spark of excitement in almost every situation. It was my Siren's call. "Because how could I not? You make even the most terrifying experiences worth it. So, I follow."

Her smile was slow and delicious. I wanted to taste every new curve and line as it appeared, knowing I put it there.

"So, speaking of exes…you seem better without Bodie."

"What do you mean?"

Her smiles came easier this past month, even with the Vegas wedding looming over our heads. "You just seem… more you. More lively. The longer you were with him, the quieter you got. I always made it a point to dig out your wild side when I was with you, but sometimes, it was harder to find."

Rae stared without blinking, the muscle along her jaw ticking, and my stomach dropped at the raw turmoil pouring from her. I was two seconds from snapping my fingers to bring her out of her thoughts, less than that from pulling her in my arms and making sure she was okay. But she blinked, and the emotion vanished.

She looked away with a wave of her hand. "You know? I am better off without him. Being in a relationship was sucking the freedom from my soul," she groaned dramatically. "I just stuck it out because it looked good for the campaign, but you're right, it did make me different, and it wasn't worth pretending anymore."

Something in her speech didn't ring true, but I didn't know what. This was the most she'd talked about her breakup and her relationship in general. She usually brushed any conversation about Bodie off, so I took advantage to maybe find some answers about what dimmed inside her with him. "How did he take it?"

"I mean, no one takes it well when they realize they can't have me."

I snorted but continued to push. "Seriously, though. He gave me a bad vibe. Like maybe he wouldn't take being dumped too well. Like maybe he'd push—"

"Nah." She waved the words away. "I made sure he knew that we were done. There was no room for doubt."

Just then, her phone vibrated again on the counter, except this time, she powered it down. I was about to push her on it when the bartender asked if we wanted another drink.

"How about vodka gimlets," she suggested, waggling her brows my way.

"I don't know. Look what happened last time."

She scoffed. "What's the worst that could happen? Wake up married to your best friend in Vegas?"

The bartender laughed. "That'd be a hell of a morning, but I'm pretty sure that only happens in movies."

"You'd be surprised," I said.

"Well, thankfully, we don't have any chapels here. So, you should be safe."

"See…" Rae jumped in with her playful smile. "We're totally safe."

"Fine," I groaned, knowing there was no stopping her. And when you couldn't stop Raelynn Vos, you joined her. Which I usually did, happily. Even if I complained the whole way. I really only did it because she tried so much harder to make me like it, and I secretly loved the way she rolled her eyes.

Three drinks later, and we'd done some dance for a TikTok and taken a dozen photos for Instagram.

"Oh, my god!" Rae squealed. "I love this song."

The band had finished, and now a DJ played music with a heavy, pulsing beat.

Rae slid off her stool and swayed her hips to the sultry tune. Her heavy-lidded eyes met mine and sent electrical pulses to my chest. My heart thudded, pumping heat through my veins. She placed both hands on my knees, pushing them wide to make room for herself so she could slowly crouch down, lining her face up perfectly with my lengthening cock before rolling back up.

Her hands slid up my chest and around my neck, causing the deep vee of her shirt to gape, dangerously close to giving me the perfect view of her nipples. My hands twitched to help and tug the neckline down for my satisfaction. Instead of risking public indecency, I gripped her hips and tugged her close, letting her feel what she did to me.

Her lips parted over a small gasp, and I took advantage, leaning in to suck her pouty bottom lip between my teeth. Her responding whimper left me aching. Before I could go back for more, she whirled around and rolled her body against mine.

She leaned her head against my shoulder, giving me the best fucking lap dance a man could ask for. Needing her to be as aching as me, I brushed her hair back, exposing her neck, and kissed up the tender flesh before nipping at her ear.

"You know, I almost gave in one time in college."

Her hips faltered but quickly regained their rhythm. "Really?"

"Yeah," I confessed, dragging my tongue along the shell of her ear. "You'd just pushed me to enter an art competition earlier that day, and we went to a party to celebrate. You were dancing just like this, trying to get a rise out of me."

"And did I?" she asked breathlessly.

"Oh, yeah. You were so fucking sexy, and all I wanted to do was bend you over right then and there and fuck you in front of everyone so they knew I could."

"Austin…"

"But you always got a rise out of me. I'm always so hard for you."

She rolled her head against my shoulder, bringing her mouth inches from mine. "Let's go."

My muscles tensed, ready to bolt, when a voice I hadn't expected interrupted our escape.

"Baby bro. Looks like you got a live one."

"Fuck me," I muttered, keeping Rae close to my side. "Hey, Johnathan."

He slung his arm over my shoulders as he gestured to the bartender for a drink. With his drink in hand, he turned back to Rae, eyeing her up and down like his next meal. "Hey, sexy."

I wonder what she saw when she looked at us side-by-side. We looked like replicas of our father. Hell, somehow, at three years apart, we looked like twins. He wasn't as bulky as I was, but that's what years of being a lazy asshole who drank too much got you. Genetics could only get you so far. But beyond that, we had the same light hair, hard jaw, and green eyes. His were just dulled by his shit decisions.

I know when I looked at us side-by-side, I saw what I could've been if I hadn't learned to not be like our father.

"This is Raelynn," I grit out, barely restraining the urge to punch him.

"His wife," Rae added, stunning me out of imagining all the ways I could rip his eyes out. She tucked herself tighter against my side, easing at least a little of the tension.

"Wife, huh?" Johnathan asked with a shit-eating grin. "Wow, I thought you'd be fifty by the time you finally found the one pussy for you. Not that I can blame you. She looks…lively."

"Ew," Rae muttered, not bothering to hide the disgust from her face.

Part of me started worrying that Rae may punch him before I could.

"Speaking of wives, how's Corinne?" I asked, reminding him of reasons he shouldn't be hitting on other women.

He grunted. "At home. Probably looking for something else to bitch at me for."

"For some reason, I don't think she needs to look too hard," Rae said with the fakest sweet tone.

"You'd think for the way she's always whining," Johnathan shot back, completely missing the insult.

"Well, why didn't you bring her with you? I'm sure a night out would be fun," Rae suggested with a smile that looked more like a grimace.

Johnathan tossed his head back and laughed. "Yeah, right. She kills my buzz every fucking time." He drained his beer in two swallows. "So, Rae. How did you meet my baby brother?"

"College," I answered.

"Yeah, she looks like one of those fancy types. No wonder you married her. You always did think you were better than this town."

"Sometimes people want different things," Rae defended. "Nothing wrong with that."

Not that Johnathan cared because a tall, skinny blonde with boobs testing the limits of the buttons of her shirt and enough makeup hiding her age walked past and sat at the other end of the bar, pulling his attention with her. "Yeah, I get that. I do love a good variety," he agreed distractedly. "Hey, it was good meeting you, Rachel."

"Rae," she corrected.

"Cool." He smacked my back. "Good seeing you, bro. I'd love to chat, but I've got some…variety to check on," he explained, laughing at his own joke.

"What about your wife?" Rae asked with disgust.

Johnathan barely spared her a glance, rolling his eyes. "We're probably going to get divorced. Gotta look to the future now."

"Just like Dad," I muttered.

## Blame it on the Vodka

This time, Johnathan did stop to scowl at me. "You know, I'd ask how much longer you're in town, see if you wanted to meet up for lunch, but I'm not up for your judgmental bullshit."

With one last slap to the back, harder than the first, he went to the blonde.

"He seems...nice," Rae said, struggling to deliver the fake compliment.

I gave her a *let's be real* stare. "He's a dick."

"And a cheater too." She winced, looking down the bar at him schmoozing the woman. "Totally gross."

I squeezed my pulsing temples before dragging my palm down my face. "Sorry, he kind of killed the vibe."

Rae offered a sad smile. "Do you just want to head home?"

My body ached at the loss of what our night should've been, but I couldn't be at the bar anymore with my brother just down the way, replicating the history I hated. "Yeah," I sighed. "Do you mind?"

She linked her arm with mine, smiling up with bright eyes. "I'll follow you anywhere, Austin Caldwell."

I almost made her pinky swear to mean it forever like we were kids. I was desperate for it to be true, and it was in those moments when she said things like that, my brain interrupted with the questions I forced back to keep from facing.

*Would you follow me into a future together?*

Somehow, I managed to shove it down and walked us out.

We made it to the car, and I was digging through my pocket for the keys when two small hands gripped my biceps and spun me. I was so shocked, I went willingly, stumbling back when she stepped into my space.

"Rae—"

I choked when she pressed her hips to mine and slid her hand up my body to pinch my nipple. "Just for clarification, no one kills my vibe. Ever." Her eyes darkened and grew heavy as her other hand started at the inside of my thigh, slowly sliding up to where I grew harder by the second.

Before she could reach me, I took control and whirled us around, pinning her to the car. She gasped, and I latched on to her open mouth, pushing my tongue inside to tangle with hers. In the flash of a second, the weight pressing in on my chest from the embarrassment of my brother vanished. She took it away—making life better, just like she always did.

"Fuck, Rae. I—" I cut the words off just in time, quickly swapping them out. "I need inside you."

Because I knew if the words I really wanted to say came tumbling free, I'd make a liar out of her. There was no way I could admit how much I loved her and not ruin the vibe.

Maybe someday, but not now. And as images of that day formed in my mind, I quickly unlocked the car and pulled us into the backseat. All thoughts of my past fled, only leaving room to lose myself in the present and imagine ways to create the perfect future—with her.

## Chapter Twenty-One

AUSTIN

THE NEXT DAY we said goodbye to my grandparents. When they asked Rae to come back soon, she sounded so convincing, I almost believed her.

I wanted to so much that I spent the entirety of the car ride back to the city running through ways to make it happen. Our weekend was over—our deals done. We didn't have a reason to pretend to be married anymore, and I was terrified we'd snap right back to where we were when we woke up in Vegas. Me wanting to be married to the woman of my dreams, and Rae looking for the nearest exit as she called her lawyers to set up the quickest divorce.

My mind scrambled through ideas but still hadn't come up with a solid plan.

It didn't help that we spent the whole drive talking. Not that I minded. I'd learned over the years to bask in every moment with Rae—to live for that second. I promised myself I'd create a plan when I got home, after losing myself in every smile and laugh I could get from her.

"I can't believe you woke up under your truck, and it was parked in a field. How did it get there?" she asked, laughing.

I pulled up alongside her building and gave her my best

innocent smile. "No clue. But apparently, I knew I was drunk enough I couldn't be in the car."

"But why under it?"

"I'm going to go with to keep myself safe. If anyone came along, they'd look for me in the bed or in the cab."

"Okay," she said slowly, still laughing.

"Listen, you had to get creative when finding entertainment in a small town. Most of the time, that included alcohol and questionable mornings after."

She shook her head as she unbuckled her seat belt. "You know, I can imagine you quite perfectly in that life. Especially since it makes more sense how you were always so good at those drinking games in college."

I huff on my nails before buffing them on my shirt. "Beer Pong champ for life."

Her brow furrowed as she looked me over. "At the same time, it was so different than I expected."

"How so?"

"I don't know." She shrugged. "I guess I have a pretty narrow thought process sometimes. I met you at college and saw you in New York, so that's where you belonged."

"It's understandable. It's easy to imagine people in this setting when you've lived here your whole life."

"Well, not my whole life."

Her admission was like tossing a marble in the wheels of my mind, halting the smooth movement with something I wasn't familiar with. "You lived somewhere else?"

"Yeah," she answered, waving her hand as if shooing the words away like an annoying fly. "We lived outside of the city a ways, in a rundown suburb."

"When?"

"Long before my mom married Kenneth."

*Ping. Ping. Ping.*

More and more marbles fell between the grooves. "What? Kenneth isn't your dad?"

"Hah! I wish," she scoffed. "But also, yes, he is my dad. He adopted me after they got married."

"How the fuck did I not know this?" Was this how she felt when she first came to the farm? I imagined my face right now, and I couldn't recall ever having her stare at me with bulging eyes and a dropped jaw.

Up until then, Rae had enjoyed my shock, but something shifted, and she looked away, focusing on her clasped hands in her lap. The dropped head and hunched shoulders were such a contrasting image from the bold woman I'd always known that I knew this was a piece of her that most likely filled in any gaps I had never been able to figure out.

Holding my breath, I waited for her to answer, shoving down the questions I wanted to ask in rapid-fire. Something urged me to dig deeper—to figure out the puzzle because maybe then I'd have the answers I needed to get the future I wanted. It sounded crazy, but I had to go with my gut.

"It's not something I really talk about," she finally answered.

Curbing my urgency, I asked softly, "How old were you when they got married?"

"Twelve. That's also when he adopted me. But we moved to the city when I was seven, after my mom *finally* left my dad. Thank God," she said, rolling her eyes upward like she was speaking to him. "I *hated* him and wished she would have left sooner."

It was like the confession tumbled free without her even realizing it.

The raw honesty hit me like a wrecking ball, knocking the wind from my lungs. "Rae…" I barely got out.

As if realizing the situation, she stiffened, closed her eyes, and took a deep breath, forcing any tension from her body with her exhale. She shut the gate, and the bold woman I'd always known tried to reappear.

"Listen, it's not a big deal," she said, trying to wave it off. "Cool?"

It wasn't cool. I couldn't stop imagining her as a child living a life that made you hate a man so much. The two didn't blend. A lasso wrapped around my chest, compressing my lungs as it tried to yank me back in time to save the little girl she was.

When I stayed silent, she finally snapped her gaze to mine. "Please," she uttered.

I loved when she begged.

*Please more. Please fuck me. Please don't stop. Please eat me. Please kiss me.*

But not this. This was a plea I could've gone a lifetime without. A plea for me to not make her face a past she wanted to forget.

I could give that to her. Maybe instead of pushing for more to discover the missing puzzle piece, I could remind her that I could be what she needed when she needed it. I could show her that being with me didn't end in a corner she couldn't get out of. I could show her that life with me wasn't what she imagined when she pictured marriage.

Forcing my jaw shut, I took a breath and a long blink, shoving aside my shock and bringing out the playful man she needed. "I'll let you drop this for now," I said with a tip of my lips. "Only because I have a meeting to prep for tonight. But later…" I looked her up and down. "I have ways of extracting information, Miss Vos."

Her eyes lit with a playful challenge. "We'll see."

I gave her one last perusing look before fully shifting away from the subject. "Thank you for this weekend."

"Of course," she said easily, taking my lead. "Ethel and I are best friends now. And I'm always here for anything you need."

"Anything?" I asked, raising my brow slowly.

"Anything."

"Hmmm…" I pursed my lips and scrambled back for any ideas I might have had earlier in the drive to convince her to not run to the nearest lawyer. We'd spent two weeks together being a married couple—but in reality, it felt the same as spending two weeks with my friend.

That I now slept with.

But it was also the same, and maybe that was what she needed to see while we were home, in our city. Our marriage lacked a day-to-day example. Hell, even the week between the weekends had been us locked in her apartment fucking like rabbits.

That wasn't the life Rae lived. Rae went out as much as she stayed in, and I needed to show her the other side—but show that side with me as her husband.

"How about you let me take you out?"

"Ooooo. Like on a date?"

"Yeah. Like a date."

"So, basically what we do all the time," she joked, grabbing her purse before getting out.

She wasn't wrong. Before Bodie, I'd been her date to almost every event. We'd gone to dinners and bars and everywhere in between. But she was missing one crucial detail that made it very, very different.

"Except this time, you're my wife."

The word hung between us, and I waited for her to react.

As expected, she rolled her eyes and opened the door.

Unexpectedly, she'd had to bite her lip to hold back her smile and looked away to hide her blush. She tried to hide what the word did to her. While I had no intention of pushing her to admit her past, I had no qualms about eventually pushing her to admit how much she truly liked being my wife.

She bent down to look in the car once the doorman had her bags. "Send me the details, and I'll be there."

"I can't wait to have dinner with my wife," I said, just to watch her blush all over again.

I stayed to watch her walk in the building before pulling away. The plans I struggled to create during the drive came together perfectly now. I'd take her on a romantic date. I'd wine and dine her like she deserved. And at the end of the night, I'd lay it all out—the perfect timeline. I wouldn't rush her—I'd only ask for a chance.

I had to at least try.

## Chapter Twenty-Two

### RAELYNN

"Shit," I hissed.

"Truth Hurts" blared, startling me so much I jerked, smudging mascara against my perfectly done brow. I glared at the offending mark because how dare it be there when it knew how hard it was to get two matching brows.

Lizzo started singing, and I turned my glare to the phone, almost grinding my teeth to dust, when I saw Bodie's name across the screen.

"You motherfucker," I growled.

He'd messaged me almost every other damn day since I got back from Vegas. And once the photos appeared of Austin and me in the Hamptons, his messages increased from one to two easily ignored comments to ten texts and phone calls.

Between the smudged makeup and the anger that had been brewing all week long, I was done with pretending they weren't there. I'd been done with him for longer than when I kicked his ass to the curb for good, but somehow, he hadn't gotten the message.

Time to make sure he did.

"If you don't stop fucking calling me, I'm going to rip your balls off and give them to the filthiest homeless man with the most STDs."

"Raelynn—baby. I've missed your voice."

I almost snort-laughed at his polite greeting that sounded like it came from between gritted teeth.

"What do you want, Bodie?" I asked, in the most bored tone I could give.

"I've missed you."

My face scrunched over a silent *ew*. I pulled the phone away and made sure it was actually Bodie that called.

"Maybe we can do dinner?" he suggested when I didn't respond.

"Hell, no."

"C'mon," he coaxed, again through what sounded like a clenched jaw. "Maybe one of your family dinners, so we can be on neutral ground to talk."

No, this was definitely Bodie—the man who downplayed every outburst or lash of anger. The fact that he called my family dinners a neutral place let me know nothing had changed—not that I thought they had. I couldn't count the times he'd smacked my thigh under the table or squeezed my arm too hard because I wasn't speaking up for him like he thought I should—or joked about our relationship that he didn't find funny. Or the times he'd been so angry by my lack of expressed devotion that he couldn't even wait until we got home and ended up cornering me in the foyer before we left.

Nowhere was safe with Bodie.

My chest ached because, looking back, I could see it so clearly. I could see his small smacks to the leg, minor pinches to my arm, and light intimidation. They'd all been so small that they'd barely blipped on my radar until it was too late—until they all slowly chipped away at my core and left me in too deep. I'd been so ashamed to be led there that I hadn't had the courage to ask for help.

Bodie's abuse was like a slow drip in a roof—sometimes,

you didn't know how bad it was until the ceiling came crashing in on you.

"You know," he kept going. "I never did get to finish pitching my goals to your father."

Like a switch to a lightbulb, everything lit up and made sense.

"Ohhhh, I see," I said slowly. "You don't miss me. You just miss harassing my father.

He sputtered before grounding out, "No. I'm just thinking of his future and what I can do to help after the fucking fiasco you caused."

Clue one to Bodie losing his shit: swearing. Usually, that was the point I backed down, doing my best to not escalate him any further.

But I didn't let Bodie's moods dictate my actions anymore, and after a month away from his dominance, confidence surged, and I wanted to prove it.

I wanted him to squirm, knowing he had no control over me anymore.

"Fiasco? You mean marrying my best friend after dumping your ass?" I asked, my tone dripping with sarcasm.

"I meant getting drunk and married in Vegas like some low-class whore."

Clue two: personal attacks.

"Oh, Bodie," I laughed. "No need to worry about that. Did you not see the articles about the Hamptons? People are eating it up. They love it." My false jovial tone turned acerbic. "So, you can go fuck off because you and your shitty proposals aren't needed here. Apparently, you didn't get the message that I'm done with you. That means move the fuck on and stop calling like a desperate piece of shit."

"Raelynn."

Clue three: animal-like noises warning of an impending explosion.

If I closed my eyes, I could clearly imagine him with a

tight jaw and clenching fists. The vein along his forehead would be pulsing, and his eyes dark.

A single tremor rattled about before I quickly shoved it down. Fuck him and fuck any fear he instilled in me. Taking a deep breath, I closed my eyes and imagined another time. A time when Austin looked at me like I was crazy for apologizing for making him mad. A time when Austin reminded me that abuse isn't my fault. Others choose how they act —not me.

"Go fuck yourself, Bodie, and get some anger management."

"I wouldn't be so angry if you weren't such a bitch," he finally snapped. "You fucking owe me."

*I owed him?* I replayed the words, trying to make sense of them, but that only made me angrier. *I owed him?* He took a year from me. He took a piece of me I said I'd never give up. I owed him *nothing*.

"Excuse me?" I asked slowly.

"You fucking owe me for dating your high maintenance-ass and having to deal with your annoying-ass friends. I made you look good at events instead of a desperate slut spreading her legs for any dumb fuck that came along. So, we are not fucking done."

His words hit the brick wall of my rage. I didn't bother to waste my time addressing his weak insults. Instead, I made one thing clear. "I don't owe you shit."

"You owe me a goddamn meeting with your father," he shouted, fully enveloped in his anger. "I fucking earned it, and you're going to get it for me because I swear to fucking god, Raelynn, I will come there and fucking force it out of you if I have to. I'll break down your goddamn do—"

"Goodbye, Bodie." I didn't bother letting him finish his tirade. Instead, I hit the red circle and sat my phone back on the counter.

I ignored how my hand trembled and shoved aside the urge to run and check my locks.

I was *not* scared. Bodie had no power over me.

Besides, I always locked my doors.

I met the dark smoky eyes in the mirror and lifted my chin.

"I'm a bad bitch," I said to my reflection, adding a smirk for good measure. "A bad bitch with a fucked-up brow."

I quickly finished my makeup before running to my closet. I imagined each outfit from Austin's point of view, trying to pick one. We'd gone to countless dinners, and I'd never worried about what I looked like for him. Maybe how I'd look if my photo got taken, but never for Austin.

No matter how much I tried to convince myself this was like any other dinner together, it felt different, and I couldn't quite figure out why. Maybe because I squeezed my eyes shut and plugged my ears while singing *lalalala* anytime the answer got too close. I was happy in our bubble, and I didn't want anything to ruin it. So rather than dig too deep into the cause of the warmth blooming in my chest, I explained the difference away as knowing we'd end up back at his place or mine by the end of the night.

That made sense. Sex always made me happy. Especially sex with Austin.

I arranged two outfits on the bed and stepped back to take a picture, sending it off to the girls for their opinion.

**Nova:** Part of me wants to say the red dress because daaaaaaamn!
**Nova:** But go for the skirt and top.
**Vera:** Agreed.
**Vera:** The red says, we're not really having dinner. We're having a drink, then going back to my place.
**Nova:** The calf-length skirt and off-the-shoulder shirt with some fuck me heels says, I'm going to torture you through this entire meal.

**Vera:** I always love a good torture. Drives Nico insane. **devil smile emoji**
**Me:** Savages!!
**Me:** I love it.
**Vera:** So, is this a date?
**Me:** Kind of…but not really. I mean, we've gone to dinner together so many times.
**Nova:** It's totally a date.
**Vera:** Definitely.

Their surety that this was, in fact, a date and not another simple meal had my hackles rising, and I rushed to dissuade them. As if making them believe it would help ease the tension and nerves like I was some teen waiting for my boyfriend to pick me up for prom.

**Me:** It's nothing special.

Not that they were letting me get away with it.
*Bitches.*

**Nova:** Except that it's a date.
**Vera:** With your husband.
**Nova:** Because you're his wife.

And there it was, laid out in black and white, impossible to ignore.

*"Except this time, you're my wife."* Remembering his parting words added a shiver down my spine to my core. I squeezed my legs around the pulse and sucked in a breath around my racing heart when I closed my eyes and remembered the blaze in his eyes when he said it.

*No.* I cut myself off. Focus on the sex. That's what had me so excited. That's what had me aching.

**Me:** Eye roll emoji.
**Me:** What? Do you guys have another bet going on and need me to admit to something?
**Vera:** Nope.
**Nova:** At least not a bet on a date.
**Me:** Bitches.
**Vera: kiss emoji**
**Nova: kiss emoji**
**Vera:** So, what does this mean? What comes next? After the date?
**Me:** Sex
**Nova:** And then ...

And then what? More sex.

At least, I hoped. I didn't know. We didn't have any more reasons to keep this ruse of our marriage going. We fulfilled our weekends with family, and now we were back at square one. There was no more forced proximity to keep us together—no excuse to keep sleeping together. I could get my divorce, and we could go back to being friends. Easy-peasy.

Except, the sharp pang in my chest didn't feel easy-peasy. It twisted and pulled, making it hard to take a deep breath.

**Me:** I don't know.
**Vera:** Have you maybe considered possibly giving it a try?

*Giving it a try...*

I closed my eyes and imagined it. I imagined him in my home—our home. I imagined him in my bed. I imagined going to events and introducing him as my husband.

My phone pinged with a different sound than the one I set for the girls' texts.

*Bodie.*

Doing what I should have done from day one, I blocked his number and deleted the message without reading it before going back to the group chat. My chest squeezed tighter while my fingers hovered over the buttons, unsure of what to say.

With a sigh, I muted the conversation and set the phone aside. I'd get hell for it later, but I just…couldn't.

I didn't want to go back and forth about it. I didn't want them to tell me I was wrong or making a mistake because this feeling clawing away at my chest was too much to ignore. They'd try to convince me it was love, but I knew myself—I knew I couldn't stay married to Austin.

I would ruin it, and it would ruin us. Hell, all I had to do was look at what I let Bodie do. If I stayed married to Austin, who knew what I'd let him do? Who knew who I'd become? There was too high of a chance that I'd become something I hated, and I'd end up resenting him for it.

No. I couldn't risk it.

If Austin and I had any chance of making it, we had to be friends and nothing else.

As much as I hadn't had enough of him—of basking in his pleasure—I knew it was better to break it off now rather than drag it out into something ugly.

I pressed my palm to my chest over the tightening pain, like a dull knife twisting and pulling at my skin. Neither solution of staying or going felt good. Both left me with my heart sinking to my stomach.

Shoving it all aside, I grabbed my phone and sent a message to my lawyer, asking him to draft the papers as soon as possible—tonight. I needed to make the decision before tonight. I needed to make the decision before anyone else tried to talk me out of it. I knew what was best.

I just hoped he agreed.

He had to.

I'd make him understand…tomorrow.

Because tonight, I planned to create a night to remember before we went back to being just friends.

## Chapter Twenty-Three

### AUSTIN

As if my heart hadn't been working overtime already, watching Rae sit across the table eye fucking me through the entire meal tripled the pace. I was surprised I could think at all with the amount of blood rushing to my cock.

I'd been a nervous wreck all day. My hands sweating and tingling. My lungs struggled to expand fully, and my heart galloped along like a speed racer. I had to keep double-checking that I was just nervous and not actually having a heart attack.

However, watching her strut out of her apartment building, her hair softly blowing in the wind across her bare shoulders, the slim length of her calves above the sexiest black heels, I hoped would be digging into my back later. I wasn't sure I hadn't died right then, and this was actually heaven.

My body almost split in two, warring over what emotion would dominate. Below the table, all I could think about was those fucking shoes and figuring out the quickest way to get under her flowy skirt. Above the table, my hands still shook, and my heart still raced.

The thing my mind had a hard time separating was that this romantic restaurant with its flickering candles, soft jazz, and decadent food was the kind of place I would have taken Rae if I had been asking her to marry me. Which I guess I kind of was.

I was going to ask her to stay with me. I was going to ask her to stick it out and give our marriage a try—give *me* a try.

However, with the way she wrapped her lips around every damn bite, my focus kept shifting below the table, only to swing back to my thoughts when I watched her smile. It bounced back and forth like a yo-yo, and I couldn't control it enough to form the words.

"I might die of blood loss, Raelynn."

She tilted her head like she didn't understand as she dragged her finger through the remaining alfredo on her plate. But we both knew she knew what she was doing because the next moment, she brought that same finger to her full lips to suck the cream off.

"All the blood is rushing to my cock," I explained anyway.

"Poor baby," she cooed with a fake pout. "Want me to kiss it better?"

I almost groaned, imagining her sliding under the table to suck me off behind the secrecy of the tablecloth. Part of me wanted to push her to see if she would, but then I remembered who she was, and I had no doubt she'd relish in the task. Instead, I walked a fine line with my control and played with her back. She may be able to seduce me with just a look, but I knew how much Rae loved when I talked dirty to her.

"I would love nothing more than to watch you take all of me between those pouty fucking lips, but we might get kicked out for that."

Red tinged her cheeks beneath darkening eyes. "It'd be worth it."

"For a chance to push past your resistance and be in your throat? Definitely."

Her chest rose and fell quicker, her cleavage pressing against the confines of her black top, and I knew I brought her at least somewhat closer to where I was. But then she shifted, leaning back in her chair, and slowly dragged her finger along the curved line of her top from one shoulder to the next, caressing the top curve of each breast along the way.

What had I planned to say?

Fuck, I couldn't wait to rip that shirt down and suck her nipples into tight rosy buds.

*Shit. Focus.*

I cleared my throat, struggling to find the words, but desperately needing to. "But first, I wanted to talk ab——"

My words choked off when something brushed past my knee and landed against my thigh.

"What was that?" she asked with false innocence.

"Fuck, Rae," I grunted. Her foot grazed my balls, and I almost came from that alone.

"Yeah," she said, her smile growing. "I can't wait to get home so you can do just that—Fuck Rae."

My fists clenched against the tabletop to keep from gripping her foot and forcing more pressure. If anyone looked over, they'd probably assume something was wrong. Not because Rae showed any signs of distress. No, if at all possible, her smile grew while she sat back, relaxed, sipping her vodka gimlet. Meanwhile, I stared so intensely, my face stern and focused on not embarrassing myself.

"Dessert?"

We both blinked, breaking our staring contest, but not bothering to look at our waiter, who waited for our answer.

"No," we said in unison.

"Thank you," Rae added.

As soon as the waiter walked away, I gripped her foot and pulled it tight against me, causing her to slip an inch down the chair. Her gloating smile vanished when she gasped and rushed to grip the arms of the chair to hold steady.

Fuck it.

Now, it was my turn to gloat—to be in control. I pushed

against her and let her read the promise in my eyes of every filthy thing I planned to do to her tonight.

We'd talk tomorrow because tonight? Tonight, I'd show her a different side of me. One I'd kept mostly to myself because we'd never crossed the boundary of friendship, and when we had, I'd been scared to push too hard.

Rae spent most of our friendship pulling me out of my shell—always the one to create exciting experiences. I knew she feared settling down would bore her. She claimed that life had too many experiences for her to miss out on because she was too busy being tied to one place—one person.

Tonight, I'd show her I could be wild like her, that there would never be a boring moment with me, and life would always be exciting. I'd lay it all out there for her tonight—every hidden desire.

I didn't share that side of myself with many women, but I knew Rae was strong enough to want it as much as me. The few times I'd pushed her and let bits and pieces slip free, she flourished under the dominance.

I couldn't wait to see what she did when I fully let go.

## Chapter Twenty-Four

### RAELYNN

"Austin, I'm going to fall."

I tried for an offended tone, but it escaped on a needy exhale instead.

The lips I'd been staring at for the better part of an hour quirked up, and a flare of something powerful glinted behind his green eyes. Something I'd only spotted glimpses of over the last month, but now it blazed, and I was useless to do anything other than sprint toward the light.

"Good. Then you'll be on your knees. Exactly how I want you."

I almost melted to the floor right there, a puddle of aching need, but I refused. Instead, I narrowed my eyes and tugged my foot away. Or tried to, but he just pulled me back harder and laughed.

"I love watching you try to act like you don't want to be there just as much as I want you to. All that pride trying to cover up all that want."

"You think you know me so well," I challenged, hanging on by the skin of my teeth in this battle of wills. I'd been winning all night until, all of a sudden, I wasn't. I'd been on the edge of victory until he transformed into the big, bad, sexy beast.

"Oh, I know you better than you think. I *see* you, Raelynn Vos."

My nipples pebbled tight, sending a shot of electricity straight to my pussy, shocking my heart on the way. More often than not, it was never straight arousal with Austin. My heart always jumped in and clung to the excitement.

Which was how I knew ending it was the best choice.

But not yet. Not until after tonight.

This time, I pushed my foot against him, earning a bit of control back when he jerked in his seat. "I think it's time we head back to my place."

"I think so, too. Except, tonight, we're heading to mine."

Austin's place was nice—clean, modern, and perfect for him. We just usually went to mine since it had luxury and a view. But I had no plans to object. Hell, we could've booked a hotel down the street, and I would have been more than fine. As long as I got him undressed and inside me, I'd be happy. So, without objections, I rested my hand in his and followed him out, doing my best to appear calm when the adrenaline flooded too close to the surface, and I sat on the edge of exploding.

I thought I'd known need before, but it all paled in comparison to the desperation that clawed just under the surface to get to Austin. By the time we stood at his door, I was ready to mount him like my favorite ride. I practically vibrated behind him while he took his sweet time turning the key.

The lock clicked into place, and before I could rush in, he turned, pinning me to the spot with the weight of his own need. His eyes scanned my face, neck, shoulders, chest, and everything in between before finally landing on mine.

"Do you trust me?"

The question sent up a warning sign, but I quickly erased

it, too eager to get inside, and offered up a flippant response. "Yes, Aladdin, I trust you."

His lips quirked, but his eyes stayed serious. "Raelynn?"

"Of course, I do."

I was too busy matching his sincerity that I missed his hand dropping to deliver a sharp pinch to my nipple. "Good girl. Now follow me."

I gasped but arched forward, chasing the fingers that pulled away, desperate for more of that sharp sting before the warming pleasure. I chased him past the leather couch in the living room, past the kitchen I'd seen a thousand times, all the way to his bedroom.

*Perfect. Right where I wanted him.*

Zeroing in on his broad back, pushing the restraint of his dress shirt, I took a step and then another.

"Stop."

Immediately, I obeyed. His words sharp like a whip, almost delivering their own sting and warmth. My spine tried to stiffen under the command but quickly softened with curiosity, needing to know how much more bite I could take before I lit on fire.

"I want you to go to my side of the bed, kneel, and pull out the box underneath. Then, place it on the bed and open it."

My heart thundered, the unknown and excitement warring on the edge of a cliff, and everything swarmed around me. I just walked, not really being able to identify what had my breaths coming so quick and short.

"Is this where you confess you're a serial killer?" I taunted. Deciding to break the rules, I stroked my fingers along his back on my way to the bed. He grumbled at my disobedience, but the way the muscles twitched and rippled under my touch made it worth it.

"Not quite."

Hairs on the back of my neck rose as I met his gaze while

I dropped to the plush rug covering the dark wood floors. Everything about him screamed control, but something dimmed the green I saw before. Something hesitant.

Holding his stare, I lifted the heavy box to the bed, rose to my feet, and hesitated. Just a moment to wonder if maybe I should shove this box back where I found it and demand he fuck me.

*Thump. Thump. Thump.*

Had my heart ever beat so hard? Had I ever stood on the edge of the unknown with uncertainty playing out before me. He always complained about how I forced him to skydive with me, but *this*? Skydiving didn't come close to this.

"Open it."

"What if I don't want to?"

"Is *the* Raelynn Vos scared of a little box?"

"Hardly," I scoffed. "Maybe I just don't want to play your game?"

His smile was slow and nowhere near sweet. "Trust me, Rae. I think you do."

"Why do you think that?"

"Because you've spent so much time poking fun at the way I *blush* when you flirt with me—like I can't handle you."

Harder. Faster. Maybe this was what a heart attack felt like? If so, then bring it on because I could die happy watching Austin prowl toward me like an animal.

"But maybe I was just hot from imagining *you* trying to handle *me*."

The gauntlet was thrown. The challenge there in his eyes as he closed in. Meeting it with a stare of my own, I flipped the box open and rolled my eyes before looking down.

Of all the things I expected, a blue stack of balls atop a flat base was the last thing I expected. It was right up there next to everything below it.

Black leather cuffs.

Tiny clamps. I didn't even know what they were for sure,

but my nipples pulled tighter just imagining being pinched between the metal.

A small bar.

Rope.

A flogger I recognized from a porno I watched once.

And a handful of other toys I couldn't put a name to.

"You asked me why my ex and I broke up. We weren't compatible. In more ways than just sex. I don't need this kind of sex, but I want it, and she wasn't strong enough to handle it."

Somehow throughout his speech, he'd managed to make his way behind me without me noticing. Soft fingers brushed my hair back, and a breath of a kiss landed against my neck.

"But you are, Raelynn. You're the strongest woman I know. And I want you." I sank into his touch, rolling my neck to give him room. "You know I want you any way I can get you, but will you try this with me?"

"Anything."

The whispered word fell from my lips before I could consider anything else—any consequences.

In a flash, his hand gripped the back of my neck and pushed me down on the bed, shoving the box of toys aside just before my chest hit the mattress. The silk of my skirt brushed up my thighs, but I barely felt it. Every sense zeroed in on the fingers digging into my neck.

This time the sharp bite of pain didn't soften to a sensual heat.

This time my heart didn't race in excitement.

This time when I whimpered, it wasn't in pleasure.

This time I didn't see Austin. All I could see was Bodie behind my squeezed eyes. All I could feel was the same paralyzing fear when he lost his temper.

"Austin," I cried, pushing up with all my strength. "No." Unlike with Bodie, the hand holding me in place immediately released.

When I turned around, I couldn't look up. Shame and embarrassment like I'd never experienced crawled over my skin.

"Fuck, Rae. I'm so fucking sorry. I should have explained more. Fuck. *Fuck.* I can't—"

"No, it's okay." Now I looked up and met the gentle eyes of my best friend, and it really was okay. My heart slowed down and the tension pinching my skin too tight eased. Austin had been rough with me before when he had sex, but I always knew it was him. "It's okay. I'm sorry I freaked."

I said I trusted him, and I did. I just hadn't been prepared for the damage that Bodie had done to intrude on our moment. It pissed me off, but I was done letting him ruin anything else—especially my last night with Austin. Shoving embarrassment and frustration aside, I took a calming breath and closed the gap between us. Holding his gaze, losing myself in the mossy green forest, I gripped his hand and pressed it to my stomach, dragging it up over my breasts and to my neck.

"I just need to see you."

"Rae…" He hesitated, his fingers stroking the sensitive skin, sending chills racing over my skin. "We don't have to do this."

"I want to," I whispered, squeezing my hand over his. "I want you to fuck me, Austin. I want to play with you. I want *you* to play with *me*. I want it to hurt because you make it so fucking good." When he still hesitated, I did the only thing I did for him. I begged. "Please."

## Chapter Twenty-Five

### RAELYNN

IN A FLASH, his hand tightened again. But this time, I was right there with him and nowhere else. This time, when I whimpered, it was from the grip around my throat, controlling the pulsing heat flooding my veins. This time the pressure ebbed to a warm goo sliding from my stomach to my pussy.

In every relationship, it was me who suggested the next adventure, but to have someone else—to have Austin—take the lead left me desperate to follow.

"Anything?" he asked softly.

"Anything." I gripped his wrist, holding on tight while he leaned into my space, swallowing my air. My eyes slid closed, and I tipped my head to the side, making room for his nose to brush against my skin. Giving him access to my neck—to everything.

"And if I said I wanted to claim your tight little virgin ass? Would you let me?"

I moaned. How could I not? His words weren't just simple words. They were living things that crept into my darkest fantasies and made themselves at home. They coiled around my need and refused to let go. "Yes," I barely whispered.

I've had a lot of sex in a million different ways, but I'd

never let anyone fuck my ass. I always thought a certain level of trust needed to be established first, and I never stuck around long enough to do it. Even with Austin's teeth scraping along my skin, I couldn't imagine anyone I trusted more.

His hand clenched for a fraction of a second before letting go. "Strip," he ordered, stepping back.

*No* sat on the tip of my tongue, so used to being spit out just because I could. However, not a single part of me wanted to put one more obstacle between our night. So, instead, I lifted my chin, doing my best to look down on him, despite being almost a foot shorter, and did as he ordered. He stood back and watched as I slid each piece of clothing from my body, his eyes stroking my skin more firmly than the fabric. I felt it all, and we hadn't even started.

"Get on the bed and lay back against the pillows."

"Yes, sir," I said, eager to comply.

Once I positioned myself in my best Playboy model pose, he prowled closer. With each step, my breaths grew shallower under the anticipation. He said nothing, gave no hints as to what came next, and I wanted to scream from the tension pulling me apart from the inside out. How did it get more intense than this? How did I survive?

He leaned over, reaching past my head to pull out two straps on either side.

"Do you use these often enough to keep them out?" I asked, hating the idea of another woman in his bed.

As much as I tried to hide the pinch of jealousy, I knew I failed when his lips twitched while he wrapped the soft velcro strap around each wrist.

"I've never had them out, but I was hopeful for tonight," he finally answered after making sure I was secure. "Fuck, you're stunning."

Pride from his admission, pride from his scorching stare and compliment, swelled. My body was out of my control.

Too tight but too full. Every emotion pushing and pulling until my mind struggled to keep up.

"Maybe you can show me how stunning you are," I suggested.

He hummed soft and low, looking like *no* was on the tip of his tongue too. But he must have come to the same conclusion as me and instead opted to start undressing. Thank god.

Each rippled muscle he revealed pushed me closer to the edge of insanity. I squeezed my legs together, trying desperately to gain any friction. When I'd finally found the perfect angle, he shoved my knees apart and crawled between them.

"I don't fucking think so."

"Then fuck me," I panted.

"Oh, I will," he promised, dragging his palm over my wet pussy. "Just not yet." My jaw dropped, ready to argue, but he distracted me with his hand gripping his thick length and stroking himself. "First, I want to paint your silky skin with my cum. Then, I want to bring you to the edge again and again while I get your little virgin asshole ready."

With each word, he stroked himself harder, looking so close to losing control. And I laid there sprawled out, ready to lose control with him.

"Are you going to be able to take me? Am I going to be able to fit inside that tiny virgin hole?"

"Yes," I panted. "Austin, please." My clit pulsed, and he wasn't even touching me. Other than the hand gripping my thigh, holding it wide, as if it was the only thing to keep him from flying away. He sat up on his knees, between my legs, and stroked his cock with a strong pace, wrapping around the head to collect the pre-cum slipping free.

"Don't worry, sweet Rae. I'll get inside you one way or another. I can't fucking wait to watch your little hole stretch around me, to watch you wince in pain but still take me. I can't wait to hold your sexy ass cheeks in each hand and pull them apart so I can watch the way my cock looks fucking you."

I was going to come from just his words. The prospect terrified me and fascinated me. How could he have so much control over my body? I pulled at my restraints, needing to touch myself to regain some control, but I could barely move. My hands never made it below my head.

"You're not going anywhere," he moaned. "Now lay back. I'm gonna come all over you."

His strong grip released my thigh as he fell forward and caught himself, continuing to stroke his length fast and hard. His eyelids dropped, too heavy with pleasure. His lips parted, and I yearned for him to be a bit closer so I could taste them. Then again, if he was any closer, I would miss the sight of thick, creamy ropes of cum stretching across my stomach and breasts. I'd miss the sight of him squeezing the last drops from the slit and rubbing them up and down my pussy.

"Oh, god," I whimpered when he brushed over my clit and held himself at my opening to finish. "Austin, please. I want you inside me. Just fuck me."

He exhaled like he'd been holding his breath the entire time and fell back to his heels with a soft chuckle. "Oh, Rae. We're just getting started."

I managed half a growl in frustration before it cut off into a gasp of pleasure. Austin dropped over my body and sucked my nipple between his lips while his hand played with the other. He feasted back and forth from one nipple to the next like a starving man, uncaring of any cum he collected on the way.

"I should tell you to wait until we wipe your cum off me, but it feels too fucking good to care."

"We've already established I don't mind my cum when I get to eat it off of you."

"Then the least you could do is share," I taunted.

His lips tipped in the most devilish smile. "Gladly."

He collected a streak from the bottom curve of my breast and brought it to my lips. Meeting him halfway, I arched up and sucked the salty liquid from his tongue. He let me have my fun, sucking and playing like I wanted to do to his cock, but he eventually took over, kissing me like a savage. I pressed up, giving just as hard as I received, losing myself in the moment.

Until a sharp bite of pain around my nipple yanked me back to reality.

"What the fuck?" I cried.

While Austin kept his eyes on me, I looked down to find a small clamp fastened on either side of my nipple. Before I could barely process it, another sharp pinch pierced my other nipple.

"Mother fuck."

"Such a filthy mouth," he chuckled.

"Yeah, let's see how well you take two little clamps pinching your nipples when you least expect it," I bit out through clenched teeth.

"What? Do you not like it?" he asked, working his way down my body. He hovered just over the swollen tips and blew gently before flicking his tongue across one.

"Oh, my god," I cried. "That's—that's—"

"Intense? Perfect? Painful? Warm?"

"It's—yes."

"You're welcome."

"Ther—there's no need to be coc—cocky." The words barely escaped between gasps. Each sensation new and exciting. The pain really did fade to an oozing warmth, following the same path his tongue was taking down my body. The first swipe of his tongue over my clit sent me to hell and back because surely, nothing in heaven could ever feel this good. Not when you had nipple clamps, bound hands, and the world's sexiest man working magic between your thighs.

I dug my teeth into my bottom lip, trying desperately to

hold back any more begging. I should be ashamed. I would've been if it hadn't felt so fucking good. And when a thick finger dipped into my pussy only to pull back out and lower to my ass, I lost it. My whole body vibrated like one large nerve ending, stimulated past thinking.

One hand held my thigh wide as his mouth latched on to my clit and his finger slid deep in one go.

"Fuck, Austin. Yes."

He chuckled, only serving to add sensation upon sensation. The next thing I knew, a second finger joined the first. It stung, but I couldn't differentiate pain from pleasure anymore. I was so consumed by the euphoria that I didn't even acknowledge the rustling. It didn't register until something other than his fingers—something harder and bigger—pushed against my opening.

I jerked up to try and see what it was but only encountered the top of his head. "Austin," I whimpered.

Part of me wanted to lie back and let it happen, but I wanted to remember every second. I wanted to see it all.

He looked up, sliding his tongue over his damp lips, and met my gaze. Seeing the need, he edged back enough to let me see the smooth but wide dildo pressing against my asshole.

"I'm big, baby. I need you to relax so I can get you ready."

I nodded but didn't fall back. I wanted to watch. Readjusting so I had plenty of room to see, he began to work the toy inside me. It stretched me—stinging—but I knew it would be nothing like how Austin would burn me. He pushed and pulled, slowly sinking it in deeper after each pass.

"Good girl," he crooned once it was seated as deep as it could go. "Now lay back."

This time he didn't give me the option. With a hand to my chest, he flicked one of my nipples, sending a sharp zing straight to my core. When it clenched tight, another shock came from my tight hole, pulled tight around the plug. All of it made my clit pulse with need. So, when he finally leaned down, licking from the base of the plug to suck on my clit, I exploded. I tried to hold back the screams, to cling to reality, but then he removed a clamp and sucked harder. And then the other.

My world exploded and collapsed all at once until I lost sight of who I even was. I writhed in a ball of pleasure, spread wide for him to do whatever he wanted.

Before I could even get my bearings, the plug shifted. I'd barely pulled myself together enough to watch him slowly ease the plug from my ass. It was its own form of foreplay, watching him squeeze lube along his dick and grip himself to rub it in. When he shifted and lined himself up with my hole, I made sure to focus, not wanting to miss a second of him painstakingly slowly easing himself inside.

As soon as I whimpered, he would pull back only to push in again, this time further.

"You're doing so good, baby. Relax and push out." I did as told, and we both groaned when his fat head made it inside me. "Fuck yeah. Let me in. Let me inside your tight little hole."

He slid in from there, taking his time but pushing me hard.

"Yeah, Rae. You're so fucking sexy," he grunted. "Take all of me."

"Please. Yes."

Once his balls pressed to my ass, he stroked his thumb over my slit, circling at the top. "You have no idea what it does to me to see your swollen, wet, pink pussy above where your little asshole is stretched around my fat cock." A pull out with a harder push in. "You have no fucking clue what it does to me knowing I'm the only man to be inside your ass—to know how tight you are. To know you're mine." A quick thrust this time. "All mine."

In that moment, I wanted to be. I wanted to fall at his feet and never leave. I was addicted. But like an addict, I knew I had to stop. I knew it was good that tonight was it. I knew it was good that I set in motion to cut myself off before he could talk me into staying.

Earlier, I'd been so confident in my decision, but staring up at him now and hearing him call me his. It didn't feel nearly as right as before.

"Austin," I barely whispered. I didn't want to think about anything anymore. I wanted this. I wanted now. I wanted him. I wanted us.

"Shh, baby. I'll take care of you."

My only warning was a hum of vibration before something pressed to my clit. I thrashed wildly and fucked up onto the thumb, pushing into my pussy as his hand held the vibrator mercilessly against my over-sensitized clit. He pushed his cock in and out, and I spiraled out of control, screaming in endless pleasure.

"This pussy is mine," he growled when I lay there exhausted and sweaty. "I want to fuck you with every toy under the sun—fill every hole you have—but I'll never share you. This body is all mine. You. Are. Mine." He enunciated his proclamation with a thrust over each word. "Now, come."

"I can't," I whimpered. "I can't anymore."

He leaned down, holding the vibrator between our hips, and gripped my jaw, sucking on my swollen bottom lip. "You'll come as many times as I tell you. I love the feel of your little virgin hole squeezing me for more."

When he sucked on my bottom lip again, I lashed my tongue out to meet his, like an animal desperate for a taste. "Please. Please."

"Please, what?"

"I don't even know," I whimpered.

He huffed a soft laugh against my damp neck before dragging his tongue along a bead of sweat. "Poor, sweet Rae. Begging for mercy."

"No," I protested, pulling at my restraints. "I'm begging

for you. I want you." I knew what I wanted now. "Let me touch you."

His rocking hips paused a moment as he studied me, and right then, I shoved it all aside, letting him see inside me. No matter what came tomorrow, I wanted this—now.

In a blink of an eye, he snapped into action, ripping the restraints off and tossing the toy aside. I wrapped my arms around his broad back and held him to me. His large hands pushed my sweat-dampened hair back off my forehead so nothing could come between the way he watched me. His eyes never strayed, taking in every reaction I had to his body, claiming mine so thoroughly.

My hands roamed into his hair, scratching down his back, hoping I left a mark for more than tomorrow. His hands skimmed over my breasts, playing with my tender nipples before slipping between our hips and sliding back and forth across my soaked clit.

"Come for me, baby. One more time. You can do it. Let me feel you."

I nodded, pressing my forehead to his, clutching him through the storm, and gave in. He rocked into me harder and held me just as tightly, both of us making our own symphony as we came together. It was chaos and beauty all at once. Everything swirled around us, but we clung to each other through it all.

When the dust finally settled, we panted into each other's space, surviving on the same air. He slid out, and already, I wanted him back. I feared I would always want him back.

"Rae—"

"Shh." Everything was too raw, and I had no clue what he would say, but I knew I wouldn't survive it. "Just be with me," I begged.

His eyes flashed with a moment of indecision before they softened. Taking my chance, I leaned up and kissed him softly, slowly. I luxuriated in every curve and taste, taking my time to memorize it all.

When he pulled back, he gave me the same promise I gave him when we started. "Anything."

And that was Austin. Always willing to give me anything.

Hopefully, he'd be just as willing to say the same thing tomorrow when I officially ended our marriage.

## Chapter Twenty-Six

### AUSTIN

WHEN I ROLLED over the next morning to find Rae perfectly stretched out beside me, her long dark hair splayed against my white pillows, the sheet barely covering her full tits, I knew we could make this work. We could make *our marriage* work. Hell, I almost laughed at how far we'd come since I'd rolled over to find her naked in my bed in Vegas.

I'd always known I loved Rae, but last night confirmed it. There was no letting go. And feeling her body react under me, watching her eyes ignite with so much passion, I knew she felt it too. She may not be ready to hear it, but she was there, and if we could move this far in only a couple months, then it was only a matter of time before she accepted how right we were for each other.

Last night had been the wedding night we deserved, and today would be the first day of the rest of our lives—as husband and wife. No more denials, no more doing it for other people. We'd be married for each other.

First, I just had to wake her up.

Giving in to the sweet temptation, I tugged the sheet down enough to bare her rosy nipple. My mouth watered as I watched it harden in the cool morning air, and I didn't hold back. Leaning down, I swirled my tongue around the bud before sucking it between my lips. When she stirred awake with a moan, I latched on with my teeth, delivering a gentle nip.

"Austin," she whimpered, her voice sexy and raspy. "Please."

"Please, what? Tell me, Rae." I loved hearing her beg.

"Please, fuck me."

I brought my hand to join in and rolled her other nipple, delivering one last lash with my tongue. "I would, but I need to shower first. Someone wouldn't let me leave the bed last night."

She groaned before slapping my shoulder. "Then stop fucking teasing me."

I laughed, watching her tug the sheet over her chest. Her attempt at a glare only made her look all the more sexy. Most men would cower under such an intense glower from a powerful woman, but it just made me love her more. It made me want every morning like this for the rest of my life. Playful and sexy and perfect.

"Don't laugh at me because I'm dick deprived. It's been a whole six hours since you've been inside me, and here you are, getting me all wet for nothing."

"Oh, you're wet, are you?" I asked, slipping my hand under the sheet.

"Don't you fucking dare," she threatened, slapping my hand away from her thigh. "Go shower. I want to sit on your cock until I come."

"I want you to sit on my face."

"I can do that, too."

I almost laughed again at her regal declaration and pursed lips.

"Good. Let me shower, and I'll be right back."

I leaned in to snatch a kiss, and when I pulled back, she chased me. It was painful, but I didn't let her catch me. I

## Blame it on the Vodka

wanted to tease her every second I could. I hoped if I left her wanting enough, she'd join me in the shower. I was sure she'd come. Especially after the way she groaned about my tight ass being too delicious to resist as I strutted naked to the bathroom.

But she never came.

When I came back out, I found her propped against the headboard with pillows, the sheet pulled over her chest while she scrolled through her phone and drank a coffee. As soon as she noticed me enter, she set the phone aside and smiled.

Again, I was hit with how perfect it all was. This perfect blend of my best friend being playful and fun, but also the seductive woman watching me with heat and need. In the mix, I saw the want—the love—but I ignored it, too scared to give it more attention and sink in deep before she saw it herself.

"I got you a coffee. I even added all the sugar and disgusting snickerdoodle creamer you love," she scoffed. "How does a man as big and masculine as you like such a sweet drink?"

I stripped out of my towel and crawled into bed beside her, mirroring her position, and grabbed the coffee she made just for me. With a cocked brow, I looked down at her cup. "How does a girl like you end up drinking coffee black?"

"Black like my soul," she said with waggling brows.

"Ha. Ha," I mocked, rolling my eyes. "See, I drink coffee out of necessity which means adding an obscene amount of sugar to it. No one drinks coffee black because they need to."

"I don't know. I just always did." She looked down at the cup, studying the black liquid with furrowed brows. "Maybe because my mom mentioned that my dad loved sugary coffees, and I never wanted anything in common with him, so I never added anything. My stubbornness forced me into drinking it black."

"Sounds like a super valid reason," I conceded sarcastically.

She laughed but didn't add anything besides a shrug. Seeing an opening to get to know a deeper side of Rae, I latched on and gently prodded.

"You never talk about your dad."

"There's not much to talk about."

"I could list a million things to talk about."

"A million?" she asked with exaggerated shock.

I laughed at her dramatics, loving everything about this moment. I craved every second I could have inside her, but these small conversations are what made us, us. These were the moments that had me believing we could make it as husband and wife. Early morning conversations, naked in bed with coffee, and getting to know each other with playful banter.

"For instance, I know your dad isn't your biological father, but I have no idea how he and your mom met."

She smiled, but it didn't quite reach her eyes before she looked away. While she studied her coffee, I studied her, holding my breath, silently begging for her to open up. Rae told me a lot—unfortunately, more than I wanted to know. Like every detail about her period or how her dates went, but she brushed off anything about her past.

Maybe now that she'd seen my past, and we had a future stretched out in front of us, she would be comfortable enough to tell me.

"It's nothing romantic or anything," she muttered, shrugging. "They met at a women's shelter when we were all there volunteering. Dad always volunteered because it was where his grandma stayed when she needed help. And Mom made it a point to give her time to them once we got back on our feet because they took us in when we had nowhere else to go after my mom finally left my abusive father."

*Whack*: A blow to the plexus, knocking the wind from my chest.

*Thump*: Me mentally falling flat on my ass.

Each impacted my body so thoroughly, I had to shift my weight against the bed just to remind myself it wasn't real.

I should've known, but how could I? Rae distracted you with her open honesty while never giving away anything too deep. No one avoided their past so thoroughly if they actually had good things to say about it.

"Rae..." I struggled for words, knowing damn well she wouldn't want pity or even empathy, but unable to pretend I wasn't affected.

She waved her hand. "It's not a big deal."

"It is, though." Usually, I let her get away with the brush-off, but this time, she was my wife. Not Rae, my best friend I've loved for years, but my *wife*. I wanted to know her inside and out, and I needed her to know she could be vulnerable with me without me ever seeing her as weak. "It had to be hard to go through. It just makes your strength all the more amazing."

Finally, like I guessed the winning numbers to the lottery, she turned and smiled. "It was hard," she admitted, accepting my sympathy with grace.

I figured that would be the end of the conversation, but with a deep breath, she shocked me and kept going.

"I don't really remember much since I was so young. Kind of like flashes for the most part. I remember one time walking in to find him pinning my mom to the bed, and when we tried to run, he cornered us against the door until she promised to stay. It was when he lost his temper on me and slammed a textbook on my hand that she finally decided enough was enough. I guess trying to explain a seven-year-old with a broken hand from a falling book really puts things into perspective," she tried to joke.

But I couldn't even fake a laugh. I had nothing left in my

lungs. My heart thundered in an attempt to compensate for the lack of oxygen. "Jesus, Rae. I'm so sorry."

The words barely escaped. If it wasn't for the quick shake of her head and slim bare shoulder rising in an attempt to shrug, I would've thought she hadn't heard me. Hell, I barely heard myself past the throbbing rush of blood blotting out everything but her and her confession. Again, I wondered how had I *not* known? Why had I let her brush it off so many times? If only I'd known….

If only I'd known, what? What would it have changed?

*Click.*

Knowing that bit of information changed everything. It slid into place, filling the crucial gap to understanding Rae. She went on about wanting to be free, but maybe she didn't want to *really* be free. Maybe she held back because she was scared—because she didn't want to repeat what her mom went through.

I'd been focused on convincing her of the wrong thing all along. I'd been showing her we could be wild and free together, but maybe I needed to show her how safe she'd be with me.

All of it made so much more sense.

The way she avoided anything serious without even trying.

The way she acted scared of me and accused me of being someone I wasn't when I lost my temper in Vegas.

The way she panicked last night when I pinned her down.

*Shit.* I cringed, terrified I'd fucked up, and she was just waiting for a way to tell me.

"Is that…" I started, scared to even ask, but needing to. "Is that why you pushed me away last night? Because of your father?"

"Hah," she barked a laugh that held a bite as ferocious as a rabid dog. "No, that was all thanks to Bodie."

Have you ever ridden one of those giant rocking ships that swing back and forth on a pendulum, dropping your stomach to your feet just for it to shoot back up into your throat? The emotions from this conversation reminded me of that ride.

Except, the ride was also spinning.

And also jerking.

And going upside down.

And was on fire but also being dunked in an ice bath.

While being electrocuted.

"What?" I whispered.

"Oh, I mean..." she backtracked. "It was nothing."

Blackness crept around my vision, and I struggled to breathe.

Her eyes widened with the truth written all over her face. Realizing what she admitted, her beautiful brown eyes clouded similarly to how they had over the past year she dated Bodie. I could never figure out what plagued her, but I saw it clear as day now—*shame*. Like a well-oiled machine, she blinked, trying to drop down the same wall she hid behind every time I looked too closely.

Not this time.

*Hell. No.*

This time, I wedged my way under and pried it wide open.

"All this time. This whole year. I fucking saw it. I watched it happening, and I let it." I barely whispered the words, but the truth scratched its way up my throat as if I screamed.

"No, Austin," she denied, shaking her head fiercely. "You didn't let it. You didn't know."

"I did," I said louder, all of it bubbling up, searching for a way out. The obvious signs clawed at my skin, banged against the door I tried to keep her behind to save myself. My limbs ached from forcing the door closed—from holding still for too long. Needing to move, I thrust my mug onto the side table, ignoring the hot coffee sloshing over. I flung the covers back and stood, pacing, uncaring of my nudity. "I saw it this whole time. I fucking *saw the signs, Rae*. I saw them and let it happen because I refused to look close enough." I shoved my fingers into my hair and tugged. Anything to release the pressure. "All because I was too hurt to watch you with someone else. All because I just didn't fucking look close enough."

She set her mug aside more gently than I did and rose to her knees in the middle of the bed, clutching the sheet to her chest. "Austin, I hid it, okay?" When I moved to object, she shook her head. "It was a slow progression, and it wasn't like he beat me up or anything."

I jerked to a stop and stared her down. My nostrils flared like a bull ready to charge. "Don't you *dare* brush this aside as nothing," I threatened.

"I'm not. It's just that it wasn't the same as my dad. Bodie was just rough and pushy."

With a growl, I went back to pacing and ripping the strands out of my skull. "The bruises. I fucking saw the fucking bruises. And I just let them go."

"Austin..." she called, but I could barely hear past my rage. Rage at Bodie. Rage at *myself.* "Austin!" Her voice cracked over the plea for me to hear her. But all I could imagine was that same sound coming from her beautiful lips when she was left alone with Bodie and pleaded with him to stop.

I snapped, making a decision. I stomped to my dresser and yanked out a pair of pants, almost tearing them in my haste to get them on.

"Goddammit, Austin," she yelled, but I was too focused to listen anymore.

"I'm going to fucking kill him."

"What?" she screeched.

"I'm going there right now, and I'm going to fucking kill him."

"Wait. No. Stop. Austin, we broke up. I know you're mad, but I handled it, okay?" she explained as if that would calm me down. "I don't need you to do this. I don't *want* you to."

"Tough shit, Raelynn. I'm your husband." I punctuated

each declaration with a stab against my chest. "You are my wife—*mine*, and I protect what is mine."

I waited for her to agree, to tell me she understood. Instead, as if in slow motion, her body curled in on itself. Sitting back on her heels, her eyes dropped, and a different kind of warning punctured my bubble of rage.

"But I'm not your wife," she declared softly. "Not really."

I stumbled back, my ass hitting the edge of the dresser, wishing I hadn't heard it. Wishing I could rewind and never hear it ever again.

The ride was no longer swinging. It was in a straight free fall.

"No," I begged, barely managing to mouth the denial.

"Austin, this was all just an accident—a great one, but…" She stared at the sheets we crumpled last night. "It was an accident we knew we had to fix eventually. It was an accident that never really made us husband and wife."

Each word threatened to take me to my knees. I clung to the edge of the wooden dresser as if it was my last grip on sanity. "No," I muttered. Her eyes lifted, and I saw every ounce of sadness and grief storming through my veins mirrored in hers. "No!" I stood, ready to fight. "It's all bullshit, and you know it. I get it, Rae. I get it now. You're scared, but it's us—it's *me*. We can make this happen. We can make it work."

"No. This has all been us *pretending* to make it work."

"I haven't been pretending. And neither have you," I declared. Maybe if I said it firmly enough, I could make her believe it. "I've seen how real it is with every look and every touch. I *know* you feel it. Just let it happen, Rae. Jesus," I threw my hands out, begging. "Give it a chance."

She shook her head before I'd even finished. "I can't. I'm no—" her words cut off as if even they'd rather choke in her throat than be said. "I'm not that girl, Austin. I'm not the wife you've been holding out for. It was nice to pretend that maybe

I could be that girl for a while, but I need to be honest for both of us. I can't be her forever. It's not me."

"Raelynn, just—"

Delivering one last blow, she held up her hand. As quickly as she looked on the edge of breaking, she snapped back together, lifting her chin in the most regal, final way. "I already filed for divorce. Yesterday, before dinner."

This wasn't a sucker punch knocking the wind from my chest. No, it was a freight train to the balls while Rae reached her bare hand into my chest and ripped out my heart. Just like that, I was back to clutching the dresser for support. I'd barely made it to my knees to fight for her, and she knocked me back down.

And this whole time, I was fighting a losing battle. She hadn't even given me a fair chance. "What about last night? Why did you still go on the date if you knew? Why did you fuck me?"

Her mouth opened and closed like a fish out of water, searching for words. I ached to save her, but I deserved the truth. "Because I selfishly wanted one more night with you."

"So, you decided. What Rae wants; Rae gets. Right?"

"Austin, please. I just—"

"No." With nothing but a gaping hole in my chest, frustration and defeat crept in, taking up the free space. "Just like before—just like always. You decide what's best for you, not even thinking about me."

"That's not it," she pleaded, her eyes welling with tears and spilling over. "I don't want to keep pushing and wait for it to fall apart, because *it will*. I know it will. It always does. I want to end it now and at least give our friendship a chance to stay intact before too many emotions rip us apart."

I ached to go to her and wipe her tears. Rae rarely cried, so when she did, it utterly destroyed me. The problem was that I was already destroyed. I stood there, battle wounded, with nothing left to give.

How much longer could I fight for her?

I studied the floor, unable to watch her suffer from the sadness she created. I searched for something to say but only found the memory of when this all began. I remembered the conversation with King. I remembered how sure I'd been that this was it—that I could convince her to be mine.

And if I couldn't, I'd walk away.

I didn't want to walk away.

But I also didn't want to keep fighting.

I didn't want to have to work so hard to make her stay and love me—even if I did love her enough for both of us.

Even worse, we weren't friends. Not anymore. Not after this. Not after knowing how good it felt to call her mine. The realization piled on top, and I hated the weight—I hated her for putting it there. I hated her for giving me hope, just to take it all away—*more* than all of it. She was a smart woman. She had to know we couldn't come back from this, but she pushed for it anyway.

It was too much, and I was so fucking tired.

"Austin…"

Swallowing the pain clogging my throat, I forced a blank stare and met her pleading gaze. "I want you gone by the time I get back."

"What? Austin, no. Please."

I ignored her, pulling on a shirt and somehow stumbling my way through the door.

"Dammit, Austin, no. This isn't what I wanted," she cried.

I turned back, taking her in one last time. Kneeling on my bed, perfectly backlit by the morning sun, still utterly beautiful despite her pain. It gutted me. "You've made all the decisions up until now, and I've gone along with every one. Now you will go along with mine."

"Goddammit. I ju—"

Falling back on my old tactics, I became a dick to help

preserve the last shred of myself. "Just stop fucking talking and get out."

Not bothering to look back, I slammed the bedroom door and bolted, reminding myself there wasn't anything to go back for, despite the way my body ached with the need to turn around.

The way my heart begged me to go to her.

I had to remind it that she didn't want us, making it hurt all over again.

Unfortunately, I wasn't sure it would ever stop.

## Chapter Twenty-Seven

### RAELYNN

Somehow, I found myself in the back of a cab. I wasn't even sure how I managed it. The last thirty minutes swirled around me in a blur of tears, shock, and so much unbelievable pain I didn't know how I fucking stood. Everything inside me ached. My muscles strained with each movement. My legs resisted every step away from Austin's apartment. My heart, a murdered mess on his bedroom floor.

The worst part ... I was the one who ripped it out and left it there.

My head thudded against the glass, matching the same repetitive throb in my skull. I hated my brain. It was all its fault. While every other part of me rioted, it stood tall along a precipice. My mind ruled with the fragile confidence of sticking to the plan. No marriage. No falling in love. Never. Ever. Meanwhile, everything else raged, shredding the pillar of strength until nothing was left except a toothpick.

"Fuck," I whispered, hitting my head again.

"We're here," the driver announced.

I looked out at the curved driveway and regal front doors just outside the city. It would have been closer to go to Vera's penthouse. That's where I should have gone, returning the favor for all the times they'd shown up brokenhearted and crying at my doorstep.

Yet, somehow, I stood at the front door of my family home. Or the house I'd called home since I was twelve. I raised my fist but only managed to make it hover inches from the door, hesitating.

I could turn back. I could head to my girlfriends and cry and eat ice cream and threaten to kill whoever hurt us.

But I had questions. Questions only one particular person could answer.

Something broke open inside of me this morning. I'd never talked about my father with anyone. I shoved it aside, making myself believe that because it was in the past, and I couldn't change it, there was no need to think about it. I believed it couldn't hurt me anymore. Instead, I opted to power through any doubt, refusing to be anything other than a strong woman all on my own.

In the unknown territory of confessions and revelations, I'd babbled on, accidentally slipping about Bodie, too.

The flash of sympathy—*pity*—before he could mask it still left me cringing. It still left me feeling weak and stupid. And when Austin's pity morphed to a raging superhero, I panicked, spiraling into a hole I was sure I'd never dig my way out of. The thought of him confronting Bodie, of people finding out and splashing it across the news, had bile rising from my stomach. It was bad enough I had to live with the shame of letting myself get there when I swore I never would, but to have everyone else know too?

I'd panicked, spewing the words I always said—the ones that made me, me, but this time, they felt wrong—foreign. This time they left me questioning my foundations. This time they left me alone, watching Austin leave me behind.

And now I stood outside my mom's door, without a heart and too much pride, unable to knock.

What if the answers I got only made it worse? What if I stood on the brink of opening Pandora's box?

*What if you feel this hollow and empty forever?* A voice whispered underneath everything else.

"I am Raelynn Vos," I muttered through the tears I kept choking back. "I don't fucking run."

Sticking with my decision, I hammered against the door. With the click of the lock, tears welled to the edge. When the door swung wide, revealing my mom, I lost the battle, and they spilled over.

"Mom," I cried before flying into her arms just like I had as a little girl.

She held me tight and let me soak her in tears, stroking up and down my back, rocking us back and forth. "I'm right here. Shhh. Shhh."

As soon as there was a break in the tears, the questions came pouring out.

"Why did you marry him?"

"Kenneth?" my mom asked, surprised. "Why would you a—"

"Why did you stay with him for so long?" I didn't have it in me to stop and explain the flood of questions. "Why when he hurt us so much? Was he always that way? Did he change somewhere along the way? Did you see it coming?"

Realization replaced the confusion, followed quickly by acceptance as if she'd been waiting for these questions.

"Raelynn, I didn't think we were supposed to—" my dad's greeting came to a screeching halt when I raised watery eyes to his shocked ones. Behind his glasses, I saw the caring dad who loved me from day one harden into a man ready to do battle. "Who do I need to kill."

"Kenneth," my mom scolded blandly.

"Is it Bodie?" he asked, uncaring of the reprimand. "I'll fucking wipe the floor with that piece of shit."

More tears built over his knight in shining armor dad routine. Unable to get words out, I shook my head.

His brows lowered more while he worked the puzzle out in his mind. Realization dawned. "Shit. Is it Austin?" Disappointment flashed before he hardened again. "Well, then, he can wipe the floor with me, but I'll get enough hits in to make it count."

A garbled laugh choked its way through the tears, watching my dad try to pump himself up like he was about to hop into the ring right there. With a swallow, he relaxed enough to offer a sad smile. "I'm sorry, kiddo. Do you, uh, want to have a drink and talk about it?"

While Dad and I always managed to sneak a joke in here and there to ease the tension in any situation, he still struggled with handling all the "girl stuff," as he called it. But he always tried, and I loved him for it.

"It's okay, Kenneth. I've got this one. We'll be upstairs."

After a slight hesitation, he nodded. "Okay. But let me know when the ass-kicking part is needed."

"Thanks, Dad, but the only ass that needs to be kicked right now is mine." I pressed a quick kiss to his cheek before following my mom upstairs to my room.

"Have a seat," my mom suggested once we entered the room. I almost protested, thinking I'd need to pace, but the past few hours hit me, and I climbed into the mountain of jewel-tone pillows atop my white bed.

"What are you doing?" I asked when my mom went to the closet instead of climbing in beside me. She fell to her knees and shoved clothes aside. "Mom?"

"I'm getting a drink," she answered as if that was supposed to make sense to me.

"From my closet?"

She fell back on her heels with a sigh, giving me a look that said, don't judge me. "I like to come in here to relax and hide away sometimes."

# Blame it on the Vodka

"But you have a sitting room."

"Yeah, but no one thinks to look in here for me."

I laughed at her devious smile, watching her dive back into the closet. "Either way, it's too early for wine."

"Obviously," she scoffed before whirling around, clutching a glass bottle full of clear liquid. "I got the vodka."

"Hah. That's what got me into this mess."

"Hey, don't blame it on the vodka," Mom joked, joining me in the bed. "You don't have to have any if you don't want to, but if we're talking about your father, I'll need a drink."

She produced a glass from the bedside drawer, and it was so absurd, I figured why not join the insanity. "Fuck it. I'll take a drink."

"Atta girl."

She poured two glasses and passed one over. We clinked our drinks together and tossed them back. I tried to hand my glass back to her, but she just refilled it.

"This one is for sipping," she explained. Setting the bottle aside, she leaned back and released a heavy sigh. "So, what do you want to know."

"Everything."

"Rae, I thought we covered this," she said slowly. "Babies are made when a man and wo—"

"Mom! Gross." I shoved her shoulder with mine and laughed. In the chaos of pain consuming so much space inside me, I found a small piece of gratitude. How lucky was I to have parents who knew exactly what to do to make me laugh even in the worst of times?

Our laughter faded out, and we took matching sips from our glass before returning to stare up at the ceiling, lost in thought. Her bracing for impact, and me trying to figure out where to start.

"How did it happen?" I finally asked, shifting my head against the pillow to study her profile.

"Which part?"

"How did you—a woman so strong—end up married to a man like him?"

Her lips pinched as she thought. "He wasn't always that way."

"I know. You've told me that before, but what does it mean? You always stop after that, and I don't get it. Did he just change? I mean, how am I supposed to trust anyone when I'm always worried that they'll end up like him in the long run? How do I...How do I love someone?" I finished quietly. I hadn't even realized that was a question I'd wanted to ask until it came spilling out.

She jerked her matching dark brown gaze to mine, concern and understanding swirling in their depths. "Oh, Raelynn. I'm sorry I never talked about it before. I wanted to protect you from dealing with more than you already had. I never meant to cause you to be scared of letting someone in."

"I'm not sc—" The lie sat on the tip of my tongue. I almost said it, but this was Mom, and I needed a moment of honesty if I wanted to fix anything. So instead of saying anything, I just shrugged.

"I wasn't always so strong," she explained sadly, brushing a strand of hair from my shoulder. "When I met your father, we were in the last few months of college. He was handsome and endearing, with a personality that sucked you in. I came from a modest upbringing, and it was so easy to become enraptured by him. So much so that I blotted out any signs that something darker lurked under the surface. When he lost his temper because some guy stared at me too long? I thought it was romantic because he was jealous and wanted me so much. When he didn't want me to go home so I could stay with him? It was romantic that he couldn't stand to be away from me for a second. When he lost his temper? He explained it was because I made him feel so much passion like he never had before. I was special whereas before I was plain."

"You've never been plain," I cut in. I couldn't imagine the

vibrant, strong woman who taught me everything as anything other than a beacon of hope and love.

"Thank you." She smiled and then paused for another deep breath. "It wasn't always the way you experienced it when you were young, but the signs were always there. I just ignored them because the closer I got to the end of college, the closer I got to going back to the restrictions of my hometown, and I didn't want to. By the time the signs became too big to ignore, I had you, and I somehow needed to make it work. My mother passed away a couple years before, and I had nowhere else to go. He controlled everything, and I figured if I could just bide my time, I could keep him calm, and it would all work out in the end. Then he hurt you, and it was too much."

She looked away before turning back with watery eyes. Hating to watch her cry, I reached between us and held her hand in mine, squeezing tightly.

"I'm so sorry, Raelynn. I should have been stronger. I should have walked away at the first sign. I regret not leaving sooner. I regret ignoring the signs. I regret so much, but I can't regret that it happened because he gave me you, and you are worth everything."

"Mom." Tears burned the backs of my eyes, and holding hands wasn't enough. Rolling to my side, I clutched my arms around her and buried my head against her shoulder just like I did as a little girl. "You don't ever need to apologize. You did the best you could, and look at us now. Two bitches crying in a mansion, drinking high-class vodka you stowed away in a closet."

As intended, we both laughed through our tears, wiping them away like we always did.

"Did…did Austin hurt you?"

Just like that, the reprieve the laughter offered vanished. Now it was her turn to ask questions and my turn to talk.

"No." I rolled to my back. "Not physically. Actually, not at all," I confessed with a sad laugh. "I set it all up. It's me hurting both of us."

"Rae..."

"I just...I always said I wouldn't get married. Even as a girl. I used it as a mantra to build a foundation of my character, and somewhere along the way, it became all I knew. I didn't even question it. It was just who I was."

"Until him."

"Until him," I agreed. "Until he made it feel wrong to not be with him. Until telling him over and over again that I didn't want to be his wife felt...wrong. The whole time I filled out the paperwork for our divorce, my body shook. I assumed it was because I was nervous of losing his friendship, but it was like I had to force myself to do it. Like my body was trying to tell me how wrong it was, but my mind was too conditioned to hear it. I was too focused on the mantra."

"And now?"

"And now I've lost him completely."

"Do you love him?"

"I've always loved him."

"Rae," she chided my easy answer. "Do you love him?"

I closed my eyes to focus on the thudding in my chest. I listened to the useless organ pumping pulse after pulse of pain through my veins. I hated it. But I had to be honest about why it hurt so damn much.

"Yes," I whispered.

"Do you want to be his wife?"

I cringed over the word. My mind gagged while my heart jumped an extra beat.

"Okay, we'll come back to that one," my mom said, reading my face. "Do you think he'd hurt you?"

I didn't even hesitate. "No. Even in the moment of justified anger with other people, he always remained calm. Just a little mouthy."

When Mom didn't respond, I peeked out the corner of my

eye to find the are-you-fucking-kidding-me stare she perfected just for me. "I know someone else who's a little mouthy too."

"Nonsense," I denied.

"Pfft."

I'd heard that sound so many times I didn't even need to look to know an eye roll came with it.

"So, don't answer if you want to be his wife," she said, moving on. "Sometimes making a decision isn't about what you want. It's about what you can't live without. It's easy to walk away from something when you're surrounded by pain and confusion."

"What if nothing *feels* right?" I asked.

"Rarely does any decision feel all good or all bad. So, instead of focusing on the pain right now and doing whatever you need to get away from it, ask yourself if you can live without ever calling him on the phone again. Can you live without your *Bachelor* marathons together? Can you live without meeting up to share disgusting ice cream together? Can you live without dancing with him again? Can you live without holding his hand? Can you live without kissing him—without ever waking up next to him ever again?"

"No." The word escaped on a breath, the truth too big to hold back.

"So, what are you going to do about it?"

*What am I going to do about it?*

The question cambered around my brain, struggling to find purchase, struggling to find an answer. Before I could dwell on it, the door flung open.

Almost jumping out of my skin at the intrusion, I slapped a hand to my chest and looked over to find my two best friends standing at the foot of the bed. Both women stared down at us, clutching our half-full glasses of vodka. They couldn't have looked more different, yet somehow, we all found each other and fell in love so fiercely that they managed to make it here without me even having to call.

"I can't believe you guys are here," I said, tearing up again.

"And miss returning the favor of supporting you through your first heartbreak?" Vera asked.

"You mean, judging her through her heartbreak like she did ours?" Nova joked.

"That too. You do owe us this."

I let out a watery laugh.

"I messaged your dad while we walked up here to call them," Mom explained before holding up her glass. "Vodka?"

Nova's brows rose to her hairline. "Well, at least we know where she gets her love of vodka from."

"She does get it honest." My mom batted her lashes as we sat upright to make room on the bed for the girls. "So, would you like one?"

"How bad is it?" Vera asked.

My mom hissed a breath in through her teeth and winced. "It's been a rough morning."

"Might as well," Nova answered first with a shrug.

Both Vera and I looked over with wide eyes. "Wow, Parker is having a bad influence on you. You used to hesitate at least a second before accepting a drink at any time of day. Let alone one before noon."

"Meh, it's more like the whole band is having a bad influence on me," she explained, accepting her drink.

"Oh, I bet." I waited until she started to take a sip before asking, "Any five-ways lately."

As expected, she choked on her sip. Vera and I broke down laughing. "That's gross," Nova grumbled.

"C'mon, Naughty Nova. Spill all the deets," I cajoled. She gave an unamused stare that only made me smile harder. "Still my sweet Nova."

"All right," Vera cut in. "Don't try to focus on us. Spill."

I looked from one person to the next for an out. When I didn't find one, I released a heavy sigh and gave in, going over it all. I opted to leave Bodie out of the equation because we had enough to focus on.

And I wasn't ready to admit what had happened to anyone. Least of all, my mom. I just…couldn't.

By the time I reached the end, three pairs of unblinking eyes watched my every reaction.

"Well…" Vera asked.

"She was about to tell me what she was going to do about it before you got here," my mom explained.

"And?" Nova asked.

"I don't know."

"Yes, you do," my mom assured. "You're a smart woman. Now, close your eyes and trust your gut. Not your mind, but your gut."

As uncomfortable as it seemed to close my eyes while three people watched, I did as she said. I thought about all the things I didn't want to live without. My friendship with Austin flashed behind my closed lids like a highlight reel. I remembered every time he was there for me. I remembered all the times he stood up for me. I remembered all the times we laughed. I remembered every time he'd be the one to go with me on any adventure I wanted.

I remembered the way he kissed me, the way he held my hand. I remembered the way he looked at me like nothing else existed. I remembered the way he made love to me.

"I want him," I admitted, opening my eyes. I hadn't meant to say it out loud, but there was no way to keep it in. "I want him so much it hurts. And I can't not have all those things."

"Then you know your answer, and you can call being married to him whatever you like. You could be his missus, his woman, or even his consort."

"Mom," I laughed.

"His partner," Vera chimed in.

"His uxor," Nova added.

"What the fuck is uxor?" I asked, thoroughly confused. But she didn't get a chance to answer because they kept going.

"His dame," Vera crooned.

"His other half," Nova exclaimed.

"More like his better half," I joked.

"Whatever you want to call it," my mom cut in before we lost control. "Just have *it* with him."

*It.* What was *it* for us? At the baseline, I guessed I would be his wife, but it didn't sit right. It didn't sound like a word to describe what we had between us when we had so much more.

"His friend," I said softly, adding my own ideas to the list. "His love."

Three hands rested on me—my hand, my knee, and my shoulder. All of them supporting me.

"You know what to do," my mom encouraged.

"I need to go to him."

"Yes," Vera agreed. "But maybe wash your face first. Your mascara is smeared…" She paused, gesturing all over her face. "Here."

"And one more drink," my mom said.

"Here, here," we shouted in unison.

Even if things didn't work out with Austin, which created a crater in my being that wanted to swallow me whole, looking around at these women, I knew I'd be okay.

I just wanted to be more than okay. I wanted to be all the names they said and so much more. I wanted to be Austin's everything, and I wanted him to be mine.

But first, a drink.

## Chapter Twenty-Eight

### AUSTIN

"So, should I have brought ice cream and a Taylor Swift CD or what?" King asked, looking me up and down.

"Fuck you," I muttered with a scowl before heading back to my spot on the couch. He could make himself at home, I was in no mood to entertain a guest. I wanted to sit on this single cushion until it swallowed me into oblivion.

"Thanks for the offer, but I'm good." He closed the door behind him and followed, falling onto the other side of the couch. "Besides, you and Rae have been going at it like bunnies. There's no room for anymore fucking."

"Not anymore."

"Ohhhhh. The moping, calling off from work, and not answering the phone makes more sense now."

I didn't bother responding, instead glared while I grabbed a beer from the floor and popped the tab.

"So testy," he joked.

"If you're going to mock me, then get the fuck out."

"Nah, I think I'll stay."

"If you're going to say I told you so, then get the fuck out."

"C'mon, Austin. I should get at least one I told you so."

This time I bared my teeth when I glared. He held up his hands in surrender and settled back, not looking like he planned to go anywhere for a while. I wanted to demand he leave—to let me wallow in my misery alone, but I was too fucking tired. Everything ached even though I'd done nothing but come back to my empty apartment and sit on my couch.

I couldn't bring myself to go back in the bedroom. I couldn't go back to where everything imploded. The memory of her tears was permanently embedded behind my eyes and haunted me even though I tried to avoid it by sleeping on the couch. No matter where I went, her announcement of already having filed for divorce followed me like a shadow, and I was terrified I'd never be rid of it.

Each knock at the door, each ping of an incoming email, left me shaking on the edge of a cliff, wondering if it was the papers being delivered—the final shove that toppled me down. Part of me wanted to get it over with, to put me out of my misery, to just fucking end this. Maybe the clean break would allow me to heal.

I doubted it, but it was the only hope I had right then.

"Okay, bro. Talk to me."

"Nothing to talk about," I answered before downing half my drink.

"Says the man clutching a beer like it's the last one he'll ever have, despite the case sitting next to him, while he stares at a blank TV screen."

Like nails on a chalkboard, his depiction scraped along my solitude, forcing me to acknowledge him—to acknowledge everything when all I wanted to do was hide away. "What the fuck, King?" I snapped, slamming my bottle on the coffee table and unleashing the full swell of my emotions on the only available target. "What do you want me to say? That I fucked up? That you were right? That Rae didn't want to be married to anyone, and now I've got fucking nothing? Huh? You wanna hear how you were right when you said she'd break me? Because I am. I'm mother-fucking-broken."

My chest heaved like I'd run a marathon while King sat back with wide eyes under pinched brows. I waited for him to lash out, to shout back and tell me to fuck off with my misplaced anger. But he didn't. He remained calm, despite my verbal assault, and his lack of reaction sucked all the fight out of me.

I dropped my head to my hands and fisted my hair, trying anything to relieve the headache that took up residence as soon as Rae left.

"For what it's worth, I'm fucking sorry," he finally said.

"Me, too."

"Wanna tell me what happened?"

"Not really."

"Wanna pass me a beer and tell me anyways?"

I pulled myself up and glared but grabbed a beer and passed it to him. We each took a sip, and then I laid it all out. All of it except the part about her past and Bodie. I knew how much Rae didn't want anyone to know what she'd gone through. While I wanted her to shout it to the world, smear his name, and let everyone know she survived, it wasn't my choice.

Although, I still planned to visit Bodie and give him a taste of his own medicine and more. She may not have plans to destroy him, but I fucking did.

By the time I finished with how I stormed out after demanding she be gone, King had finished his beer and shook his head. "Shit, Austin. I'm sorry. For what it's worth, I didn't want to be right."

"Yeah. I didn't want you to be right either."

He had the decency to wince. "So, what now?"

The million-dollar question.

Now, I sat there and hated myself forever and ever. Now, I lived with regret for the rest of my life. Now, I wondered how many beers it would take before even a modicum of this ache eased. Not that I said any of that, unwilling to bare the raw parts of my soul for consumption.

"Now, it's fucking Monday, and I'll watch *The Bachelor* alone because I can't go over there like I usually do. I'm the guy that watches *The Bachelor* alone because it gives me at least some connection to her."

"You could always not watch it," he offered gently. "I mean, the screen is already blank. Why not just keep it that way?"

I glared like his suggestion was the greatest insult.

"Or not."

"It's not the point," I explained. "I want to watch it *with her*. I want to go to her house, have pizza and beer, and make fun of everyone. I want to watch her laugh and then take her to bed. I want my friend. I want *my wife*."

I wanted every last single part of it. It was how I got into this mess in the first place. My greed took over, and I wanted more and more even though I knew she might not be able to admit she wanted it, too. I kept pushing, and now I was left with nothing.

"Could you...be friends?" King offered, but I could tell even he didn't believe it was an option.

"How the fuck would I do that?"

"I don't...I don't have a good answer for that."

"I figured. Which leads me back to the plan I thought was a good one before we went to my grandparents. I said I'd back off if it didn't work out."

"Yeah..."

"But the problem is that I don't want to back off. I'm standing back after storming away, looking at both options with the experience of going through it, and I don't like it. I fucking hate it. The problem is that I was a dumbass for thinking I'd rather be without her than only be her friend again. I was so damned mad before, wanting to shove it all away and make it not true. All I am now is sad, and I hate it."

"Then go be her friend," he suggested like it was as simple as saying five little words.

"How?"

"Act like you did before Vegas, I guess."

I laughed. "I'm not sure I know how the hell to do that."

"I sure as shit don't know either, but all you can do is try. All you can do is show up and do your best to leave all this behind. You can't go in clinging to these past few months, hoping it will come back. You have to go in knowing it's only for friendship."

"Yeah," I agreed, but it lacked any conviction.

I knew he was right, but it didn't make it easy. However, the alternative was even harder. My chest ached with shards of pain prodding against every organ, but at least one small part around my heart avoided the jabs, holding tight to the idea of seeing her.

"So, you going to go over and give it a try? It is *Bachelor* night."

I closed my eyes and imagined showing up with pizza and her favorite wine. I imagined her wearing another small top and tight jeans.

I imagined dropping it all to pull her in my arms, only for her to pull back before I could get too close. What if she didn't want me there. What if she decided she didn't want to be friends after the way I kicked her out?

Doubts plagued every thought until they piled on so high I couldn't move.

"Not yet," I answered like the chicken I was. "I'll make a better plan tomorrow. Maybe an extra day of space will be good."

"Whatever you say, man. Either way, I'm not watching *The Bachelor* with you."

I gave him a side-eyed stare as I turned on the TV and started the show.

With his every grunt and question about the contestants, I missed Rae more, locking in the peace of mind, knowing I was making the right choice.

Like I said before everything happened. I'd take a lifetime of friendship over nothing at all. And I'd tell her tomorrow.

If she'd let me.

## Chapter Twenty-Nine

### RAELYNN

After more than our fair share of drinks and a night to sleep it all off, I finally made my way home. If I moved quickly, I figured I could shower and get ready before grabbing dinner from Austin's favorite restaurant and surprise him with it. If nothing else, I could order a pint of ice cream and bring it to him.

"You don't need to bring anything but yourself," I muttered as I unlocked my door.

But I wanted to. Just something to show I made an extra step. It was *Bachelor* night, and I couldn't think of a better time to show up like everything was normal. Maybe I could confuse him enough to give myself some time to talk quickly. And if he ended up slamming the door in my face, he'd at least have to think of me while he ate whatever I left for him. I'd take any win I could get.

I was so consumed with my plan that I didn't notice anything off when I opened my door. I didn't notice the man standing just inside, waiting for me. Before I could react, he gripped my wrist and jerked me inside, slamming me back against the door to close it. I looked up and met cold, blue eyes.

"Bodie." I tried to spit his name, but it lacked any power from my breathless lungs.

His lips curled into a sneer that washed over me like a bucket of ice water dripping from my head to my toes. I watched in horror as he yanked the keys from my weak grip and shoved them in the special top lock by my head, locking us both inside before tossing them across the room. Bile churned in my stomach, watching them disappear under the couch.

He chuckled. "Don't worry, Raelynn. You won't need those. It's just you and me for however long I say."

The stench of putrid alcohol burned my nostrils, and I jerked back, hitting my head against the door. I refused to flinch, instead lifting my chin in challenge. His eyes always reminded me of a barren blizzard, but they looked even more haunting with the dark circles and bloodshot corneas.

I tried to twist my way out from the door but didn't make it far before he slammed me back, pressing his weight into me and slipping his hand around my throat. "You won't pick up my calls, so here I am, and you're going to fucking listen to everything I have to say."

"Fuck you, Bodie."

He squeezed painfully tight, baring his teeth like an animal. I watched him, unable to remember why I ever found him attractive in the first place. Although the patchy stubble shading his hollowed cheeks wasn't there when I first met him.

"Maybe I'll let you fuck me later. *Maybe*. I know you've been with that low-class fuck, Austin, and who knows who else you've whored yourself out to."

"I'd rather stitch my vagina closed than ever have sex with you again."

"Don't worry, I'll just fuck your filthy mouth."

I was like Pavlov's dog, automatically reacting in fear from months of training. But I needed to remember my time with Austin and how he built me up. I needed to remember the woman I'd created before Bodie—the one who didn't take shit from anyone. I copied him and bared my teeth, letting him know he wasn't the only animal in the room. Even if mine was a false bravado in a desperate attempt to cover up the tremors shaking me from the inside out.

"You, my fucking slut, have cost me a job."

"You cost yourself a job by making promises you couldn't keep." I almost added that he did the same thing to me when he promised me I'd scream his name, and I never did, but while I wanted to be strong, I also wanted to make it out of this intact.

"Well, if you would have supported your boyfriend and put in a good word with Daddy, none of this would have happened. So, here's what we're going to do. You're going to take me back, and we're going to get married. Daddy will have to help his son-in-law out."

"Ha," I shouted. "I don't fucking think so."

"Goddammit," he screamed, finally making me flinch when he raised his fist to slam it down against the door inches from my head.

I turned my cheek, trying to avoid the bad breath from his angry pants. As if on a wild pendulum, his demeanor softened along with his voice, but this alternative only infused me with more fear.

My muscles contracted, trying to pull in on themselves to avoid the hand dragging down my neck, over my breast, curving around my hip to grip my ass. "Or maybe, I'll fuck a baby inside you. Then you'll really be stuck."

The mere mention of sex with him—of having his baby—left me lightheaded. Panic compressed in on my chest, creeping up my throat. I needed to get out of here. I needed to...*Fuck.* I could barely focus.

Out of the corner of my eye, my purse lay on the floor a few feet away. If I could break free just long enough to grab it and run, it would buy me time to call for help. With a few deep breaths, I recalled enough self-defense training from college and acted.

Jerking my head upright, I muttered, "Fuck you, Bodie." I slammed my forehead into his face, kneed him in the balls, and gripped his wrist, torquing it to bring him to his knees, and then I ran.

I snatched my purse and immediately turned to leave but remembered the missing keys. "Fuck," I hissed. My mind scrambled through places to hide that would give me the most time.

I grabbed my phone out of my purse and pressed the buttons to call my emergency contact, not even remembering who it was until Austin's name appeared on the screen. Relief washed over me only to be followed by dread. What if he didn't pick up?

One ring.

With Bodie still clutching his groin, I held tight to my phone and made a break for it.

Two rings.

I focused on my bedroom door and made a plan. I'd lock it, and then I'd lock the bathroom door before barricading myself in my closet. Hopefully, three doors would be enough.

Three rings.

If Austin picked up.

Four ri—

Before the fourth ring could even complete, a hand latched around my ankle and jerked my feet out from under me. I smacked the ground, each point of collision sending its own thudding vibration through my bones. I took the brunt of the fall with my hands and cried out, pain shooting from my wrist up my arm.

Fingers dug into my legs, and I squirmed to break free, but it was useless. The fall knocked the wind from my lungs, and the room spun, making me wonder if I'd hit my head. I didn't even hear the ringing anymore.

## Blame it on the Vodka

*I didn't even hear the ringing anymore.*

I forced myself to ignore Bodie, pinning me to the ground, and looked for my phone. I caught sight of it less than two feet away—still connected.

"Austin," I shouted.

"Rae?"

His voice was faint but there. Unfortunately, it caught Bodie's attention too. I reached for it, but he lunged, beating me before I had the chance to even try.

"You fucking bitch," he growled.

Before he could hang up, I shouted out the most pertinent information, hoping Austin would understand. "Bodie. My apartment. Help. Police. Crazy."

"Nice try, Raelynn, but it's just you and me. Douchebag Austin isn't going to come save you. If he does show up, you're going to be a good girl and tell him you're done with him and that you're with me now. Or else, I'll fucking kill you. I'll kill your whole fucking family."

"You're too weak, Bodie. My grandma could fight you off."

The smack of his hand against my face registered before the pain did. In the year I'd managed to stay with him, not once had he actually hit me. I wasn't sure I'd ever been hit in the face. With the way the world turned black at the edges and fire exploded along my cheek, burning its way through my skull, I never wanted it to happen again.

But I also needed to create enough time for Austin to get here.

"What do you think will happen, Bodie? You're not always going to have a big fish to bring in. *If* you managed to sign my dad over to the sleazy lawyers you worked for, you'd have to keep him. You'd have to bring in more."

"I would," he proclaimed. "Once I had your dad, they would all come crawling. All I need is one."

"And if they don't?"

"Then you can help me get more. You can use your tits to sign them on. I can parade you around and maybe even let them play with you a bit as a signing bonus."

My stomach convulsed, and I prepared to spew vomit. It was too much.

I couldn't stand another second under his weight. Despite knowing I hadn't wasted enough time for Austin to get here, I gave in, spewing my words instead of vomit. "I'd rather fucking die, you trashy piece of shit."

"You dumb fucking bitch."

He adjusted his weight to gain leverage for another blow. When he moved, it left enough room for me to take my chance at freedom. I shoved him off and scrambled to my feet, preparing to run.

Except, I barely made it two steps before he gripped my ankle all over again. This time sending me flying headfirst into the end table.

Right before I hit, all I could think about was how I hoped the girls let Austin know how much I loved him.

## Chapter Thirty

### AUSTIN

*Austin.*
 *Bodie. My apartment.*
 *Help.*

The last words she said to me played on repeat over and over again. They mixed with the beeps from the various machines until I thought I'd go insane. If they weren't the only things letting me know the love of my life—my best friend—was okay, I'd smash them all for even a second of silence.

I leaned forward, resting my elbows on the edge of the bed, digging my fingers through my hair, recalling the frozen panic sliding through my veins when I picked up her call. When I saw her name on my screen, I hadn't known what to brace for. Hell, I almost didn't answer, scared she was calling to tell me off since she never got the chance before I kicked her out. I waited until right before it went to voicemail, holding my breath—bracing for impact, but there was no preparing for her shrill cries for help. King had just left, and I'd thankfully stopped drinking. However, even sober, I knew there wasn't a chance in hell I'd make it to her on time.

Bodie's growled slur had been the last thing I heard before the line went dead, the silence slapping me into action.

As much as I'd wanted to be the one to kick down the door and beat him to a bloody fucking pulp, I couldn't take the chance and called nine-one-one, praying for a miracle.

"Austin?"

The soft scratch of her voice calling my name slid across the bed and around my heart, squeezing until I feared it would burst. Releasing the death grip on my hair, I looked up into Raelynn's stunning brown eyes, grateful for the chance to see them again.

When I stormed into her apartment, finding her limp body being loaded on a stretcher, time stood still, filling it up with every memory and every dream I'd never get to experience with her again. Starting with the first time she met my gaze across the room at a crowded frat house.

"You weren't here earlier," she murmured, sleep clinging to her words. She blinked, her soft lips pulling down into a pout. Raelynn could pretend pout like a pro, but this one tugged at the corners of her eyes.

As if my absence truly hurt her.

As if I hadn't been the world's biggest asshole and kicked her out of my life.

Maybe she had amnesia, and they forgot to tell me.

I didn't know, but I didn't want to remind her what a dick I'd been. Knowing I didn't deserve it, I latched onto her sincerity and offered an apologetic smile.

"I'm sorry I wasn't here. I had to meet with the police."

When I'd finally made it to Rae's apartment, the police had already broken down the door and apprehended Bodie. Which was probably good because I'd been ready to pummel him since the first day I met him. The entire drive, I imagined —in extensive detail—all the ways I wanted to beat him to a bloody fucking pulp. Then I walked in, taking in the decorations shattered on the floor, the blood spilled on the carpet, and her unconscious body, and nothing I imagined came close to how I wanted to torture him to the point of begging for death just to revive him and do it again.

Blinding rage slid down my spine, shrinking my sight to nothing but him, and I charged. It took three officers almost as big as me to hold me back, and I still kept trying to get to him. He looked like shit, sitting there crying in his wrinkled and tattered suit. I wanted to rip him limb from limb. I wanted to break every single bone in his body slowly. It wasn't until the paramedic asked me if I knew any information about Rae that I finally stopped my fight.

"I'm her husband."

*The woman blinked, looking to Bodie and then back to me, probably imagining some soap opera drama, before asking if I wanted to ride to the hospital with my wife.*

"Yes," I answered without a second of hesitation. Before I followed them out, I turned back to Bodie. "So help me, God, if you even think of her ever again, I'll find a way to send you to the worst hell hole of a prison, and then I'll find the biggest motherfucker there and have him kick your ass every goddamn day until you wished you were dead. Understood?"

*I hadn't waited for an answer from the sniveling cunt. Rae needed me. She'd needed me before, and I hadn't been there because of my pride. I wasn't going to* not *be there now.*

A soft hand on mine brought me back to the present. I stared as her slim, delicate fingers curled over my rough, larger ones, wondering if I imagined it. I expected her to thank me for being there but then ask me to leave. I deserved for her to repeat my words back to me from that morning, telling me to get out. I'd planned on begging her to forgive me, and yet, she clung to my hand like she needed me.

"I was here when they brought you in, too, before they called me away."

"They told me. I'm just glad you're here now," she confessed.

How the hell had I ever thought I could never see her again? How the hell had I even considered a life without her friendship? How the hell had I gotten so lucky that she'd be glad I was there with her after everything I said? How the hell had I been graced with this second chance to make it right?

I looked her over, reminding myself she was okay—or as okay as she could be with fractured ribs, a concussion, and more than a few bumps and bruises. The dark split on her lip was the only mark she wore of this nightmare. I hated it. I hated looking at it. But then it ceased to exist when her lips tipped into the most beautiful smile that tugged and pulled at my heart until it hurt.

My love ached inside my chest because I knew I couldn't give it to her. Every part of me wanted to turn my hand and hold hers in mine. I wanted to kiss the tips of each finger, making it all better. But I couldn't—not anymore. Not even like I would have as her friend before Vegas.

Before, I would have held her hand and smacked a kiss against every cut until she laughed. If I did that now, we'd both remember all the times I kissed her when we weren't friends.

So, what did I do?

Did I hold her hand?

Or did I not?

If I wanted to be in her life, I had to make sure she knew I would never push for more than she was willing to give. The problem was that I didn't know how to go back? Now that we'd crossed the line, how did we go back to being just friends?

"Can I get you anything?" I asked, the question croaking past my tight throat. I needed to distract myself from the inner turmoil pulling me apart.

"Ugh," she groaned, rolling her eyes. "They gave me dinner when I woke up a few hours ago, but it was gross. Even the pudding."

She scrunched her nose, apparently not struggling with the situation like I was. Maybe she did have amnesia. Maybe that was why she slid into the role of my playful best friend like the past two days didn't exist.

As confused as her reaction left me, I again decided not to question it. Maybe this was the opening we needed, and I wasn't going to be stupid or prideful enough to turn it down.

Already knowing what she hated about it, I played along. "What flavor?"

"Vanilla." She sneered the word as if the flavor was as offensive as a pile of shit.

"How dare they?" I gasped.

"I know," she exclaimed. "Everyone knows chocolate is the only way to go."

"We'll make sure the manager hears about this."

Her soft laughter blotted out the beeping that had put me on edge earlier, sinking between the cracks of my heart. The need to brush her hair back from where it covered her shoulder, lean forward, and gently feast from the perfect curve of her lips bubbled so close to the surface that I almost acted without thinking. I imagined if I had followed through and the thought of her pulling back with a look of confusion, rejecting what came so natural, rattled me.

Back and forth, back and forth. My faith that we could make this work—that we could be just friends—swayed on unsteady ground, leaving me with doubt and questions pressing in.

I needed to get out, if only for a second, to regroup. I needed space to add these new interactions into the future I was trying to imagine for us. When I talked to King, I only had our friendship, pre-Vegas, to build from. We could do that. I could lock my feelings up like I had before. It would take time, but if she let me, we could make it the same.

Now, I had to factor in our friendship with the weight of post-Vegas dragging behind every action and every word.

Now, I had to factor in the way she'd looked at me and knowing it meant more. Now my feelings had blossomed into something too big to fit in the same box as before. They clambered for freedom, and I needed out of that room to try to compose a new box.

I rose from the chair, hating the instant her hand no longer touched mine but knowing it was for the best. "You know, I saw a vending machine down by the waiting area. Want me to get you a Reese's and Dr. Pepper?"

Her whole face lit up as if I offered to get her a trip around Europe instead of a simple candy bar. "Really?"

"Yeah," I laughed. "I'll be right back."

"Austin," she called just before I walked out.

"Yeah?"

She hesitated, taking her time. "Thank you."

Two simple words filled with more meaning than thanking a friend for getting a snack. Continuing with meaning so much more than was said, I returned one word of my own.

"Anything."

Even if we fell apart after this, all she had to do was call, and I'd be there for anything.

My pacing steps echoed around the empty hall while I took deep breath after deep breath, refocusing my mind to the friend she needed. I could do this. I *wanted* to do this. Even if it was hard or it hurt. Pre-Vegas or post-Vegas, Raelynn Vos would always be my friend.

When I made it back to her room, a nurse stood by her bed checking her vitals. She gave me a bored assessment before focusing back on Rae. I hated how small and fragile she looked against the stark white sheets of the hospital bed with the large machines towering around her.

"Sorry, sir. Visiting hours are almost over, so you'll have to leave soon."

I flicked my gaze to Rae, looking for direction. I hadn't thought about visiting hours when I told her parents I'd stay with her tonight. I'd have to call them to come back. I couldn't leave her alone. Not tonight.

"I'll just drop these off. Is it okay if I wait for her mom to get here before I go?"

"Listen..." the nurse sighed. I was sure she'd worked enough night shifts to last her a lifetime and didn't have the patience to deal with another pushy visitor.

I braced for the denial, but Rae blindsided me out of left field. "He's my husband. Is he not allowed to stay with me?"

A soft breeze could have knocked me on my ass. Had Rae actually ever called me her husband? Out loud? To another person?

And she hadn't even cringed or stumbled through it.

*My husband. My husband.*

I wanted her to say it again so I could record it and listen on repeat like some lovesick teenage girl.

*Jesus*, what the fuck was wrong with me?

I blinked, shaking myself back to reality. There I was, mentally ordering monogrammed towels and planning our family photo while she would have called me Jesus himself if it meant I stayed over her mom, who was bound to smother her with love and concern.

It didn't mean anything. I needed to remind myself of that if I wanted to make it.

"Of course," she answered Rae, barely offering me an annoyed side-eye. "If you need to sleep, the chair folds out in a cot. Although, it'll probably only hold half of you."

Rae snorted. "I can't wait to see him try."

This time the nurse laughed with her. Once she finished up, she offered me good luck and left us alone. I handed Rae her treats and retook my seat on the edge of the chair by the bed.

She hummed her pleasure with the first bite into the candy. "God, that's so good."

Just like that, my mind flashed to the last time she made

that noise and told me how good I made her feel. I wanted to growl and smack my head to knock the memory free. Not that I wanted to get rid of it either. I just needed to find a safe space to keep it locked away—to keep it from bursting free to instigate a yearning I didn't know how to get rid of. How was I supposed to go back when I'd already had her?

I had no fucking clue, but the one thing I did know was that I had to try. I'd fucked up kicking her out. I fucked up even more when I didn't fix my mistake as soon as I knew I made it, and she paid for it. I knew I would spend the rest of my life trying to make up for not being there for her.

Even if it meant giving her the space she'd craved her entire life. As much as I wanted to hold her to me and never let go, I knew Rae craved her freedom.

"Listen, Rae, if you only want me to stay until you fall asleep, that's fine. Just let me know when you want me to le—"

"No." She reached past the edge of the bed for my hand.

I stared down at the white-knuckled grip before looking up to find wide eyes holding a whole storm of emotions. A hell of a lot more than the simple smiles she had when she first woke up.

"Please don't leave me."

Again, the words sounded so simple, especially after the trauma of the day, which I had no doubt would plague her for a while. But being scared because she was attacked was something Rae would handle with her chin held high, denying any and all fear whether she felt it or not.

This was different. This had nothing to do with Bodie. The only thing left was me—*us*.

All over again, guilt crashed against me, stirring my stomach into knots. I'd been so determined to save myself from the repeated jabs of pain that I missed the knife I stabbed into my own back. And that knife twisted each time I saw that same pain reflected in her gaze.

I rested our hands on the bed between us and settled,

letting her know I wasn't going anywhere. Looking down to where she held onto me, I took a deep breath, needing to get at least one thing off my chest. "I'm sorry I wasn't there tonight," I muttered so low I wasn't sure if she heard me. But then her hand tightened in mine, and I knew she had. "I should have been there."

She didn't say a word as she shifted, staying silent until I met her dark eyes. "It's not your fault, Austin."

I winced at her easy dismissal of my part in this. "It was our night to watch *The Bachelor*. I should have been there."

"And I should have never let Bodie into my life," she countered.

"This isn't your fault," I snapped, ready to fight her if she dared try to take the blame for Bodie's actions. "You have no idea the man he was, and you never would have let him in if you did. You're too strong."

"Exactly." With one word, she knocked the wind from my sails. "It's not my fault, and it's not yours. Bodie did this."

I met her gaze, weary but so strong. Every day she amazed me all over again with another facet of her personality. Even now, with a slow blink, a new emotion rolled across her face, pulling me in.

"I was so ashamed, Austin," she whispered.

Her confession pierced my heart, and I ached for her. I *hated* the way she looked away. Before I could correct her, she held up her hand and continued.

"I know it wasn't right. I know it wasn't my fault, but it's the one thing I never wanted. It's the one thing I swore from when I was a little girl that I would never get caught up in. Hell, I even denied the thought of marriage just to avoid this. I'd done everything to avoid it." She laughed softly. "Yet, somehow it happened. Even now, I'm not sure how it happened. It was like the first few times happened so fast, and he was so quick to apologize that I was left wondering if I'd imagined it. Then it went further and further until I couldn't brush it off. But I'd already allowed so much to happen it left me questioning myself. It left me wondering if I was as strong as I said. He crept in and stole a crucial piece of my confidence, and I began to wonder if anyone would believe it or if they'd think I was being dramatic for the publicity. He'd broken me down enough that I believed him when he rolled his eyes and said no one would care about a bruise or two. I believed him when he said my father would be disappointed if I cried wolf when there were women who were heavily abused."

"I'm so sorry I didn't see it earlier, Rae."

"I didn't let you. I was so embarrassed—*ashamed*. I wondered if you guys would believe me because I was the strong Raelynn Vos, the maneater. I was the last person who should have ended up in an abusive relationship. I guess I didn't want to lose the way you looked at me. I didn't want you to see me as the weak woman I'd become."

"You were never weak," I assured, but she stared down at her lap. "Look at me." I waited for her to raise her gaze to mine, pouring every ounce of strength I had behind my words to make her believe them. "You. Are. *Not*. Weak. You survived, and I'm in awe of your strength."

"Thank you," she said with a soft smile. "I realize that now. Thanks to you reminding me."

"How did I do that?"

"Just the way you look at me. As if I'm on top of the world."

Because that's where she always stood in my eyes. It was where she would always be. Even if I wanted more, I couldn't hurt her anymore. Even if she shot me down, I had to buck up and let her know I couldn't not be her friend—*just her friend*—if she'd have me.

Turning my hand in hers, I gave in and held onto her, using my other hand to gently trace the veins until she relaxed, realizing I wasn't going anywhere.

"Do you remember the first time you came up to me at that frat party?"

Her face softened as she relaxed against the pillows, but she didn't let go of my hand. She laughed gently but still watched me cautiously, not understanding where I was going with this. "How could I forget? You were the first—and only—guy to turn me down."

I hadn't been sure what I planned to accomplish with this walk down memory lane, but once I started, I figured it out, realizing the confession I needed to make. I needed to let her know how much she meant to me, so she knew I couldn't ever walk away. With a deep inhale, I prepared to share the secret I'd carried with me all these years.

"Raelynn, I've loved you from that very moment." Her brows rose high. "That's why I wouldn't sleep with you. I saw how special and bold and unique you were even from across the room. And when you came close, it was like being able to stand beside the sun. I knew I would always need more than a one-night stand."

"Austin," she whispered, her eyes growing wet.

But I couldn't stop, worried that if I did, I'd never finish, and I was so damn tired of pretending I didn't love her. And I could never watch her beg me to stay again. I never wanted to make her question my friendship.

"You're my friend, Raelynn Vos. My best friend. And I'll always be here. Even if I'm not your husband anymore—I'm still here. It was wrong of me to force it. I never want to make you feel trapped because you'll end up hating me for it. So, if being your friend is what you'll allow me to be, then I will gladly stand by your side. I just can't not have you in my life. So, send me whatever papers you want, and I'll sign them."

"No," she said, her voice cracking.

Tears built on her lashes before spilling over. I wanted to wipe them away, but I couldn't move, the two letters holding me frozen. Had she decided she didn't even want my friendship either? Had I read this all wrong?

"No, Austin Caldwell," she said, brushing her own tears away. "I want you to throw the papers away."

"What?" I asked softly, too scared to think what her words meant.

"Burn them. Shred them, Ruin them. I don't care. I love you too, and I'm sorry it took me so long to admit it. I'm sorry I was so scared. I'm sorry I tried to push you away. I'm sor—"

The words reached across the space between us, holding me in their grasp, and yanked me across the bed. I leaned over, burying my hand into her hair and not wasting a second before latching on to her lips. I needed her. "Say it again," I ordered, barely pulling up for a second of air.

"I love you. I don't care that this is unconventional. I love you, and we can make it work."

"Are you serious?" I asked, too scared to believe my ears. "We can get it annulled and try it the right way?"

"Fuck the right way," she said, laughing against my mouth. "When have I ever done anything the right way?"

I smiled slowly. "I can think of a few things you do exactly the right way."

"Oh yeah, and what is that?"

"Beg."

"I would never dare beg," she gasped between pressing kisses anywhere she could reach.

"Oh, you do for me. So beautifully."

"Only for you. Always."

Fuck, I loved the sound of that. I knew I'd always love her. I just never thought I'd be lucky enough to have her always love me in return. I wasn't sure what I'd done in life to deserve her, but I did know how we got here.

We blamed it on the vodka.

# Epilogue

### RAELYNN

"All you have to do is say the words, and we can make a break for it," Nova said, tucking a stray piece of my hair back in place.

"I can distract them with Camila's adorableness while Nova gets the getaway car," Vera jumped in.

"Yup," Nova agreed. "You don't have to go through with it."

I laughed, taking in the two stunning women I loved like sisters. They studied me with shrewd eyes, dressed in beautiful black dresses, looking ready to karate chop anyone's head off if they dared try to stop me from running—if I wanted to run.

"Thanks, you badass bitches. But I'm kind of already married to him. I'm not sure running now will do anything."

"True," Vera agreed.

"But still...we'd find a way to get you out of it," Nova promised just as Austin and the other guys came up.

"Are you trying to kidnap my wife?" he asked.

"A girl has to have options," Nova explained.

"I'm not sure it's called kidnapping if she wants to go," Vera defended.

Austin raised a questioning brow and gave a pondering look

for all of two seconds before he growled, making me laugh. "No, I don't want to go," I assured, stepping into his open arms.

"Good."

I raised my mouth for a kiss, stealing them every chance I could get. How had I been around him for so many years and missed out on his delectable mouth? I had to make up for lost time.

"Besides, where would I go? I'd be lost before I hit the end of the driveway."

"And you don't know how to drive stick shift, which is the only thing up here on the farm."

"I don't know, I think I was getting the hang of it last week," I defended.

Austin barked a laugh. "I think you might have wrecked the engine. Thank god we got a rental instead of driving Grandpa's classic."

"Let's try the classic next time," I said, batting my lashes.

"You're lucky I love you," he grumbled.

"You're lucky we like you," Vera cut in, looking damned scary despite the chubby baby on her hip with a fistful of her hair.

"Yeah," Nova agreed. "You may already be married, but if you hurt our girl, we'll mess you up."

Vera gave Nova a confused glance.

"I can't swear in front of Camila."

Vera passed Camila to Nico and went toe to toe with Austin. "If you hurt her," she started in a deathly quiet tone, "I'll fucking skin you alive."

Austin swallowed audibly before nodding. "Yes, ma'am."

I smiled like a proud mama at Vera's terrifying threat until Nico cut in.

"If you hurt her, we'll never hear the end about how she was right about marriage all along," he deadpanned.

"You love me," I said with exaggerated sweetness.

"Who would have thought," Nova said, curling up to Parker's side, "all three of us—married."

"Does this mean no more wild nights out?" Vera asked.

"God, I hope so," Nova said.

"Nah. I've got plenty more party left in me."

"Which is wilder?" Parker asked. "A night out with a rock star or a night out with Rae?"

In unison, everyone said, "Rae."

"You're welcome," I responded with a bow.

"Speaking of a night out, did you ever hear from Oren?" Nova asked.

Parker's brows furrowed. "No. Not yet. Brogan and Ash are looking for him."

"They'll find him," I added. Nova had let us know that she may need to leave early. Apparently, Parker got a phone call from the rest of the band that their fun-loving drummer, Oren, had gone missing last night after an argument. "And if you need to leave, we understand. No worries."

"No way," Parker objected. "There's no way I'm making Nova leave her best friend's wedding because Oren is being a baby."

"Besides, shouldn't we be getting this show on the road?" Nico asked, looking at his watch?

Parker looked at his before glaring at Nico. "Nah. I think we could wait a couple more hours before we get to the actual I dos."

"Uhhh…" Austin looked between the two. "We kind of have a schedule to follow."

"Yeah, but we could push it until at least five, right?" Parker asked.

"No, *Parker*," Nico said. "It's set for before five."

"Okay, what the fuck is going on?" I asked.

Vera rolled her eyes. "We made a bet on if you'd actually have a wedding or not, and these two idiots picked the same day, so we made them pick a time. Obviously, Parker said the evening, and Nico said at least by three."

"This is bullshit," I declared.

"Yeah," Austin agreed. "I at least want in on the next bet."

"What?" I screeched.

"I mean…"

I narrowed my eyes. "Fine, I want in on it too so I can kick my husband's ass."

"On that beautiful note, it's time to start the wedding," my dad deadpanned, joining the group.

"You look beautiful," my mom said, pulling me in for a hug.

"Thanks, Mom."

"Only you could get a designer wedding dress tailor-made in less than two weeks."

"What can I say? I have connections. All I had to do was promise a few pictures, and they were basically fighting over me."

"I'm proud of you, Raelynn. You're an amazing woman."

Fire burned the back of my throat, and I struggled to swallow it down. I didn't want to ruin my makeup. "Thanks, Mom. I learned from the best."

"Ida, can I walk you to your seat?" Austin asked.

"Of course."

"I'll see you out there?" he asked me over his shoulder before walking away.

"I wouldn't miss it."

My cheeks hurt as I watched him crest the hill and disappear where the makeshift altar stood. The girls fussed over my dress and hair before lining up to make their way down the aisle. All that was left was my dad and me.

I linked my arm with his, and we waited for our cue to go.

"The paper came out today," he said.

I was wondering if anyone would mention it or if they'd try to ignore it on my wedding day. Not that it mattered. I'd rolled over in Austin's small bed and saw my phone waiting on the bedside with a million notifications. Despite Austin distracting me before I could pick up my phone, I still saw the article.

*Raelynn Vos Speaks Up About Domestic Violence.*

*Raelynn Vos, New York socialite, and daughter to senator candidate, Kenneth Vos, bares all in an exclusive interview where she shares her emotional truth about her experience with ex-boyfriend Bodie Forrester. Mr. Forrester stands trial for breaking into Ms. Vos's apartment last month and assaulting her during a dispute over their separation. Ms. Vos explained that she had originally wanted to sweep the incident under the rug to hide the shame she felt for finding herself in that situation but later changed her mind because there was nothing for her to be ashamed of. She didn't choose to be assaulted—no one did. She wanted to be an advocate for other men and women who struggled to find their voice under the shame society puts on them.*

*Senate candidate, Kenneth Vos, is vowing to pursue the highest punishment possible for Mr. Forrester's trial. He has always been an advocate for women's rights, volunteering and donating to local women's shelters as well as creating his own charity. Pressuring the law to make stricter decisions only stands to enhance his platform.*

"You know you didn't have to do that for me," he said before we started walking.

"I didn't," I clarified. I stopped, and he turned to face me. "I did it for me."

I was unprepared for the way my dad's eyes filled with tears while he studied me. "I'm so damned proud of you."

Life hadn't played out the way I planned or the idyllic way most people assumed it had, but I wouldn't change a damned thing if it meant I ended up here every time. "I'm proud of me too," I said, my eyes starting to water. "I needed to remind myself that there's no shame in being caught in that situation. It wasn't my fault. I didn't do anything wrong."

"No, you didn't."

"And I want to help others know that, too," I declared, swallowing back my tears and standing tall.

He blotted his eyes with a handkerchief and matched my stance with a smile. "Damn, you'd make a good politician. I'm glad I'm not running against you."

"Ha. I wouldn't waste my time on Senate. It's presidency or nothing."

"That's my girl."

"Thanks, Dad."

With one last smile, we looked over to the wedding coordinator, who looked one second away from performing smoke signals to get our attention.

"We better get going," Dad said. "I can only imagine Austin thinks you actually ran."

I laughed but started walking. "It'll be good for him to sweat a bit."

It was all talk because as soon as we reached the top of the aisle, I met his eyes just like I had years ago, and it took everything I had not to run down the aisle into his arms.

Halfway down the aisle, seeing all the love and support around us, I couldn't hold back the tears anymore. They slid down my cheek, and I did my best to blot them away. As soon as Austin took me from my father, he kissed each cheek, making them disappear for me.

I loved this man.

I loved my husband.

I loved my best friend.

And I couldn't wait to spend the rest of my life laughing with him.

A whole future flashed before my eyes while we listened to the pastor start the ceremony, but one memory from the past pushed its way to the front.

## Blame it on the Vodka

Holding his gaze, I mouthed the same words I said when this all started.

*Wanna fuck?*

He snorted, causing the pastor to stumble over the words, which made me snort. But I wasn't laughing anymore when, unlike that first time, he mouthed back, *hell yes.*

The rest of the ceremony blurred together with more tears and promises of forever. By the end, I was a ball of emotion, ready to explode. When the pastor claimed Austin could kiss his bride, he delivered a chaste peck and had me tossed over his shoulder, heading down the aisle before we were even presented as Mr. and Mrs. Caldwell.

Catcalls and my mom's embarrassed face were the last things I saw and heard before Austin rushed us inside so he could make good on his promise.

When we came stumbling out, no one commented on our rustled appearance. They greeted us with open arms and a beautiful reception.

In between dances, the girls pulled me off to the makeshift bar.

"For you," Nova said, passing me a shot of vodka.

Vera poured a shot of tequila and passed it to Nova. "This is for you, Naughty Nova."

I joined in, pouring a glass of champagne for Vera. "And for you, my dear."

We raised our glasses, looking back at our men talking around one of the tables. "To the lucky men in our lives," I declared.

"And to the alcohol that brought us all together."

---

Don't forget to check out Nico and Vera's hate-to-love, marriage of convenience romance. The tension and heat are sizzling!

Read for free with your Kindle Unlimited subscription.

---

If you're looking for something a little more forbidden, check out this student-teacher romance, VOYEUR. It's book one of six in the best-selling series.

Read for FREE with your KU subscription.

---

Want more angst in your books? Check out my new adult, second chance romance, SHAME. Find out how Anna and Kevin discover each other and learn to understand their unique sexuality.

Don't miss out on any of my upcoming books, giveaways, and important news by signing up for my newsletter... Fiona Cole Newsletter.

You can also join my Facebook reader group, Fiona Cole's Lovers, for exclusive sneak peeks and teasers.

## Afterword

This story turned into so much more than I anticipated. When I started writing Raelynn and Austin I hadn't planned to delve into such a deep topic, but domestic abuse can happen to anyone. I've known many men and women who survived an abusive relationship, including my mom. When I started writing I never intended to slip in personal details, but each memory of Raelynn's past was one of my own. I decided to share to release a part of my past and to also let people know that they are not alone.

If domestic abuse has affected your life, please know that you are strong and powerful. I am proud of you for surviving each day.

If you need assistance, you can use the website https://www.thehotline.org. There are multiple ways to contact support privately.

> *"I now see how owning our story and loving ourselves through that process is the bravest thing that we will ever do."* — **Brené Brown**

## Acknowledgments

**My family:** Thank you for always understanding and being supportive. Thank you for the cuddles after a hard day and laughs when all I want to do is rip my hair out. I couldn't do this without you being the foundation holding me up. I love you.

**Serena.** You're the lady behind the scenes making this all work. Thank you for everything you do and keeping me sane and always talking me down. Thank you for loving my characters and pushing me to be the best writer I can. Best. PA. Ever!

**Kelly.** Thank you for being an amazing editor. Thank you for being an even better friend! I couldn't have finished this book on time without your knowledge, skills, patience and understanding. You worked with me through it all and I don't have words to share my appreciation.

**Karla.** Thanks for always being there every step of the way. Dream Team!

**Najla Qamber.** As always, you always do the most amazing work and I'm so lucky I found out all those years ago! Thank you for working through every minor detail until it's perfect.

**Valentine PR.** Thank you for all your support and making sure everything is taken care of so I can write.

**Review team.** You ladies are wonderful, fun, kind, and beyond supportive. Thank you for every share, every review, and everything in between. You guys are the real MVPs!

**Lovers.** You are my safe place. You make me laugh and give the best book recomendations. You're more than I could ever ask for. I can't tell you how many times I've scrolled through your comments and have been brought to tears. Thank you for being such an awesome group.

**Bloggers.** You all work so hard and take beautiful pictures and write such amazingly kind reviews. I couldn't do this without you.

**Readers.** You guys rock my socks off. Thank you for taking a chance on my words. Thank you for taking the time to read something I've created. You're the best.

## About the Author

Fiona Cole is a military wife and a stay at home mom with degrees in biology and chemistry. As much as she loved science, she decided to postpone her career to stay at home with her two little girls, and immersed herself in the world of books until finally deciding to write her own.

Fiona loves hearing from her readers, so be sure to follow her on social media.

authorfionacole@gmail.com
Newsletter
Reader Group: Fiona Cole's Lovers
Bookish Shop + Swag

www.authorfionacole.com

## Also by Fiona Cole

### The King's Bar Series
Where You Can Find Me

Deny Me

Imagine Me

### Shame Me Not Series
Shame

Make It to the Altar (Shame Me Not 1.5)

### The Voyeur Series
Voyeur

Lovers (Cards of Love)

Surrender (A Lovers Novella)

Savior

Another

Watch With Me (A Free Liar Prequel)

Liar

Teacher

### Blame it on the Alcohol
Blame it on the Champagne

Blame it on the Tequila

Blame it on the Vodka

### Standalones
Just for a Little While

# Free Newsletter Story

The Guardian and the Escort

Printed in Great Britain
by Amazon